A Beautiful Sound

A BEAUTIFUL SOUND

Ellen Harris

Guideposts

NEW YORK, NEW YORK

www.guideposts.com
(800) 431-2344
Guideposts Books & Inspirational Media

Cover and interior design by Cindy LaBreacht
Cover art by Gail W. Guth
Map by Jim Haynes, represented by Creative Freelancers, Inc.
Typeset by Nancy Tardi
Printed in the United States of America

For Myrl Buckelew Bonner, whose selfless service
to others is an inspiration.

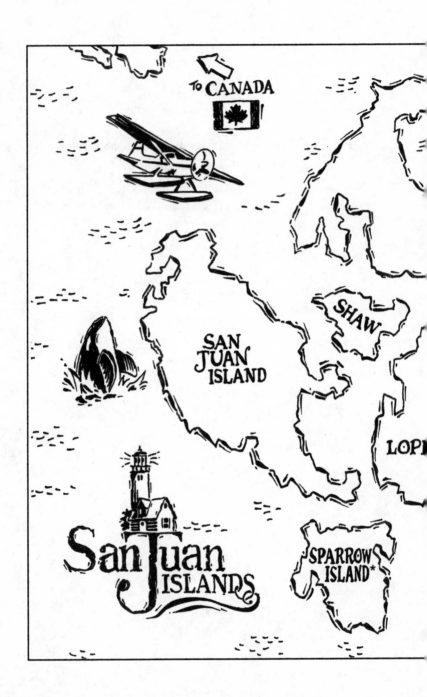

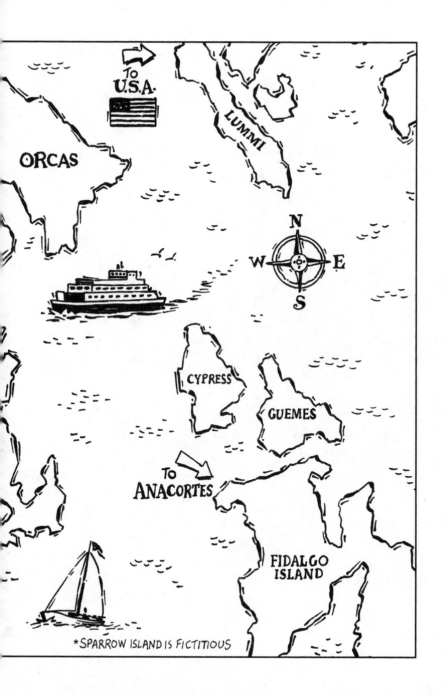

CHAPTER ✿ ONE

Isn't he a good dog? What's the sign for good dog?" Bobby McDonald asked his new friend, Dustin, as they both ran their hands along the sleek fur of Mary Reynolds' very happy companion dog, Finnegan.

Dr. Abby Stanton smiled and wondered if she should try to slow the conversation a bit. Her young friend Bobby sometimes got carried away by his enthusiasm for learning new things, and he could be a little overwhelming at times. Bobby had called last night—at the insistence of his mother Sandy, Abby was sure—to ask if he could bring his friend by today to introduce him and to have him meet Finnegan. "And you and Mary too," he'd added quickly.

Abby had already promised Mary she would help her put all her completed scrapbook pages into albums this morning, so it had worked out fine. She and Mary worked on that rote task while they visited with the boys in Mary's den.

Abby realized that Bobby's new buddy seemed to be going with the flow. She could tell Dustin Parker and Bobby were going to get on famously.

"*Good* is this," Dustin said as he formed an arc with his right hand and brought it down from his mouth and into the open palm of his left hand.

"I thought that was *thank you,*" Bobby said, studying Dustin's movement and repeating it.

"It's pretty much the same, except you end up in the other hand instead of stopping in midair. You can't just pay attention to what one hand is doing. It's about everything you do in, like, this space," Dustin said, forming a bubble around himself with his outstretched arms.

"Dustin knows sign language really well," Bobby said, obviously proud of his new friend's expertise. "That's American Sign Language, or ASL for short. He's teaching it to me."

"I know it because of my grandmother," Dustin said quietly, and Abby sensed that perhaps Dustin wasn't too crazy about Bobby's calling so much attention to him.

"So, does your grandmother have a hearing loss," Mary asked, "or does she teach signing?"

"She's deaf," Dustin said, flatly, making no attempt to match Mary's delicacy. "She used to be able to hear, but then something went wrong and it started to get harder and harder for her to hear things, until finally she couldn't hear anything at all."

"Well, I'm sure she appreciates your learning to sign so you two can still talk to one another," Abby said. "How often do you get to see her?"

"Every day," Dustin said, continuing to stroke Finnegan's coat. "She lives with us. She takes care of the house and looks after me while my dad's at work."

Abby wondered what had become of his mother, but she couldn't think of a tactful way to ask, so she inquired instead about where his father worked.

"He works at the Sparrow Island Medical Center," Dustin said, "on Sparrow Island in the San Juan Islands, Washington State."

Abby smiled to herself. It sounded as if Dustin had memorized the answer.

"Well, Dustin," Mary said, "Abby and I haven't had the opportunity to meet your dad or your grandmother. We would love to meet them and welcome you all to the island."

"Sometime," Dustin said, hunching one shoulder, "but my grandmother says right now's a busy time. She's working a lot on the house we moved into over by the Medical Center, and my dad works—a lot. We don't have a car, and anyway my grandmother doesn't drive 'cause of being deaf, so we stay at home a lot."

As the conversation went on around him, Bobby had been practicing signing "good dog" and Finnegan wagged his tail enthusiastically each time he did it.

"I wonder if he understands sign language," Bobby said, testing again by signing "good dog" and again getting Finnegan's happy response.

"Maybe," Mary said. "You know, the lady who had Finnegan before me had a hearing impairment."

"Do you think she signed to him?" Bobby asked.

"Quite possibly," Mary said. "I know I talk to Finnegan all the time, and not just to give him commands. Why, the two of us have big conversations about all sorts of profound things. Of course, I do all the talking, but Finnegan gets my meaning, I can tell. And he always, *always* agrees with me!"

The boys found this funny, and Abby noticed that Dustin

actually laughed for the first time during the visit. Then he seemed to catch himself and turned somber again.

"You know what?" Bobby asked.

Abby knew better than to answer Bobby's most famous rhetorical question, and sure enough, he rushed right ahead. "Dustin and me are both interested in all the same things."

"Dustin and I," Mary corrected automatically.

"You too?" Bobby said.

"No—" Mary started and then noticed Bobby's devilish grin. He bent over and touched his forehead on the carpet, laughing. After one last giggle, he continued. "Dustin and I," he said slowly, "both like to read about nature, and he likes birds, too, Abby. And airplanes and boats, and most especially, *especially*," Bobby emphasized, "Native American culture. He's like an expert in everything about all the tribes from every place he's lived."

"Have you lived a lot of places, Dustin?" Abby asked.

"Six," Dustin said, frowning and rolling his eyes toward the ceiling as if counting in his head.

"Wow, that's a lot," Abby said, wondering what had precipitated that many moves in his young life. "Well, we'll have to get you started learning about our tribes here," Abby said. "In fact, I hope you'll come out to see the Native American exhibit at the museum where I work—the Sparrow Island Nature Museum. I think you'd enjoy it."

Dustin nodded his head enthusiastically. "I would. Bobby's told me all about it. And he told me you're like a *real* scientist."

"I'm an ornithologist, Dustin," Abby said. "Do you know what that means?"

"Yes, you study birds," Dustin said.

"That's right. I study birds," Abby affirmed. "And I've been doing that for a lot of years. I worked back on the East Coast at Cornell University, and they have the best ornithology department in the country, in my opinion." She smiled. "Though of course, I may be a little biased. In any case, I am a real scientist, but only in my field. I'm not an expert on Native American culture."

"Oh, you're not?" Dustin said, seeming to deflate before her eyes.

"I'm not," Abby said. "But I'm certainly interested, and I've done a lot of study on my own. And my boss at the museum, Mr. Hugo Baron, has done a lot more than me. I think he definitely qualifies as an expert. And there's my friend Wilma who is herself a Native American. She also works at the museum."

"I told him that too," Bobby said. "And I told him I'd introduce him when he gets to come to see the museum."

"Well, I hope that will be soon," Abby said.

"I hope so too," Dustin said, turning almost morose. "But I don't know."

"Maybe you could come along with Bobby when he does his junior <u>docent</u> duties one day," Abby said. "I've got plenty of chores you boys could help with."

Dustin hesitated and Abby wondered if he was afraid she was going to put him to scrubbing floors or some other disagreeable task.

"I'd like that," Dustin said at last, "but my grandmother, well, she'd probably like to go with me to see the exhibit."

"How about if I came over and drove you two out one afternoon after school?" Mary volunteered.

"You drive?" Dustin blurted, staring at Mary's wheelchair. He seemed to realize, too late, how the question had sounded and his face reddened. "I'm sorry, I didn't mean—"

"It's okay," Mary said, holding up her hand. "The truth is, it's pretty miraculous that I can drive. I have a special van that I drive with my hands."

"It's really cool," Bobby volunteered. "She works the brakes and the gas and everything with her hands and, it's got a lift that goes up and down so she can get right in. It's even got a place where she buckles Finnegan in."

Dustin's eyes widened as Bobby went on to describe various buttons and whistles on the van.

"Wow," Dustin said at last. "That sounds neat."

"It's very neat," Mary said. "And I'm really lucky to have it. Some very kind people got it for me as a gift after my accident, and I just love using it to help other people who need a ride. It makes me feel like I'm giving a little something back. So it would make me happy if you'd let me drive you and your grandmother out to the museum one day. You just let me know when you'd like to go."

Dustin hesitated again, but before he had time to answer, a ringing sound filled the room and he jumped up and dug a cell phone out of his pocket. He didn't say hello. Instead, he stared at the screen display for a moment, then worked his thumbs quickly over the keypad.

"Excuse me," he said, as he put the phone back in his pocket. "That was my grandmother. I have to go home now. It was very nice to meet you, and, Bobby, I really liked seeing good dog Finnegan," he said, signing to the dog. He and Bobby laughed and bumped fists.

Abby and Bobby walked him to the door and watched as he jumped on his bike and rode off into the fine May afternoon.

"Your new friend seems like a really nice boy, Bobby," Abby said, watching him pedal furiously down the road.

"Yeah, he's cool. And we've got lots of projects we want to do together this summer, but I don't know. His grandmother wants him home like nearly all the time. And she says he can't have people over, not just yet anyway."

"Maybe after she gets to know people on the island better she'll lighten up," Abby said. "They're new here, and she doesn't know yet that this is a safe community. She's right to look out for him."

"Yeah, I guess," Bobby said, "but she sure seems to go overboard with it. When I rode my bike over to get him today I overheard her tell Dustin's dad she didn't think they should let him be friends with me. Maybe she doesn't like me—but she just met me, and I don't think I did anything rude or anything. She said it was the price they had to pay for what they'd done. I think she talks louder than she means to 'cause she's deaf. I guess I wasn't supposed to overhear that. What do you suppose she meant?"

"I have no idea," Abby said, frowning. "But I'm sure you didn't do anything wrong, Bobby."

She couldn't imagine what Bobby could have done to earn such disapproval. He was a very polite, caring boy. And what in the world could that mean, "That's the price they had to pay for what they'd done"? What had they done?

"Maybe she just meant she didn't think it was good for him to be going off with friends they don't know. I bet it'll be better by the summer," she assured Bobby. "Once she realizes people here watch out for one another, she'll feel better about letting him have more freedom."

"Maybe," Bobby said, but he sounded doubtful.

As they walked back into the den, Bobby stared down at his tennis shoes and hardly said a word.

Mary was stacking up the finished scrapbooks to be put on the shelf in her craft room. She frowned at the sight of Bobby's sad face, then looked over at Abby and raised a questioning eyebrow.

Abby nodded her head in the direction of the driveway to let Mary know Bobby was upset about Dustin's leaving. If there was one thing she and Mary had perfected since she'd been back on Sparrow Island, it was their sister-shorthand.

"Well, I guess I'd better go home too," Bobby said, glumly. "I've got Saturday chores to do. I might as well get them over with."

"Before you go, would you have the time to take Finnegan out for a romp in the backyard and then give him a good brushing?" Mary asked, winking at Abby. "I mean if it wouldn't be too much trouble."

"Sure thing," Bobby said, perking up. "I don't have that many chores, and I can get them all done this afternoon. Come on, Finnegan!"

As the dog rose, tail wagging, he looked over at Mary as if for permission. "Go on, Finnegan," Mary said, "off the clock. Go with Bobby."

Finnegan trotted forward and Bobby seemed to be searching his memory, then signed "good dog," before turning to head for the yard.

"I'm not sure which of them needs that romp the most," Abby said with a laugh. "Poor Bobby. He's so excited about spending time with his new friend, but I gather Dustin's grandmother has him on a pretty short leash."

"I think they must be in the McCrary house, the one over on Harbor Seal Road," Mary said.

"I didn't know anyone new had moved there recently,"

Abby answered. "In fact, I'm not sure I even remember which house it is. McCrary, you say?"

"Yes," Mary said. "Maybe you don't remember them. They were summer people."

"Oh yes, I do have a vague memory," Abby said, "but I never knew any of them very well."

"I got to know the children pretty well because they were both in my Sunday school class at one time or another over the years. I've heard the girl, Paulette, is in graduate school overseas somewhere. I want to say London, but maybe it was Edinburgh. Anyway, the son, Randall, is doing his residency in oncology at a hospital in Virginia, and I hear he and his wife have newborn twins. So it's no wonder they don't have time to use the house right now."

"Will they sell it, do you think?" Abby asked.

"I don't think they plan to," Mary said. "Janet said she heard Paulette had told someone who'd approached her about it that she and her brother inherited it together, and neither of them could bear the thought of selling because they have so many fond childhood memories here. But they didn't want the house to sit empty either. You know how houses decline when they're empty. Houses need people."

"True," Abby said, and something clicked in her memory. "Oh, I remember now which house you mean. Oh my, no wonder Dustin's grandmother's working so much on the house. It's been empty for quite a while, hasn't it?"

"Yes," Mary said. "Too long. I'm glad someone has moved in who'll give it some TLC. I'll have to remember to tell Rev. James about Dustin's grandmother being hearing impaired. He'll want to pay a welcome visit like he always does, and he should know that before he goes."

"Yes," Abby said, tapping her chin with her finger. "Do we know anyone on the island who signs?"

Mary frowned. "I can't think of anyone. Maybe he can go when Dustin's there to help interpret."

"Maybe," Abby said. She glanced at her watch. "Oh my, I need to get going."

"It's too bad you have to work on a Saturday," Mary said.

"I don't mind," Abby answered. "Actually, I don't mind at all. We're coming up on our busiest time. School will be out in June and the summer vacationers will start to arrive. I'm just as eager as Hugo is to have everything in tiptop shape. Today we're doing a walk through to make a list of everything that needs to be replaced or repaired. I have a hunch that between Hugo's vision of always making things bigger and better and my attention to small details, we'll end up with a mile-long to-do list."

She kissed Mary on the head and walked toward the garage, grabbing her bag and jacket off the rack in the laundry room.

She pressed the button to raise the garage door and caught sight of a car approaching. She recognized Janet Heinz's mini-van and tried to remember if Mary had mentioned that Janet was coming over today.

Then she caught sight of other figures in the car. She recognized the person sitting in the front with Janet and knew for sure this was a surprise visit. This was *not* something Mary would have neglected to mention.

She stepped back and called excitedly for Mary to come outside.

"What is it?" Mary said as she wheeled down the ramp. "Is something wrong with your car?"

"No," Abby said, smiling broadly. "Come look."

Janet's van came to a stop. Janet turned off the ignition and sat grinning from ear to ear as two young children bounded out of the backseat and made a beeline for Mary, enveloping her in hugs. "Grandma, are you surprised?" seven-year-old Emily asked, bouncing up and down on her toes.

"Yeah, did we surprise you?" three-year-old Nicholas echoed.

"Surprised?" Mary said, breathless. "I'm flabbergasted!"

Abby went to greet Mary's daughter, Nancy, who got out of the vehicle more slowly. Nancy had a smile on her face, but Abby noticed as she hugged her that she'd gotten very thin since her last visit. And there were dark circles under her eyes. Of course that could be chalked up to travel fatigue. It was a long trip from Florida.

"I've been keeping this secret for two weeks," Janet said, as she came around the van in a little shuffling run. "I thought I was going to burst." She laughed and bent down to hug Mary.

"I'm just overwhelmed," Mary said as Nancy kissed her cheek. "This is such a wonderful surprise!"

"We'll be here a week and a half," Nancy said. "But don't worry, Mom. We don't expect you to disrupt any of your meetings or plans. We'll visit around them. Some friends of ours had frequent flier miles that were about to expire. They couldn't use them, so they offered them to us. It was too good to resist!"

"Oh, I'm so glad you're here," Mary said. "It's good to have you home."

"It's good to be home, Mom," Nancy said, smiling down at her mother.

There it was again, Abby noted as she watched Nancy, that smile that didn't make it all the way to her eyes.

CHAPTER ✿ TWO

ABBY WAS ALREADY rearranging her upcoming workweek as she drove toward the Sparrow Island Nature Conservatory. On paper she was listed as Associate Curator, but practically speaking, her self-defined job duties ranged from handywoman all the way through to advanced ornithological fieldwork. And anything in between she desired to take on.

She loved her job and it sometimes gave her pause to realize how close she'd come to passing it by. Hugo Baron liked to tease her about how she'd played "hard to get" when he'd initially tried to hire her.

But of course, as he well knew, a negotiating strategy had been the last thing on her mind at the time. It hadn't been that long since Mary's accident. She had just gotten out of rehab then, and Abby had been afraid to leave her for more than short periods of time.

But Hugo had persisted, and Abby was eternally grateful he had. He'd made the position so attractive, and he'd let her fashion her own hours and do a lot of the work from home in those early days. And as Mary got stronger and more independent, Abby had been thrilled to have such interesting work to do right here on the island.

She tried to remember what Hugo's calendar for the week contained. She'd want to spend as much time as possible with Nancy and the kids. Florida was about as far from Sparrow Island as it was possible to go and still stay within US boundaries, so it was a rare treat to have Nancy visit, especially when it wasn't a major holiday with all the attendant rushing around those times demanded.

Cards, letters and e-mails were fine, and Abby was always cheered to get them from her niece. Plus, she and Mary usually received a fresh packet of "refrigerator art" from the children every couple of weeks. But none of those things were a satisfying substitute for time together.

Abby had always treasured her relationship with both Nancy and Zack. Her niece and nephew were as close as she would get to having children of her own. And she had the advantage of being once removed from parental authority, so when they were growing up, the children had often confided things to her that they were reluctant to tell their parents. It had brought them very close.

Abby saw less of them these days than she had when she still lived in New York. Of course, they'd been living here on the island through most of that time and Abby had come home frequently for visits. Now with Nancy in Tampa and Zack on the road with his jazz combo, arranging reunions got increasingly more complicated.

Abby thought of how elated her mom and dad would be.

As she pulled into the parking lot, she took out her cell phone and called the number at Stanton Farm.

As she'd expected, her mother immediately went into a litany of all the dishes she would prepare—all Nancy's favorites. One of the many ways Ellen Stanton showed her love was by her labors in the kitchen. So much so that Abby had lately noticed her waistbands getting a little snug. She'd been hoping to cut back, so she tried to keep from audibly groaning as her mother chattered on about key lime pie, Apple Dapple Cake, au gratin potatoes and smothered chicken.

"Is Benjamin going to be joining them?" her mother asked when she'd finally come to the end of her menu.

"No, Nancy says this time it's just to be her and the kids."

"Is everything okay?" her mother asked.

"Yes, fine," Abby answered and gave her the explanation Nancy had offered about the gifted tickets and Benjamin's crowded work schedule. She gave her mother firm assurances, but in the back of her own mind she was wondering if everything really was okay. She recalled the image of Nancy's hollow smile that didn't quite cover the anxiety and stress Abby thought she detected.

She was brought back to the phone conversation by her mother's voice asking, "Abby, can you hear me?"

"Sorry, Mom," she said. "What was that?"

"I said, Do you think I should bring over supper tonight? I can get something out of the freezer."

Abby did a quick mental inventory of the refrigerator's contents back at Mary's. "No, I think we'll be fine. I have a feeling Nicholas is going to want me to make my famous Silver Dollar Pancakes. That's normally his first request. And Emily likes them too. And there's plenty in the fridge for us big girls."

"Okay," her mother said. "Then I'll get going on Sunday dinner for tomorrow after services. You'll all come here, right?"

"I'll check with Mary and Nancy, but I expect they're already planning on a Stanton Farm Sunday dinner. Just waiting for the invitation."

"Oh, Abigail, don't be silly. Since when do I have to issue an invitation to family? But please tell Mary to invite Henry and anyone else you girls would like. Just call me with a count so I can make sure we have enough food."

"Enough food has never been an issue at Stanton Farm, Mom," Abby said with a laugh. "But I will have Mary call you to coordinate the menu. You have to let us bring some things. And don't wear yourself out. We can all help when we get there tomorrow."

"I won't dear," her mother said, though Abby doubted she'd heed one word. "I'm just so excited, it will be a joy to have so much family here."

"Yes, we're very blessed" Abby said.

"Oh, Abby, I almost forgot. We have new kittens from one of the barn cats. Emily will love seeing them. And Nicholas will want to see all the downy little baby chicks we have running around. Do you expect they'll come over this afternoon?"

Abby opened her mouth to answer, but Ellen rushed on. "No, probably not. They'll want to get settled in. I imagine they're tired. That's a grueling trip, that long flight and then the ferry from the mainland and the time change and all, but I can hardly wait to see them. Wait until I tell your father. He'll be beside himself."

Abby laughed. "I don't think he'll be alone in that."

"Pardon?" her mother said. "Oh, Abby, you're teasing me. Well, that's okay, how can I help but be excited?"

"I know, Mom," Abby said. "I'm excited too."

"Was Mary surprised?"

"Completely! And the most amazing part of all, Janet's been in on this for almost two weeks now and has managed to keep mum about it. Not a peep!"

"Well, will wonders never cease!"

"HUGO," ABBY SAID in a warning voice.

They were walking the museum, clipboards in hand, making inventory of repairs and improvements. It was a quiet day, but a few visitors were gathered around the Native American exhibit. Hugo, Abby knew, was itching to go over and give a personal tour.

"I know, I know," he said. "I'll stay on task. But there's so much I'd like to share. This exhibit only hits the highlights. There's more rich history here."

"I know, Hugo," Abby said. "But today—" she tapped the clipboard with her pencil—"is for practical matters, remember?"

"Yes, I do," Hugo said, sounding resigned.

This museum was a dream realized for Hugo Baron. He took great pride in it, justifiably so in Abby's opinion. Of course she was not exactly objective. She'd come to feel a sense of ownership almost equal to Hugo's. And they surely had a shared vision of all it could be one day.

"I'll tell you what," Abby said, giving Hugo a smile. "How about we start at the Native American exhibit and you can show me where you plan to put the new multimedia booth."

"Capital idea," Hugo said, his white mustache curving up along with his smile. "This is going to be a wonderful addition to our museum."

The visitors who'd been admiring the dioramas in the

Native American exhibit had moved on to the Wonderful World of Wings. Hugo strolled over to the area and started motioning with his hands to indicate an area on the floor between the Native American exhibit and the Birds of Prey exhibit that was nestled in the corner.

"The booth will be constructed right here," he said. "It will be long and narrow, and people will be able to walk either around it or through it. There will be a small bench for seating for those who'd like to stay for the entire presentation and standing room for those who'd rather wander in and out."

"The configuration and the proportionality of the dimensions is critical here," Hugo continued. "An architect friend from Seattle is coming over later in the week to look at the rudimentary plans I've drawn up and give us some guidance. Then he's going to give them to one of his young interns to draft out for us free of charge. Isn't that splendid?"

"It is splendid," Abby agreed. "I especially like the free part. It will give us more money to spend on the multimedia presentation that goes *inside* the booth."

"My thoughts exactly," Hugo said with a chuckle.

"I know you've been working on the script for the presentation, and I'm eager to see it," Abby said, "but for now I'm afraid we've got to press on with this." She held up the clipboard.

"Yes, yes, ever the practical one, Abby," Hugo said. "Let's march on."

They stopped in front of the Native American exhibit and Abby started scanning the dioramas looking for anything that might look shopworn or need repair.

"Oh, for pity's sake," she heard Hugo mutter and her eyes followed to the spot where he was looking. Someone had thrown two good luck pennies onto the small resin "lake" in one of the dioramas. One had come to rest flat on the shiny surface of the resin, but the other had lodged in between the dugout canoe of a Salish tribesman and his paddle. "What are people thinking when they do things like that?" Hugo huffed. He leaned into the exhibit and tried to pluck the penny out, but it was stuck. He leaned a little farther and almost lost his footing.

"Hugo!" Abby said, "Leave it. That's why we're making the list. We'll do everything at once. Rick's going to rig us a scaffold so we can go in and clean and do repairs. We'll get the coins out then."

Hugo let it go, but he continued shaking his head and making tsking noises.

"While we're on this part of the museum, Hugo, it reminds me I've been meaning to ask when you want to schedule the special Salish days. For the past couple of years we've done one in June and another in July, but I was thinking maybe we'd do three this year. They're very popular with the tourists and especially with the locals."

"I think that's a stupendous idea!" Hugo said, obviously pleased. Abby was happy she'd been able to offer something to get him to stop obsessing about the pennies.

"Shall we do one a month then?" she asked.

"Yes, let's do that. When we've finished up here, we'll go to my office and look at the master calendar."

Hugo's eye wandered back over to the troublesome pennies and he started to shake his head again. *So much for my masterful attempts at distraction*, Abby thought.

"Oh, Hugo. I guess not everyone takes the educational component as seriously as we do. But look at it this way. If that little lake in the diorama looked realistic enough for people to try to throw pennies into, that's a good thing, right?"

Hugo threw his head back and let out his trademark booming laugh. "Yes, you're right. That's one of the many things I love about having you around, Abby. You always find some good in every situation." He patted the rail. "Ah, maybe I do get too serious about it sometimes."

"I know one young patron who'll appreciate every effort you've made, Hugo," she said. She told him about Bobby's new friend, Dustin, and his passion for all things Native American.

"Well, I'll look forward to meeting this young man. Is he visiting the island?"

"No, his family moved here recently. His father works over at the Medical Center. I don't know what he does. And Dustin's grandmother lives with them and sees after him while his dad's at work. I'm not sure whether the mother is in the picture or not."

"I believe I heard someone new moved in, but I hadn't heard anything about them."

Abby told him what Dustin had said about his father's working a lot and about his grandmother's staying close to home. "She's deaf, so I'm wondering if that's part of it," Abby mused aloud. But in her head, she still had that phrase Bobby had overheard rattling around. *That's the price we have to pay for what we've done.*

"Could be," Hugo said, snapping her back to the conversation.

"You don't happen to know of anyone around who signs, do you?" Abby asked.

Hugo pursed his lips. "No, not right off hand, I can't say that I do. You know my mother-in-law lost a lot of her hearing capacity in her later years and it caused her to become more reclusive. We certainly do take that sense for granted, don't we? I shudder to think of all the things I'd miss if I couldn't hear. Just imagine, right here in this moment, what we'd miss.

Abby stood still and became aware of everything her ears were taking in. Hugo's sonorous voice coming from the voice-over on one of the video presentations, the murmur of conversation and laughter coming from the small clique of visitors, the birdsongs coming from the bird exhibit as a little boy who looked to be about Nicholas' age went along the exhibit pushing every button.

Yes, so much, she thought. And she did take it for granted. She made herself a promise she'd add the blessing of good hearing to her gratitude journal that evening.

"You're absolutely right," Hugo," she said. She gave him a sly smile. "Now hear this: Let's finish our list!"

CHAPTER ❦ THREE

ABBY PULLED UP AT RICK DeBow's workshop just before three and found him cutting small slats of wood into uniform strips. There were several stacks sitting on his long workshop table.

"What's all this?" she asked.

"For the Bird Nest," he said. "Four of the shutters have rotted out, and I can't find exact replacements, so I'm building them to match the old ones. The rest are in good shape, there's no sense replacing them all."

"I'll bet Martin and Terza appreciate that," Abby said. "I'm sure it's saving them a lot of money."

Rick nodded and pursed his lips. "A fair amount," he said. "I've never done anything like this before. This kind of spills over into the historic preservation area, and I'm just an everyday handyman, you know? But I'm enjoying the challenge."

"You're far from an ordinary handyman, and I think you know it, Rick," Abby said. "Speaking of which, I've got the list of repairs for the museum here. We haven't done the walk through for the conservatory yet. I'll get that to you later. We cut it short today. Nancy and the children are in town."

"No kidding. When did they get here?"

"This morning. It was a big surprise," Abby said. "We didn't know they were coming."

"I'll bet Mary's flipping out," he said. "I hope I get to see them. How long they gonna be on the island?"

"I think Nancy said a week and a half, so I'm sure you'll see them around. But anyway, I've got to get to the market. I want to get home so I can visit with the kids a little while, so I'm just going to drop this off and let you look it over. I think most of it's pretty self-explanatory, but I'll call or come by Monday. Then we can go over it and also the plans for the multimedia booth. Has Hugo talked to you about that?"

"Yeah, some," Rick answered. "That! Now that's going to be a big challenge. I mean, I can build the booth, but we're going to need some serious gearheads to come in and install all that equipment."

"Yes, I know," Abby agreed. "Hugo's got someone. There's a graduate student from Bellingham who's taken the technical stuff on as his class project. And we've found someone willing to fund at least a portion of it, so it's all coming together. I think we'll actually get it installed before midsummer if all goes as scheduled."

"It sounds really cool," Rick said. "I'm clearing the decks to do my part. I've been putting in what for me are some long days. I want to get the church and the Chois and all my regulars taken care of before I need to start in on this. 'Course, there's always emergencies that have to be tended to, so I can't guarantee my time. Not ironclad."

"I know," Abby said. "We'll just pray for no broken pipes or electrical outages or anything around that time." She looked at her watch, "Okay, I need to get going."

"I'll walk you out," Rick said, brushing sawdust off his flannel shirt and jeans.

"You don't need to do that; I don't want to interrupt your work here," she nodded toward the stacks of slats.

"I need to see the sunshine," Rick said. "I've been in here cutting these things practically all day."

As they walked toward Abby's car, they saw Bobby and Dustin Parker ride by on their bikes.

"Bobby's new friend, Dustin, must have finished his chores and earned a little free time this afternoon. I know Bobby's thrilled," Abby said. "Those two are going to be thick as thieves."

"I don't recognize the other boy," Rick said.

"His name's Dustin Parker," Abby told him. "He and his family are new to the island."

"Oh, he must be John Parker's boy," Rick said.

"You've met his dad?" Abby asked.

"Yeah, a few days ago," Rick said. "He came by the shop. He makes inlaid chessboards—beautiful pieces, so intricate you wouldn't believe it. Anyway, he wanted to know if I could cut him some bases and sand them out. He was over early this morning to pick them up."

"*Hmm*," said Abby, "I understood he works at the Medical Center."

"Yeah, he does," Rick said. "He's some kind of technician or assistant or something. He didn't mention having a kid. I guess we just never got around to that in the conversation."

Abby told Rick the little she knew about the family. "I don't know what the situation is. Maybe his wife died, or there was a divorce or something. Maybe family talk is a painful subject," she said.

"Maybe," Rick said. "Anyway, the chessboard thing, I'm guessing that's just a hobby, but his are the best I've ever seen.

Working with wood veneers isn't as easy as some people think. You've got to have a steady hand and patience by the bucketful to get them to fit together perfectly, and his are spot-on. The ones he showed me had to have at least two thousand pieces in them. Honestly, they looked like somebody found a magic seed and planted it and these things just grew up out of the ground as one piece of wood with a design in it."

"They sound incredible," Abby said.

"They are," Rick said. "I told him if he was interested in selling any of them, he should take them over to the craft co-op in Friday Harbor. He could get a pretty penny for them, I'm sure. He seemed hesitant about it, but he was going over to Friday Harbor for something else this afternoon and said he might take one in and just see how it goes. Maybe he can at least get enough to pay for the materials to keep making them —then he wouldn't have to feel guilty about it. He said he should quit making them altogether, but it's the one thing he does just for himself and he can't bring himself to give it up."

"Sounds like this is more than a mere hobby for him," Abby said.

"Yeah, I guess. I think he's a guy under a lot of stress."

"What's he like?" Abby asked, remembering again the cryptic remark Bobby had overheard.

"He's sort of quiet, low-key, but I like him," Rick said. "I think he's an okay guy."

"Well, with that recommendation, I look forward to meeting him," Abby said. "The boy seems very sweet and bright. He and Bobby have really hit it off. Heaven help us, now we'll have two curious boys asking twice as many questions!"

"And you love it," Rick said. "You know you do."

"Yes, yes, I do," Abby admitted. "Sometimes, though, I wish he could be a little less intense. Bobby always wants to know everything all at once."

"I suspect you were like that when you were a kid too," Rick said with a grin. "Shall we ask your mom and dad about it?"

Abby laughed and crisscrossed her hands. "No, no. Let's not do that. I confess. I was *exactly* like that. I can only aspire to having as much patience as my parents had with me."

"I think it's a family trait," Rick said.

"I hope so," Abby said. "By the way, I've been asking everyone I've seen today, you don't happen to know of anyone who signs do you?"

"Signs?" Rick frowned.

"Sign language," Abby said, motioning vaguely with her hands.

"Oh, no, I don't think I do," Rick said, still frowning. "But surely there must be someone."

"Yes, you'd think," Abby said slowly, "but so far I'm striking out." She glanced at her watch again. "Now, I really need to go. I've got a three-year-old who's going to be hungry for some silver dollar pancakes." She got into her car and Rick leaned down.

"Guess this is one time when money—or a facsimile anyway—really *can* bring happiness." He gave her a grin, then tapped the hood of her car a couple of times as he walked away. "Drive safe," he called back over his shoulder.

ABBY WAS SURPRISED to find Mary's van gone when she got home. As she went into the kitchen everything was quiet. She smiled to herself, thinking her mother must have won out over fatigue and enticed them all over to the farm.

As she put the groceries away Abby started to notice the sounds in the house, things she never gave any thought to in everyday life. She started to separate them one from another. There were birds chirping softly at the bird feeder attached to the kitchen window and Abby's ear naturally went to them first. She could easily distinguish the bubbling note of the purple martin from the nasally yank of some variety of nuthatch and the bright warbles and trills of a song sparrow. Her father had taught her early in her life to pay careful attention to the sounds of nature, early training that had put her in good stead in her chosen profession.

She realized in that moment that she didn't always carry that over into domestic situations. She listened for other sounds, man-made sounds she'd have to call them, for lack of a better word. A ship's bell in the far distance, the refrigerator kicking on, the ticking of the grandfather clock she'd brought with her from New York, the rustle of the plastic on the package of noodles as she slid them onto the pantry shelf. The creak of the stairs?

She tilted her head to one side and listened, frowning. *Was* that the stair? The one near the top? She slotted the milk into the refrigerator door and went to investigate. She found Nancy coming down, her hair tousled and her eyes puffy.

"Oh, Aunt Abby," she said. "I thought I heard someone down here, but I didn't hear your car. I forget how quiet your hybrid is."

"Yes, it lets me sneak up on people," Abby said, smiling. "Where are the kids? Where's Mary?"

"At the farm, naturally," Nancy said with a tired smile. She followed Abby back into the kitchen and began helping stow the groceries. "The kids slept on the plane, so they were full of energy. And Grandma dialed here the minute she got off the phone with you this morning. The second Emily heard the words *baby kittens*, she could think of nothing else. Mom took pity on me and left me here for a nap. I did *not* sleep on the plane. Or much of the past few nights, for that matter."

"You aren't sleeping well? Is everything okay, Nancy?" Abby asked.

Nancy stiffened. It was a slight movement, and she immediately turned and busied herself with rearranging the things in the pantry to accommodate the rest of the groceries, but Abby had noted it. "Oh sure, everything's fine," Nancy said, casually. Perhaps too casually, to Abby's ear. "I meant I had to get packed for the trip and I wanted to make sure I had everything caught up at work and at home before I left. So it was a hectic few days."

"Well, I'm glad you were willing to make the effort. And fond as I am of Benjamin, it'll be great for us to have a just-us-girls week. With the notable exception of Nicholas, of course."

Nancy grinned. "Yes, he's definitely a notable exception. He's enough boy for two boys, believe me. I love him madly, but that child keeps me hopping." The grin faded as she came across and hugged her aunt. "I'm glad to be here, Aunt Abby," she said and Abby felt a slight tremor in her slender body. "I need this."

Abby wanted to ask why she felt she needed the break, but Nancy turned back to her task, her voice brisk as she switched to talk of supper plans. Abby recognized the tone; it was intended to end that strand of the conversation.

"It's great that you were able to sneak in a nap," she said instead. "Now that you're well rested, we can gab for a while tonight. Catch up."

"That nap was lovely," Nancy said. "I'm feeling almost human again."

"I'm glad," Abby said. "You end up with an extra long day when you fly from east to west."

"Yes, just like when you used to come from Cornell, right? It's nice in this direction, but going back is going to be hard."

Abby saw a dark look pass over Nancy's face and she wondered if maybe she was really talking about something more troublesome than time zones.

CHAPTER ❦ FOUR

It seemed everyone at Little Flock wanted to speak with Nancy and to *ooh* and *ahh* over the children, pinching their cheeks and telling them how much they'd grown, which is how the Stanton clan ended up being the last group to file out of the church. They stopped in the doorway to shake hands and compliment Rev. James Hale on his sermon.

Abby was last in line and Rev. Hale followed her out into the sunlight as they talked. "Your sermon was certainly in perfect harmony with my own ponderings over the last few days," Abby told him. "They're always thought-provoking, of course," she told him, reaching over to touch the sleeve of his vestment. "And well delivered."

"Are you buttering me up for something, Abby?" he asked teasingly.

"No, I'm being serious," Abby said. "Your sermon today, Hearing the Lord's Voice, it's amazing how timely it is." She told him about the Parkers and how she'd been thinking about how much she took her hearing for granted."

"I'm not as prescient as you give me credit for, Abby," he said. "I found my sermon inspiration in the same place. I heard about the new islanders—the Parkers—and about her being deaf. It got me thinking about all I'd miss if I couldn't hear, and that led me to consider everything else we fail to hear, metaphorically speaking."

And perhaps everything we mis-hear, Abby thought. She hoped what Bobby had overheard had a less ominous explanation than the ones her mind had been conjuring up.

DINNER AT STANTON FARM was an event, as always. Ellen Stanton had pulled out all the stops.

"We're going to serve buffet-style off the sideboard today," her mother said as she bustled about the kitchen. "These bowls and platters are all too heavy to pass."

Abby saw her mother's point. She wasn't sure they were ever going to finish ferrying the dishes out. There was a gigantic bowl of mixed salad greens from the cold frame her father had built. Other large bowls were filled with green beans and corn from the larder stocked with last year's garden crop. Abby carried in a round crockery bowl heaped with mashed potatoes and Nancy followed after her with an oversized gravy boat. They had to rearrange the sideboard to find room for the roasted chicken, then again for the basket of rolls.

Then they stood around the table, hands joined and George Stanton gave thanks for the meal, for the hands that had prepared it and for the great joy of having family and friends to share it.

Nancy helped Nicholas serve his plate. Abby assisted Emily, who fretted over every choice as if it were life altering. She was

Nancy's picky eater, and Abby took care in serving up her food because she remembered Emily did not like the different foods on her plate to touch.

George insisted that Henry Cobb go through the line next as he was technically a guest, though since Henry had been seeing Mary, he'd become a very regular guest at Stanton Farm.

As Henry began serving his plate, he said, "You know Mrs. Stanton, you may be responsible for my having to take early retirement from the sheriff's department."

"Me?" she said, a look of concern on her face. "What have I done?"

Henry gave her a grin. "Well, if you keep inviting me to Sunday dinner, I won't be able to fit into my uniform anymore. And the department can't afford new ones, so I'll just have to quit."

"Oh, Henry!" Ellen said, flapping a hand at him. "You do love to tease me."

Henry laughed. "Everything looks wonderful, as usual."

Nancy picked up her plate and followed Henry. "Yes, Grandma, everything. Just what I need, all my favorite comfort foods."

To Abby's ear, Nancy sounded wistful and when Mary looked over and caught her eye, she knew Mary had heard it too. A frown creased Mary's forehead, but Abby could see her struggling to put aside her worries for the time being.

The table talk was lively as Nancy inquired about different people on the island and what they were all up to. She learned that Al Minsky at Al's Garage had, much to Abby's delight, gone off for a training workshop and was now certified to work on hybrid cars.

She heard from George that Frank Holloway was turning more and more duties over to his grandson, Aaron, so that he could spend time sailing and making occasional trips to the Seattle Seahawks games.

"Well, good for him," Nancy said. "That poor man has been practically living in that store for years. He's earned a break."

"Yes, I think he's enjoying himself," George said. "But more important, I think he's giving young Aaron a chance to build up his confidence. It means a whole lot to Frank that Aaron's showing an interest. Frank was really hoping the store would stay in the family. That's a big, big thing in a family business like that, you know."

"Too big sometimes maybe," Nancy said. She looked up and seemed to realize her grandfather was looking at her strangely. "I mean it's great in this case. It seems like Aaron's really into it, but I'd think it would put a lot of pressure on a son or daughter who didn't feel that was the work they were meant to do."

"Yes, yes," George said. "I see what you're saying. But in the Holloways' case, it seems to have worked out wonderfully for both of them."

"Good," Nancy said, with what Abby perceived as a too-bright smile.

"Works out in lots of ways," Henry said. "If old Frank had his way, the store would stay exactly the same, every nut and bolt in the same drawer it's been in for years and nothing new-fangled. Just like he wants the island to stay frozen in time. But with new people coming in and houses needing upgrading, Holloway's needs to expand its stock. Aaron will bring it along to meet modern needs."

"Speaking of new people," Mary said. "We got to meet one yesterday, Abby and I." She told them about Dustin Parker and his family and their move to the house on Harbor Seal Road.

"That's right," Abby said. "Henry, I meant to ask you if

you know anyone through the department who knows sign language."

"I'm not sure, Abby," Henry said frowning. "I can't recall that we've had a need for that kind of translation, not recently anyway. The only hearing-impaired person we deal with on a regular basis reads lips. He lost his hearing as an adult and has good verbal skills, so we don't need an interpreter. I'll check the list though and get back to you."

"Is the boy hearing impaired?" Ellen asked.

"Not the boy, his grandmother," Mary said.

"Buddy of mine, Luke Crandall," George mused, "lost his hearing back during the war. Got caught standing in the wrong place next to one of the big guns on the ship. Percussion burst both eardrums. He went through an awful rough time with it."

"Medically?" Abby asked.

"No, no, he got good care and all," George said. "Course they shipped him home right away. He progressed along and got so he could read lips pretty good, though it frustrated him. The Veterans' Hospital made arrangements for him to learn to sign, but he just flat out refused."

"Why, Grandpa Stanton?" Emily asked, her little face screwed up into a frown. "I think it would be cool to talk with your hands. Why wouldn't he want to learn?"

"I think it would be too, Sweet Pea," George said, reaching to touch Emily on the nose. "Ah, but it was different back in those days. Some people thought any sort of disability was something to be kept hidden. Luke didn't want to learn signing because he felt it'd call attention to him when he was out in public. And anyway, who would he have talked to? He lived with his folks when he first came back, and they wouldn't learn it."

"That's a shame," Mary said.

"Well, the story has a happy ending," George said. "One day when he went in for a checkup, there was a pretty young woman doing office work. Her name was Lila Greenway. She was beautiful and a really nice girl, and she also happened to be profoundly deaf. Let me tell you, he got *really* interested in learning to sign."

"What happened to them?" Nancy asked.

"Well, let's see," George said. "I guess it must have been about a year and a half after that first meeting that I was standing beside him at the altar as his best man, watching them sign their vows to one another. And it's now"—he looked toward the ceiling as if calculating in his head—"fifty-two years, four children and eight grandchildren later and they're still talking up a storm. Now that I think about it, I remember his telling me that the whole family signs to each other, even though all the children and grandchildren can hear. One of the granddaughters told him they have fewer misunderstandings that way since they have to look at one another and pay attention when they sign."

"Yes," Nancy said, "that would be true, wouldn't it? We listen, but only halfway, while we're doing something else. Always multitasking. No wonder we don't communicate well sometimes. We're just talking past one another."

Again Abby saw Mary's forehead creased with worry lines. This didn't sound like idle conversation to Abby either. Nancy seemed to be considering this on a very profound level. Abby saw Mary close her eyes and get very still for a minute, even as the conversation continued around her. Abby knew her sister was praying.

THE TABLE AND BUFFET were cleared in a matter of minutes, with the men and women working together like a well-practiced drill team.

Ellen loaded the dishwasher and Mary and Abby washed up the few things that wouldn't fit. Their mother was a wash-as-you-go cook and there were generally few preparation dishes left dirty once a meal was on the table.

Nancy placed the big salad bowl back onto the top shelf of the kitchen cupboard, a chore she was always elected to do since she was tall enough to reach it without hauling out the stepladder. Just as she closed the cupboard door Nicholas came into the room. He stood, rubbing his eyes for a minute, then finally said to Nancy, "Mommy, I think I need a nap. My eyes are blinking too slow."

Nancy took him to an upstairs bedroom and George and Henry excused themselves to the television room to watch the remaining innings of the baseball game.

Ellen took Mary into her bedroom to show her the quilt she had won at the spring raffle to benefit the youth group at Little Flock.

"Can we go see the kittens, please, please, Aunt Abby?" Emily asked, pulling at Abby's skirt.

"Did your mom bring clothes for you to change into?" Abby asked, looking at Emily's frilly dress and little Mary Jane shoes.

"Yes, I have them in my backpack," Emily said, pointing to a bag in the corner of the kitchen.

"Okay, then," Abby said. "I brought a change too. Let's get them on and we'll go explore."

Abby always kept a change of clothes in her car. In her line of work, and with her love of nature, she never knew when she'd need to don hiking gear.

She and Emily changed in record time and went out the back door. "I haven't seen the kittens," she told Emily. "Do you know where they are?"

"In the barn loft," Emily said. "They're so tiny, Aunt Abby," she demonstrated by holding the index finger from each hand very close together. "Grandma Stanton says we can't get too close or touch them because the mama cat will get worried and move them and we might not be able to find them again."

"Grandma Stanton's absolutely right," Abby said. "Above all else, the mama cat will keep her kittens safe. And she doesn't know us or trust that we won't harm them."

"I wish we could speak cat language, Aunt Abby," Emily said, "I'd tell the mama she's got nothing to worry about and that we just want to see her little kitties 'cause they're so cute."

In that instant, Dustin's grandmother came to Abby's mind. She was keeping her charge close, too, in this strange new place. Bobby was going to be crushed if she kept the boys apart this summer. Abby wondered if there was anything she could do to reassure the woman that Bobby was a good kid from a good family.

"We counted five of them," Emily went on, forcing Abby back to the present. The girl was chattering excitedly. "But it was hard to tell 'cause they were all just kind of squirming around and you couldn't figure out which one you'd already counted."

"Five is a big litter," Abby said, enjoying Emily's contagious enthusiasm.

"One of them crawled out of the little nest she'd made for them while we were watching," she said, skipping ahead of Abby, then turning and walking backwards as she talked. "And he started to kind of wobble across the bale of hay." Emily demonstrated by making her limbs loose and taking a few awkward steps. "But the mama cat dragged him back to the nest by the skin of his neck. And he was making this little noise like meeew, meeew. I think it meant 'Hey, no. Wait a minute, I want to see what's out there.'"

Abby looked at her great-niece with amusement "Why, Emily, I believe you do speak cat."

"Oh, Aunt Abby," Emily said, wrinkling her nose, "you're so funny."

At the edge of the yard they stopped to admire a red cross-bill at the bird feeder. They stood quietly, watching the bird. It reminded Abby of times with her father when she was Emily's age. "Look at his bill," she told Emily. "See how it's shaped? It doesn't match up like most birds' beaks. The top crosses over the bottom like scissors. They use that to pry the seeds out of pinecones."

"Wow," Emily said. "No wonder they like the bird feeder. That must be a whole lot less work."

"Yes, I expect it is," Abby laughed.

They watched the bird for a couple of minutes, until he flew off with a *kip-kip-kip* to report his findings to the rest of the flock.

Emily was taking everything in and seemed to be enjoying herself, but Abby saw her glance toward the barn every few minutes. She was eager to see the kittens, but she also knew that anticipation was half the fun.

Abby glanced down and saw a small patch of clover the lawnmower had missed near one of the rugosa rosebushes. Just in the center there was a perfect four-leafed clover.

"Emily," she said, "if you look down, you might see something that would interest you. I can't tell you what it is, but I'll give you a hint. If you find it, it will bring you luck."

Emily looked down, her head moving back and forth as she searched. "I think I know what you mean, but I don't see it."

"Just relax and look at one part at a time," Abby said, remembering how her father had taught her to train her eye to isolate some point of interest in a natural setting.

"I can't see it," Emily said, her impatience growing. "I'll never find it. Let's just forget it."

"Now, Emily," Abby said, surprised at how quickly Emily had gotten frustrated, "let's try one more time." She moved the toe of her tennis shoe to point directly at the clover. "Here, I'll give you a little help."

Emily's face brightened and she reached down to pluck the clover. As she stood the smile faded. "Here," she said, handing it to Abby. "You're the one who found it. It only counts for good luck to the person who finds it. And you are lucky, Aunt Abby. You got to grow up here. You had all these pets you could play with all you wanted."

Abby pulled a tissue from her vest pocket and carefully wrapped the fragile bit of greenery. "I'd say it was a team effort, Emily. We'll share the good luck. And yes, I was lucky to grow up here on Stanton Farm. But all the farm animals are not pets, you know."

"I know," Emily said. "That's what Grandpa Stanton keeps telling me. "But I'll bet you had a dog or a cat that was your special pet."

"Well, yes," Abby said, remembering fondly a succession of well-loved pets. "Both your grandmother and I did have pets growing up. I was the dog person; your grandmother liked cats better." She leaned over and nudged Emily, whispering conspiratorially, "But let's not ever let Finnegan get wind of that, eh?"

Emily giggled, but again her smile faded quickly. "I wish we could have a pet. But Dad's allergic to cats, and Mom says a dog's too much work and too expensive to feed and all. Nicholas and me would help, we really would, but they still say no." She picked up a stick and flicked at a few dried leaves in the grass and let out a big sigh. "Can we go see the kittens now?" she asked wistfully.

"Sure, let's go," Abby said, slipping the clover into her vest pocket.

They started toward the barn, but then Abby stopped. "Hold on, Emily," she said. "Let me run and get my digital camera. Maybe we can get some pictures of the kittens. Wait right here. It'll just take me a minute to fetch it from my car."

Abby went around the outside of the house to the driveway and popped her trunk. All the while, she was thinking about how quickly Emily had gotten frustrated and her forlorn laments about the lack of a family pet. That seemed out of character for the child. She was normally happy-go-lucky. Again Abby wondered if things were really as okay as Nancy claimed.

But then again, perhaps it was just a phase, she mused as she unzipped her field bag and found her camera. After all, she had never raised a child herself and even those she was close to, like Nancy and Zack, she hadn't been with on a daily basis.

Abby turned on the camera to make sure the batteries were strong and checked the media card to see if she still had some room. She was studying the information on the display when she heard the scream—shrill and high-pitched. Her heart skipped a beat.

She dropped the camera into the bag and ran back around to the back of the house, scanning the backyard frantically. No Emily. She ran toward the barn and spotted Emily just inside the fence. She was doubled up and was clutching her shin, crying hard. As Abby came closer she saw the blood oozing out from between her small fingers and spotted the long, vertical rip in the leg of the girl's jeans. Emily had tried to climb the fence and had gotten caught by the barbed wire at the top.

Abby shouted toward the house for help in case Emily's high scream hadn't made it over the noise of the baseball game. She rushed to the gate to get to the child.

She picked her up, shushing her soothingly and was carrying her out the gate when Nancy came running, followed closely by Henry, then George and Ellen. Mary was still at the top of the ramp, maneuvering her wheelchair.

"What happened?" Nancy shouted, her voice shaky, as she ran toward them.

"She tried to climb the fence," Abby said. "I'm so sorry, Nancy. I was getting my camera."

"It wasn't Aunt Abby's fault," Emily snuffled. "She told me to stay put and wait, but I didn't." She wailed. "Oh, it hurts!"

Henry took her and carried her to the bench in the backyard where Nancy knelt to examine her injury.

She delicately pulled the two edges of the rip in the jeans apart and peered in. Abby heard the slightest intake of breath, but to Emily Nancy said reassuringly, "Well, this doesn't look too bad. But we may need to go to the Medical Center and have them look at it, especially since you cut yourself on that rusty old fence. It's going to be okay, Honey. I know it hurts, but try not to cry."

"I'll drive you over," Henry said calmly. He picked Emily up, and she rested her head against his chest, her lips pinched tightly together. Abby could see she was trying to be brave.

"I'll stay and look after Nicholas," Mary said. "Emily, it's going to be fine, sweetheart. Dr. Dana will take good care of you."

"I'll go with Nancy," Abby said, feeling miserable that this had happened on her watch.

DR. DANA RANDOLPH MET THEM at the door in response to the call Abby had placed on the drive over. She introduced herself to Emily. Her friendly manner seemed to put Emily at ease— or at least make her less terrified about what they might do to her. She had asked at least three times on the way over if she'd have to have a shot.

Henry took a chair in the waiting room and, at Emily's request, Nancy and Abby both went into the exam room with her.

A man who looked to be perhaps in his early forties followed them into the room carrying a tray. "Abby, Nancy, Emily," Dr. Randolph said, "this is my new assistant, John Parker." She yanked a paper towel from the rack she'd cranked down with her elbow, dried her hands and snapped on gloves. I'm so lucky to have him, but I'm afraid he's wasting his talents as a physician's assistant."

"Thank you, Dr. Randolph," the man said, setting the tray on a rolling cart. "And what have we here?" he asked, smiling at Emily.

"I cut myself on a fence," Emily said, sniffling.

"Let's have a look," Dr. Randolph said, taking up a pair of scissors to cut away the leg of the jeans. Emily's apprehension returned and Abby could see her stiffen.

John Parker noticed too. "You know, I have a son just a little older than you. He likes to explore too. He's always getting scrapes and bruises. I guess that's what happens when you're an intrepid explorer, right?"

"An intre—?" Emily began, but couldn't wrap her tongue around the word.

"An intrepid explorer," he repeated. "You know, brave and daring, all that."

Emily sniffled again, but a new determination came over her face. *Ah*, Abby thought, *a much more effective strategy than all the cooing over her everyone has been doing.*

"I've met your son, Mr. Parker," Abby said. "Yesterday. He

and our neighbor Bobby McDonald have become good buddies it seems. I'm Abby Stanton," she said. "I'd offer my hand,
but I realize you're a little busy right now." She turned back to
include Emily in the conversation. "I'll bet you'll get to meet
Dustin while you're visiting."

"Good," Emily said, forcing a smile and trying not to look
down at what Dr. Randolph was doing.

"Well, this doesn't look too bad at all," she said, smiling up
at Emily as she gently swabbed the wound. Abby could see in
her eyes though, that she had concerns.

"Tell me, John," Dr. Randolph said, turning to Parker,
"what's your considered opinion?" She lowered her voice, but
Abby caught the words. "Do you think she'll need stitches or
will your technique work?"

He leaned over to get a better look at the cut, adjusting the
light and looking at it from a couple of different angles. "I
think the butterflies will do fine," he said. "Really good candi-
date for it, in fact."

"Excellent," Dr. Randolph said. "Emily, you're lucky that
you came when John and I are on duty. We'll close your cut
with a combination of butterfly bandages and a special glue
that will hold it together. You won't need to have any stitches.
Isn't that great?"

"No stitches?" Emily asked. She turned toward Abby. "I
guess that four-leafed clover did bring me some luck,
Aunt Abby," she said, her voice catching a little.

Nancy shot a questioning look at Abby, and she took the
clover from her vest pocket and slowly unwrapped it. Nancy
smiled, but Abby could feel her body shaking as she sat next to
her in their molded plastic chairs.

Abby watched as John Parker and Dr. Randolph worked

together. Parker distracted Emily again as the doctor applied a numbing agent, then gave her an injection without Emily ever spotting the hypodermic needle—her biggest terror averted.

As they began the procedure, Abby noticed that it was as if the roles were reversed. Parker was actually dressing the wound and Dr. Randolph was assisting him.

After the treatment, the doctor asked Nancy about the date of Emily's last tetanus shot. Emily heard the word and started to whimper.

"I'm sure she's up-to-date," Dr. Randolph said, louder now, to calm Emily. "We just need the date for the record. Just to write it on the chart."

Abby turned to Nancy who looked bewildered. "I-I don't know when she had her last one." She bit her lip and turned toward Abby, staring at her beseechingly. "I don't even *know*," she said. Tears welled up, but she fought to hold them back as she glanced at her daughter.

CHAPTER ❀ FIVE

I THINK SHE'S OVERTIRED and her nerves are frayed, that's all," Mary said as she and Abby prepared breakfast together on Monday morning. "Normally Nancy's cool as a cucumber in an emergency."

"Yes, I'm sure you're right," Abby said, wondering which of them Mary was trying to convince. "It wasn't like she fell apart. When she spoke to you, she made it sound much worse than it really was. I think she was just so relieved, she let her emotions overwhelm her for a moment. All it took was a quick call to Benjamin to have him locate Emily's vaccination record in her file."

"And I'm sure it was easy to find," Mary said. "Nancy's very organized."

"Yes," Abby said as she broke eggs into a bowl. "Of course, she had to calm Benjamin down a little first. He wanted to jump on the first plane up here to make sure Emily was okay."

"Oh dear me," Mary said. "It's far easier to endure hardships yourself than to see your children have to go through them. You feel so helpless."

"I think we'd all have been a little shaky yesterday if it hadn't been for John Parker," Abby said.

"That's right. Nancy mentioned that he was the one who helped treat Emily," Mary said. "What's he like?"

"Very nice," Abby said. "We had a nice conversation while Nancy was getting the care instructions for Emily's cut from Dr. Dana. But you know, at one point in the conversation he seemed to sort of—" Abby stopped, unable to describe the impression she'd had during her talk with Parker.

"Seemed to what?" Mary prodded.

"I'm not sure how to say it exactly," Abby went on. "It was almost like he was telling me to keep my distance. He was quite friendly at first, and he was polite throughout, but when I told him that we'd offered to take Dustin out to the museum and that we were very eager to meet his grandmother, I don't know, his attitude seemed to shift a little."

"I'm not sure I get what you mean. Shift?" Mary said.

"He said something like, 'I'm sure she'll enjoy meeting you, at some point.' Or words to that effect. As if it might need to be in some far, distant future."

"Maybe he just meant, as Dustin said, that she's overwhelmed with getting the house in order right now," Mary said.

"Maybe," Abby said, "but Bobby overheard something that I've been wondering about as well." She related to Mary what Bobby had told her.

"The price they have to pay?" Mary repeated. "Maybe she meant for moving around so much. I imagine it's hard for Dustin to get attached to friends when they just up and move again. Seems like he's done a lot of that in his young life."

"Yes," Abby said, "that could be it, I suppose. But still, keeping Dustin from having friends doesn't seem like the answer."

"I was talking to people at church yesterday," Mary went

on, "and no one I talked to has met Mrs. Parker. Apparently, her son does all the errands and she stays pretty much at home."

"I wonder if she prefers it that way or if it's the disability that's isolating her," Abby said. "Maybe John's over-protective, though he didn't strike me that way. He was so good with Emily—and with the rest of us too."

"Well, all we can do is try to be as warm and welcoming as we can be," Mary said. "And try to realize where to draw the line. We don't want to come off as overbearing or pushy."

"You're right," Abby said. "I just love Sparrow Island so much, I can't bear the thought of anyone here being lonely or missing out on all it has to offer."

"You're preaching to the choir, Abby," Mary said with a laugh.

"I am, I am," Abby said, whisking the bowl of eggs with vigor. "You've always loved Sparrow Island so much you never wanted to leave, and though I've always loved it too, I think I have a renewed appreciation for it since I've moved back. I can't for the life of me imagine anyone wanting to stay indoors with so much natural beauty to be enjoyed. And to keep to yourself all the time when the people here are such good neighbors and friends—that seems an awful shame. I think sometimes people in an island community just bond more deeply than mainlanders. We have to depend on one another out here."

"All true," Mary said as she poured two cups of coffee, filling the kitchen with a lovely aroma. "But I certainly know, too, that having a disability can make you want to withdraw from life. I don't have to tell you how much effort it took for me to finally realize I still had a contribution to make to the world and to get up the gumption to pick up my life again."

"But you did, Mary," Abby said, pouring the eggs into the hot skillet. "You came back with gusto!"

"Well, I like the way that sounds, though I'm not sure I've

earned it. I did my share of whining. But yes, I'm happy now," Mary said, "and grateful. I don't think I could have done it without support and an occasional less-than-gentle push from certain members of my family," she said, giving Abby a pinch on the elbow as she wheeled to her place at the table.

"Ouch," Abby said, feigning pain and rubbing her elbow. "Yes, but Mary we can't give Mrs. Parker our support unless we get to know her so we can become friends. It's a chicken-and-egg problem, isn't it?"

"Yes, complicated by the language barrier," Mary said.

Abby heard Nancy coming down the stairs. She recognized the pattern of her footfalls. Nancy still took the stairs in the same rhythm she had as a teenager racing for the telephone.

"I thought I heard you two up," she said as she came into the kitchen.

"Did we wake you?" Mary asked. "I wanted to get up early and do my devotional before the children got up."

"No, I was up," Nancy said, "I was just writing in my journal. I guess that's kind of how I handle things. I write about all my concerns and then I pray for guidance about how to handle them."

"I do that as well," Abby said. "And for the past several years I've started keeping a gratitude journal too. Sometimes I think we get so invested in our challenges and tribulations that we don't stop to give thanks for all the things that are going right in our lives. We take those gifts for granted."

"I'm sure you're right," Nancy said. "I'll try to start adding that to my journaling practice."

"Speaking of tribulations, how's Emily?" Abby asked.

"I think she's doing fine," Nancy said. "They're both still sleeping like logs. They couldn't get settled down last night. Their internal clocks haven't reset yet."

"Nancy," Abby said, "I cannot begin to tell you how awful I feel about all this."

"Aunt Abby," Nancy said firmly, placing a hand on each of Abby's shoulders and giving them a squeeze. "You have done nothing to apologize for. The same thing could just as easily have happened if it had been me with her or anyone else. Unfortunately, she made a bad decision. She disobeyed you and these are the consequences. I wish I could spare her this painful lesson, believe me, but I hope she learns something from it. It's the price she paid for being disobedient. It scares me to realize I can't protect them from every hurt."

Abby shivered. There was that phrase again—the price she'd paid.

"I'm just grateful it didn't come at a higher price," Mary said. "She could have been seriously injured."

"I know," Nancy said. "My heart just about stopped when I saw how high that fence was. She could easily have hit her head on the watering trough."

"I saw that too," Abby said. "The trough was just inches away from where she landed. She must have gotten snagged on the barbed wire and it slowed her fall, and maybe changed the trajectory. So in a way, the thing that injured her was also the thing that saved her."

Mary passed a plate of toasted English muffins across to Nancy, who took one. It seemed to Abby more an automatic response than an intentional act. She put it on her plate, but ignored it.

"Yes," she said, her voice sounding far away, "I guess we have to be grateful for mixed blessings as much as for those that are clearly what we desire." She turned to Abby. "Anyway, I'm the one who needs to apologize."

"Whatever for?" Abby asked.

"For that little meltdown I had at the Medical Center yesterday. I don't know what got into me."

"You expect to be perfect, Nancy. It's an affliction," Mary said. "Ninety percent of mothers couldn't tell you right off the top of their heads when their child had the last tetanus shot. That's why we write these things down in those little charts they give us."

"I guess," Nancy said. "It does seem like there's just too much of it to keep up with sometimes. Dates and numbers and degrees and calendars and play dates. Asking prices, closing dates, appointments, events, warranties. There's no end to it."

"And we do the best we can," Mary said. "But you have to give yourself a break. Not every bit of information that comes into your life is urgent enough to memorize."

"That's what Dr. Dana's assistant said. He was so kind and understanding about it. He has a way about him. He helped me see I was overreacting without making me feel like a wimp." Nancy looked down and frowned as if wondering how the muffin on her plate had gotten there. She got up and poured herself a cup of coffee.

"Course, then I had to deal with Ben freaking out," she said with a weak smile. "I had to get my act together or he'd have been out here tomorrow."

"I'm sure Benjamin misses you all," Mary said. "And hearing that your child's hurt or unhappy is so difficult, especially long-distance, when you're powerless to do anything about it."

"Yes, I'm sure," Nancy said, but Abby detected a flatness in her voice. She and Mary exchanged a glance. It was clear, despite Nancy's assurances to the contrary, that things were not well in the Taylor household.

AS ABBY DROVE UP Oceania Boulevard after work that day, she spotted Bobby and Dustin up ahead on their bicycles. They probably had not heard her quiet car, and she didn't want to try to pass them for fear they'd suddenly veer into her path. So she slowed to a crawl and followed them.

The boys were standing up on the pedals of their bikes to exert pressure while climbing the long slow incline. The frames of each boy's bike passed from left to right and back again while their bodies remained vertical. It was a style of riding seen only in agile kids with loose limbs and a belief they can flaunt the laws of physics.

Sure enough, when Bobby's feet were finally resting firmly on the ground by Mary's front door he looked around and seemed surprised to see Abby's car.

"Hey," he called as she pulled up and got out, "you're home early."

"Yes, I am," Abby said. "I've rearranged my schedule this week so I can spend some time with Nancy and the children. She's here for a visit."

"I heard," Bobby said. "That's why we came. I was wondering if we could say hi to Emily. I heard she hurt herself out at the farm yesterday. Is she okay?"

"She will be," Abby said. She turned to Dustin. "You see, Dustin, you're learning already, news travels fast on the island." She reached out to pat Bobby's shoulder. "It was nice of you to come by. I'm sure Emily will appreciate your checking up on her. Dr. Dana took good care of her. And your dad too," she said to Dustin.

"Your dad?" Bobby said to Dustin.

Dustin shrugged.

"How come you didn't tell me?" Bobby asked Dustin.

"I didn't know," Dustin said, shrugging again. "My dad doesn't tell me about his work stuff. He says it's not ethical and that people are entitled to their privacy. He's really strict about it."

"Oh," Bobby said. "And I guess it wouldn't have meant anything to you anyway. You haven't even met Emily yet."

"Maybe we can remedy that right now," Abby said. "As you can clearly see, I'm just getting home myself, and I don't know for sure where everyone is or what they're doing, but let's go find out."

"Oops," Dustin said, fishing his cell phone out of his pocket. "Just a minute, okay?"

He studied the screen. "Oh man, I've gotta go. My grandmother wants me home."

"Can you stay just a minute to meet Nancy and Emily and Nicholas? Just a *minute*?" Bobby asked.

"I guess, just a minute," Dustin said. "But then I really gotta go. Let me text her back." He punched a few buttons then started for the door as if he were a sprinter coming off the block.

They found Nancy and the children in the den. Nancy reported that Mary was at a dentist's appointment and that they had been having a nice, quiet day. "To make up for yesterday," she said.

Bobby introduced Dustin to the other children, then asked if Emily's leg hurt.

"Not too much," she said.

"You know, it was Dustin's dad who treated you yesterday," Abby said. "Remember Mr. Parker?"

"He was nice," Emily said.

"Yes, he was very nice," Nancy echoed. "It's a pleasure to meet you, Dustin. We've very grateful to your dad. He's a smart guy. Because of him, Emily's probably not even going to have a scar."

"No scar?" Bobby said. "Ah, it's almost like it's not even worth getting hurt, right? When you've got a scar, people ask you about it and you can, you know, tell them the whole story."

Abby and Nancy exchanged glances, each trying to stifle a laugh.

"I don't think I'd want to tell the story," Emily said, frowning. "I got hurt 'cause I did something dumb. I don't think I'd want to be telling people that."

"Oh," Bobby said, frowning. "Well, in that case, it's a good thing you won't have a scar."

Nancy had been sketching when they came in. She set her sketchpad on the ottoman, whereupon an ever-curious Bobby picked it up. "Is it okay if I look?" he asked.

Nancy hesitated, but then said, "Oh sure, go ahead. It's just something I was doodling with."

"Wow," Bobby said, "this is really good. I didn't know you could draw like his."

Abby came over behind Bobby and looked down at the sketchpad. It was a colored pencil rendering of Nicholas with his arms draped around Finnegan's neck. It was very well executed. Not only that, it perfectly captured the feeling between boy and dog.

"Nancy, this is marvelous," she said. "I didn't know you'd kept this up. You used to draw all the time. I have two of the pencil drawings you did for me years ago hanging in my room upstairs. Remember those? One was of a sandpiper and the other a tufted puffin. You were still in high school when you drew them. I'm so glad you're still drawing. I had no idea."

"I haven't kept it up, Aunt Abby," Nancy said. "It's been a long time since I've done any drawing or painting. There's just no time. I'm afraid this sketch reflects that. My hand and my eye aren't so much in sync anymore."

"Well, I think it's great," Bobby said.

"Me too," echoed Dustin who had come over to have a look. "Really good." He glanced nervously at his watch, a plastic rectangle too big for his small wrist. It was emitting a soft beep-ing sound. "I've got to go, Bobby," he said. "It was nice to meet you, Mrs. Taylor." He turned back to Emily and Nicholas. "Catch you later," he said.

"It was nice to meet you, too, Dustin," Nancy told him. "But you must call me Nancy. It makes me feel old and <u>decrepit</u> when you say Mrs. Taylor."

Dustin gave her a smile, but Abby could tell he was worried about getting home.

Bobby started for the door. "I've gotta go too," he said. "I've got homework and my after-school chores. I'll see you later."

"Bye," Emily said, giving a little wave.

"Bye!" Nicholas yelped, then dissolved into giggles and buried his face in Finnegan's fur.

Abby walked the boys to the door, but as she watched from the doorway she saw there was some problem once they got outside.

"Dustin's got a flat," Bobby called.

Dustin stood, staring at his bike's flat tire. "I'll just have to walk home. Could I leave my bike here and get it tomorrow?"

"That's a pretty long walk, Dustin," Abby said. "I'll take you home. We can put the bike in the back of my car. I've got a tie-down for the trunk."

Dustin's eyes flicked back and forth from the road back to Abby's car. "Okay," he said, finally. "Thank you."

Bobby helped get the bike secured in Abby's trunk and then jumped on his bike and took off across the yard for his own house.

Abby tried to engage Dustin in conversation as they drove the short distance to his house on Harbor Seal Road, but the boy seemed uncomfortable with her, fidgeting constantly with his watch, and adjusting and readjusting his seat belt.

The house came into view. Abby could see that it was, indeed, a little on the run-down side. She could see paint cans and drop cloths in the carport as they pulled up.

Dustin got out of the car, but then didn't seem to know what to do. "Thank you for bringing me home," he said, standing as if glued to the spot.

"You're welcome, Dustin," Abby said, "Let me help you get your bike out of the car."

"Oh yeah," he said with a nervous little laugh, "I nearly forgot my bike."

They extracted it from the trunk and Dustin pushed it toward the carport, the flat tire making a squishy sound with each rotation. "I'll—I'll go get my grandmother," he said when Abby didn't get back into her car.

Abby got the clear message that she was supposed to wait there, so that's what she did.

Normally, Abby was not at all self-conscious when meeting new people. While she was not as outgoing or as much of a social butterfly as Mary, she was genuinely interested in others. But on this occasion, she was glad to have Dustin to facilitate communication with Mrs. Parker. There seemed to be some undercurrent at work within this family that made her uneasy.

In a few minutes a woman wearing paint-stained overalls came outside. She had salt-and-pepper hair and a frown line cut her brow. When she spotted Abby she rearranged her face into a tentative smile.

"Mrs. Parker," Abby said, putting out her hand, then she realized she was already lost. "Dustin," she said, turning to the boy, who had followed his grandmother out, "could you help me out here? How do I sign my name for your grandmother?"

Dustin turned to the older woman and made a string of

very rapid movements with his hands, which Abby could never have replicated in any sequence, much less the proper one.

"It's okay, Ms. Stanton," the older woman said, wiping her hand on a rag hanging from the bib of her overalls and extending it to Abby. "I read lips. And Dustin has told me about you. I'm happy to meet you. He told me about his flat tire. Thanks for bringing him home."

"It's Abby, please," Abby said, suddenly very aware of her lip movements. She was sure she was probably overexaggerating them now, but she couldn't seem to stop.

"Elise, Ellie for short," the woman said. Her speech was clear, but Abby could see what Bobby had meant about the lack of volume control. Only this time she spoke so softly Abby had to strain to hear her.

Abby gave her the usual welcome-to-Sparrow-Island, then told her about her work at the museum. She repeated the invitation to see the exhibits and told her about Mary's offer to drive them.

"That's a very generous offer," Ellie Parker said. "We'd love to see the exhibit at some point, but as you can see, we have a lot to do with the house right now." She gestured at her overalls.

"Could you use some help?" Abby asked. "You know that's the wonderful thing about island life, or at least Sparrow Island life. If you need a helping hand, there's always someone willing to lend it."

"I appreciate that offer, too," Ellie said, her demeanor growing less friendly, "but I enjoy doing the work myself." She signed to Dustin and he turned to Abby.

"Thank you very much for bringing me home. I've got to go in now. I've got homework to do."

Abby took that as a cue that she was supposed to leave, but

she turned to Elise Parker and said, "When you're all settled, I'd love to introduce you to people on the island. I'm sure someone from our church, Little Flock, will be around to welcome you as well."

"That will be nice, but my family and I are Catholic. We attend St. Christopher's."

"That's wonderful," Abby said. "We're involved in a lot of projects together with St. Christopher's."

Elise Parker looked back toward the house where Dustin had gone, then turned back to Abby. "Thank you again for bringing my grandson home," she said. "I'd better get inside and make sure he's getting on with the homework."

As Abby climbed behind the wheel of her car, she could just see into the large kitchen window off the carport. Dustin and his grandmother were inside having a very animated conversation with their hands. Ellie Parker gestured fast, her arms moving in wide circles. Dustin signed back, then hung his head.

It was clear to Abby that Dustin was being scolded for something. Abby had the sinking feeling that she was somehow the cause of it. First Emily's injury, now this; she was certainly not a good luck charm for children to have near them these days.

As she put the car in gear and started to back out, she saw Elise Parker pull the boy to her in a tight hug. Dustin locked his arms around his grandmother's waist and she held him tight, bending down to plant a kiss on his head.

Whatever the flap had been about, it appeared to be over now.

Abby breathed a sigh of relief, but couldn't quite shake the feeling that this family might be hiding something.

CHAPTER ❦ SIX

ABBY WALKED HURRIEDLY down Shoreline Drive the next day, shielding her watch against the midday sun so she could read the time. She was trying to fit in all her errands during her lunch hour. And she'd gone in an hour early so she could take off early again in the afternoon.

Of course, she knew she could have done it anyway. Hugo certainly didn't hold her to a clock, but she still had a lot of things do for the spring spruce up.

Emily had been forced to spend Monday quietly and despite what everyone said, Abby still held herself partially responsible for what had happened. She wanted to make sure Emily had a chance to get out and have some outdoor fun later in the afternoon. The wound seemed to be healing nicely and wasn't giving her much trouble.

Abby had parked her car near the marina, intent on getting in some exercise on her lunch hour as well. She'd been spending far too many hours behind her desk.

She reached Beach Bag Books slightly winded from the brisk pace. She was surprised to see Bernadette Deasy, the owner of the bookstore, behind the counter instead of Belinda Brisbin, the part-time store manager. Abby checked her mental calendar, wondering if she'd forgotten which day of the week it was.

"Bernadette? It's nice to see you, but this isn't your regular day here, is it?" Abby asked. "Or have you changed your schedule?"

"Hey, Abby," Bernadette said. She'd been sitting on a high stool behind the counter and she alit from it with the grace of the dancer she was. "No, you're right. Ordinarily I'd be teaching at the dance studio in Friday Harbor on Tuesdays, but it's closed for renovations. I decided to take this golden opportunity to catch up on some paperwork and ordering for the store. And Belinda's been wanting some time off, so it worked out just right. How are you, Abby? I haven't seen you for a while."

"Very well, thanks. Just busy as usual. And you?"

"In a good place," Bernadette said with a wide smile and a rhythmical nod of her head. "My dance classes are full to overflowing and I'm having a great time with the children—even a few adults."

"You look great," Abby said, narrowing her eyes. "You look happy. Very happy," she said, drawing the words out. "Is there something else going on with you?"

"Well, since you asked," Bernadette said, looking at Abby coyly, "one of the adults taking my class is a hockey player from the mainland. He's with one of the minor league teams. His coach recommended he take a ballet class to increase his flexibility, and since he works in Friday Harbor, he ended up in my class. He's a great guy and we've been seeing one another—socially."

"Bernadette," Abby teased. "I do believe you're blushing. Is this the same Bernadette who vowed she was through with dating and romance and anything to do with it forever?"

Bernadette had come to Sparrow Island several years back after a very painful divorce. She had been hurt and betrayed, and as a consequence, she'd completely lost her faith in love. She'd done a lot of healing since that time, but she'd still steadfastly refused to date, though it certainly was not from the lack of invitations.

"Famous last words," Bernadette said with a laugh. "We're taking it slow, but I really enjoy his company. His name is Lawrence Griffin and he's—well, he's just very nice, Abby. He treats me with a lot of respect, and he's a great listener. I mean he really listens when we talk, Abby. Can you imagine that?"

"Well, I'd say he's a lucky fellow to have you to talk with, Bernadette. It's nice to see you so happy."

"Thanks," Bernadette said. "Now I'm sure you didn't come in here to inquire about my fledgling forays into dating. What can I get for you today?"

"I'm looking for a good book on the Salish tribes. It's for a young boy, but I think he's probably a pretty advanced reader. I'd like something with good illustrations. What do you have in stock?"

"Come on over here," Bernadette said, "I'll show you. I've got three or four good ones."

Abby made her selection, then asked for Bernadette's recommendations for books for Emily and Nicholas. Abby chose one about river otters for Emily and an insect book for Nicholas. The others Bernadette recommended all featured pets, and Abby remembered the yearning in Emily's voice as she'd told her how she and Nicholas longed to have a pet.

Abby was of the opinion that in most cases having a pet was good for a child. It helped them to be empathetic to other creatures, and it taught them responsibility. Not to mention pets could be dear friends. Nancy and Zack had always had pets growing up. In fact, Nancy had been one of the masterminds behind getting Mary together with Finnegan. Abby wondered why Nancy wouldn't let the children have a pet. Or was it Benjamin who objected?

Abby checked her watch and decided she had a little time to browse. Bernadette carried mostly best-sellers that would appeal to a vacationer's quest for a beach read. She'd also set up a "local interest" corner where she displayed a nice assortment of books on local history, tour books for the area, wildflowers of the San Juans, orcas and some birding books.

As she was walking by one of the tables, a photograph on one of the book jackets caught her eye. It was two hands, one in a fist, the other outstretched and held perpendicular. She picked it up and discovered it was a beginner's book on American Sign Language. She smiled to herself and carried her find to the register.

"I'm so happy to have found this," she told Bernadette, holding out the ASL book. "I can't believe you have it."

"I always have one of these in stock," Bernadette told her. "It was my deal with Aunt Cres."

"Aunt Cres?" Abby repeated.

"Yes, my Aunt Crescent," Bernadette said, tilting her head. "You don't know this story?"

"I don't think so," Abby said.

"No," Bernadette said, "I guess you wouldn't. You were still in New York when I first moved here and opened the store. Well, here's the condensed version. My grandparents were old hippies. Except I guess back in those days they would have said beatniks or something. They had three children. My mother was Luna, my uncle's name is Thor, and I had an aunt named

Crescent. My uncle's the only one living. I always tell him it could have been worse, he could be my Uncle Pluto or something." She laughed as she punched some keys on the cash register.

"And what does your Aunt Crescent have to do with the ASL book?" Abby prompted.

"It was my Aunt Cres who left me the money to open the store. We shared a deep love for books. She always read to me when I was little, except Aunt Cres had been profoundly deaf since birth, so she 'read' to me in ASL," Bernadette said. She held up her left hand and formed what Abby thought of as a V-for-victory sign with her right and raked it across her palm.

"I take it that's the sign for *read*," Abby said.

"Yep, some of ASL is almost like pantomiming the action, but other signs are more arbitrary constructions."

"So, do I take this to mean that you know ASL?" Abby asked.

"Sure," Bernadette shrugged.

Abby laughed. She told Bernadette about the Parkers and about how she'd been asking all around trying to find someone who knew sign language.

"Well, I'm your woman," Bernadette said. "Strange how these things come together sometimes, isn't it? It's a lucky happenstance, your coming in today."

"Ah, Bernadette," Abby said. "I don't think it's happenstance at all."

Bernadette smiled. "A few years ago I might have argued with that, but now I'm with you. In any case, I'd be happy to go with you to visit Mrs. Parker. It would have to be after closing time. I'm kind of tied down here for the next few days with Belinda away."

"There's no hurry," Abby said. "We'll find a time that works. As a matter of fact, I already met Mrs. Parker briefly. She reads lips and we got by pretty well."

"That's good," Bernadette said, "though there's some things that are difficult to get through lipreading. And if you want to tell her about the island, there will be a lot of proper names that will likely need to be spelled out. Course you can take care of that by carrying a little notepad and writing it out. But anyway I'd love to meet her. I miss Aunt Cres and it's been a long while since I've had anyone to sign with. It'll make me think of her. That's the reason I have the book," she nodded toward Abby's bag. "I promised her I'd always keep ASL books in stock. Aunt Cres thought the whole world should learn to sign and not just because she was deaf. She said people ought to look at one another when they were speaking."

"Excellent point," Abby said. She picked up her bag of books and told Bernadette she'd call her about arranging a time to visit Ellie Parker. She was thinking that her last visit had seemed a little strained, but she hadn't been expected, and she'd interrupted Ellie in the middle of a task. She hoped that was all it was.

She went out the door and glanced at her watch again. She had a sandwich, an apple and a bottle of water in her bag and headed for the park to eat while she took a few minutes to study the ASL book.

She'd just found a nice shady spot and settled in when she heard someone call her name. She looked up to see Ana Dominguez approaching, her long peasant skirt flowing out around her and catching on the gentle breeze.

"Ana," Abby called, "how are you?"

"I'm well," Ana answered, "I was just on the way to Mary's

shop to bring her and Candace some things Ida and I collected last weekend to use in their arrangements—cones and pods and such things. Are you off today?"

"No, I'm just on my lunch hour. I had a few minutes left and decided to eat out here rather than at my desk."

"I don't blame you. Who can resist this beautiful spring day?" Ana said. "What are you reading there?"

Abby showed her the book and told her about the Parkers.

"Yes, Juan has told me about John. He's worked with him some at the Medical Center," Ana said. "Juan says he's even more skilled than many of the doctors he's worked with, and is a very nice man. He really likes him."

"Well, Juan's been a nurse at the Medical Center for a long time. He's worked with a lot of doctors, so I'd say that's high praise."

"Yes, and now I have something to admire John Parker for as well."

"What's that?" Abby asked.

"He's an artist, as I found out this morning. I was in Friday Harbor delivering one of my wall hangings and some of Wilma's baskets to the craft co-op. There was a beautiful chessboard in the window and I later learned it was John's. I can tell you, it caused quite a stir."

"In what way?" Abby asked. "Rick told me he does beautiful work, but how did it cause a stir?"

"There was a man there trying to take pictures of it," Ana said. "Cecily Denning—you know her, she runs the co-op—told him there was no photography of the artwork allowed. You know the pattern and design is part of the artistry in these things, and sometimes people take pictures to steal the designs. So then he started asking questions about the artist, and when Cecily said the artist wanted to remain anonymous, the man got upset."

"Why?" Abby asked.

Ana shrugged. "I don't know. But Cecily held firm about it, and the man ended up buying the chessboard. She had a pretty price on it, too, but he didn't blink an eye. Just plunked down his credit card. I think John will be happy with what he got for it."

"That's good then," Abby offered.

"Yeah," Ana agreed. "I didn't know it was John's at the time. The whole thing seemed kind of strange. It was more like the man was after information about John rather than about the chessboard."

"Strange," Abby agreed.

"Cecily was thrilled, though. She's only had the chessboard in the window for a couple of days. She's hoping John will bring in more. Well, you get back to your lunch and your book, Abby. *Caminata en sol*," she added—her signature good-bye phrase.

"You walk in sunshine, too, Ana," Abby said with a smile.

Abby pondered what Ana had said about the incident with the chessboard. She wondered if the man really had been more interested in John Parker the man, than in his artwork. More likely he'd just been embarrassed about getting caught trying to steal a design and made a fuss about something else to divert attention.

She sighed and turned her attention back to the ASL book. She finished her sandwich and used the water bottle to prop the book open, trying to position her hands to sign some of the words. She felt awkward. This wasn't easy.

The alarm on her watch went off, signaling that she'd used up her lunch hour. She gathered her things and marched on toward where she'd left her car parked. As she neared the marina she caught sight of a woman she thought was Nancy sitting at one of the outside tables near the entrance to the snack bar and sundry shop. She started to call out, but then realized the breeze coming off the water would carry her voice in the wrong direction and Nancy wouldn't hear her. She'd wait until she got closer.

Yes, it was definitely Nancy, but then Abby noticed there was a man sitting at the table with her. He had his back to Abby, but something about him looked familiar. He and Nancy appeared to be deep in conversation. When she got closer still she saw that Nancy appeared to be crying. Abby watched as she dabbed at her eyes with a tissue. The man turned slightly as he leaned in to speak to her. It was John Parker.

Abby saw they had food containers and beverage cups in front of them. She wondered if perhaps they'd run into one another at lunchtime. Maybe Nancy was more upset about Emily's injury than she was letting on. In any case, Abby felt she'd be butting in if she approached them, as this looked like a serious conversation. She remembered how good Parker had been with Nancy at the Medical Center. Maybe he'd be helpful to her now as well. She decided she'd ask Nancy about it later.

She got into her car and drove back to the museum and worked steadily for a couple of hours. About midafternoon she began neatening her desk. She still had to enter data into her computer from the annual counts for four different species of birds, but she could work on that at home after the children were in bed. She'd promised Emily and Nicholas that she would join them on the outing Mary had planned to feed the ducks down near the ferry slip. Mary's wheelchair could make it all the way down to the water's edge there. This was one of the kids' favorite activities, and she did not want to miss it. She also wanted to take this opportunity to do a little water-fowl education with the kids as well.

When she and Mary were growing up, they'd often gone

down to the water with a bag full of stale bits of bread and crackers to feed to the birds. Now Abby knew it was the equivalent of feeding them fast food. Terrible for their health and so addictive the birds often changed their behavior, becoming aggressive toward one another as they scrambled to get to humans who might give them more of these filling, but non-nutritional treats. Even feeding them small amounts of cracked corn gave Abby pause, but the waterfowl down around the ferry slip had long ago become accustomed to being fed handouts by people, so the damage had already been done, and the cracked corn was certainly better than a lot of things people threw out for them.

On the drive home Abby thought again of Nancy and how distressed she'd looked when she'd seen her at noon. She was worried about her. She repeated aloud, glad for the quiet inside her car, her favorite verse of scripture for times like these: "Do not let your hearts be troubled. Trust in God; trust also in me" (John 14:1).

Back at Mary's, she parked in the driveway and hurried into the house. Emily and Nicholas were chattering away and Nancy was gathering up a bag of just-in-case jackets. Mary was packing a snack for the humans.

"Good," Abby said, "I was afraid I was late. I didn't want to miss going to see those ducks!"

"We're going now," Nicholas proclaimed. "We're gonna feed ALL the ducks, not just the white ones. Emily likes the white ones, but Grandma says all the ducks are hungry."

"All the ducks are hungry," Abby said. "But you know, they have plenty to eat right where they live, and we're only going to feed them a little bit of cracked corn as a treat. And anyway, it's okay if Emily likes the white ones best, right? As long as they all get a treat."

Nicholas stuck out his lower lip and frowned as if mulling this one over. "Yeah!" he announced finally, then leaned over to whisper to Abby, "I like the *gween* ones."

"Me too," Abby whispered back.

"What's everyone been up to today?" Abby asked as she pried two batteries out of the charger plugged into the outlet by the kitchen table. She wanted to make sure her camera didn't die on her during this photo-op, but she also wanted to make certain she was doing her part to watch the children this time and not distracted with the camera as she'd been on Sunday. She grabbed the snack bag Mary had packed and followed Nancy out to put things into the van.

"What about you, Nancy?" Abby asked. "What did you do with your day?"

"Well, let's see, while Mom was having her fun time with the kids, she urged me to go do a little shopping I'd mentioned I wanted to do while I was here, so I took her up on her offer."

"Great," Abby said, "Did you run into anyone you know while you were out and about?"

"Yes," Nancy said. "I did. I saw a couple of people from high school and I saw Terza Choi. She was sweeping off the front porch at the Bird Nest. I chatted with her a few minutes, and then, let's see, there was someone else—"

Abby was relieved. She hadn't been trying to trap Nancy. She'd simply thought if she asked an open-ended question, she might have more success in finding out what was troubling her. She was fully expecting Nancy to tell her about her talk with John Parker.

"I did see someone else—William Jansen. He was out taking pictures of some of the big sailboats coming into the marina."

"So, you were at the marina?" Abby asked.

"Yes, I grabbed some lunch there," Nancy said. "I can't tell you how nice it was to be out with no kids and no place to rush to."

"Sounds like you enjoyed yourself," Abby said.

"I did," Nancy said.

"That's good," Abby said. Had her eyes deceived her? No, she was sure it was Nancy she'd seen having lunch, or at the very least sitting at the same table, with John Parker. And she definitely had not looked like she was enjoying herself. She'd looked miserable. Why would she fail to mention that? Abby thought about telling her she'd seen her there and asking her about it directly, but she held back. Surely Nancy had her reasons for leaving out that part of her day.

She glanced at her watch. She'd invited Bobby and Dustin to go along on the outing to feed the ducks. The boys would be arriving any moment if they intended to come along. Then as if her thoughts had summoned them, she heard the boys' voices.

"Hey," Bobby said as Abby stepped outside the garage to greet them. "We're going to ride our bikes on down to the slip. We'll meet you there. Dustin can only stay a little while."

"Okay," Abby said. "We'll see you in a few minutes."

There was much excitement and chatter as they all got into the van and headed toward Green Harbor. But Abby was watching Nancy closely, and it seemed to her Nancy's cheerfulness was forced.

When they arrived, Nicholas was crestfallen that there were no ducks in sight.

"Don't worry, Nicholas," Abby said. "Let's just go down to the water and enjoy ourselves. There are plenty of things to look at. You might see some little fish, and there are interest-ing rocks and plants."

"Okay," Nicholas said, but his bottom lip kept its pucker.

Abby knew as soon as they got down to the water's edge a scout bird would appear, and soon they'd be rich, perhaps too rich, with both waterfowl and shore birds hoping for a bit of the action.

Sure enough, as soon as they were close enough to hear the water's soft lap against the rock on the shore, the first gull swooped down.

Abby threw a single kernel of corn from her vest pocket up onto a nearby rock. The gull swooped down and plucked it off, then continued on an arc back into the sky.

"Wow," Nicholas said. "Wow, wow," he stamped his feet and held out both hands to Mary. "Give me some, give me some! Please!"

Mary pulled out the bag of corn and handed it over to Abby. "Aunt Abby's in charge of that. She'll show you how to do it."

Abby opened the bag and put one kernel in Nicholas' out-stretched hand. "Now, just wait patiently. In a few minutes more birds will start to come."

"How do they know to come here?" Emily asked.

"Well, birds have their language too. We just don't under-stand it. You know, that's one of the things I've been working on for just about my whole life, Emily. Trying to figure out how birds communicate. Lots of animals have a kind of language, and researchers like me study to see if we can come to understand it, but we have a lot to learn yet."

"How would birds communicate? They can't talk," Emily said, wrinkling up her nose.

"No, but they can chirp, and sing and flap their wings and tilt their tails and make lots of other gestures," Abby said.

"Kind of like, ASL," Bobby said. "Hey, Dustin, what's the sign for *duck*?"

"Wait, Dustin, let me try," Abby said.

She used two fingers and her thumb to make a bird's beak and held it near her mouth. "Is this it, do I have it right?"

"Yeah," Dustin said. "This is bird," he said, using only one finger to form the beak, "and when you use two fingers, it's a duck. How'd you know?"

"I got a book on ASL from a friend of ours who owns the bookstore up the street there. And it turns out she knows how to sign. She's very eager to meet your grandmother."

Dustin again looked hesitant. "I'll tell her," he said finally.

"Dustin," Nancy said. "I understand you moved here from Florida. That's where we're from. I live in Tampa. Where did you live?"

"Vero Beach, Florida," Dustin said.

"Oh, I know Vero Beach," Nancy said. "A good friend of mine moved there a couple of years ago and we've gone over to visit them. It's beautiful there. In fact, my friend has a son about your age. Where did you go to school?"

"School?" Dustin repeated, frowning.

Abby saw him tense. She wondered if all this adult attention was making him uncomfortable. Perhaps he was shy.

"Yes, your elementary school," Nancy said. "Which school did you go to in Vero Beach? Maybe you knew Scotty. Scotty Abbott is my friend's son's name."

"I . . . I was homeschooled then" Dustin said. "My grandmother taught me at home."

"Oh my," Nancy said, "that's a big commitment."

Just then Nicholas caught sight of a teal swimming over and Abby went into teaching mode. "Now wait until he gets closer," she told him. "And throw the piece of corn out into the water as close as you can get it to him, otherwise it will sink before he has a chance to get it."

She gave Nicholas a little assistance with his aim, and he and Emily both squealed with delight as the duck gobbled up the corn and cruised away.

In a short time the teal was joined by other ducks. Abby went around rationing out kernels for the children to throw. Dustin was standing with his back to her down at the water's edge.

"Dustin, would you like some corn to feed them?" she called.

He didn't turn around. He was staring out at the water, watching and laughing at the ducks' antics. She waited a moment and repeated the question a little louder. Still he didn't respond.

"Dustin," Bobby said, nudging his friend and jerking a thumb back in her direction, "Abby's talking to you."

Dustin looked around, seeming surprised, then came over to take the corn she offered. She wondered if perhaps Dustin might have some hearing difficulties himself. She watched him closely for a few minutes as he interacted with the other children, but he seemed to have no trouble hearing them.

When the bag of corn was gone Nicholas was greatly disappointed. "But they're still hungry," he protested.

"They won't go hungry," Abby said, "I promise. They'll just have to work a little harder for their food, and that's a good thing for ducks."

"People too," Mary said. "But I think we've worked pretty hard today, so let's have the snack I brought for us, okay?"

After Bobby and Dustin helped Nancy spread out the blanket Mary had packed, the kids settled in for crackers and cheese, fruit and juice. Bobby began telling Nancy about how he and Dustin shared so many interests and how they planned to do some study on their own this summer.

"That's great," Nancy said. "That shows real initiative. What do you plan to study?"

Abby had to suppress a smile as Bobby told her, with all seriousness, "Well, Dustin here is the Native American specialist. I myself specialize more in biology and aviation."

"I see," Nancy said, and Abby saw that she, too, was biting her lip in order to maintain the expected amount of gravitas in her answer. "Well, Dustin," she said, "being a Native American specialist *and* a former Floridian, you must know a lot about the Seminole."

"Yes," Dustin said, "they're an interesting tribe."

"I especially like how they construct their houses," Nancy said.

"Yes, the wigwams," Dustin said.

"I think they call them chickees, is that right?" Nancy said.

"Oh yeah," Dustin said. "That's right. I . . . I didn't really study that tribe that much. We . . . we didn't live in Vero Beach, Florida, for very long."

Abby wondered if perhaps Bobby had overplayed his friend's expertise when it came to Native American studies. She didn't want him to feel he was being quizzed, so she tried to gently move the conversation in another direction.

"Where did you live before you moved to Florida, Dustin?" she asked.

"Mt. Pleasant, Michigan," he answered immediately. "They have the Ojibway tribe there."

"How long did you live there?" Abby asked.

"We lived there, I think, two years," Dustin said. "Yeah, Mount Pleasant, Michigan, two years. Then we moved to Vero Beach, Florida."

Abby noted his repetition of both the city and the state almost as if he'd memorized the information. And perhaps he had. It sounded like Dustin and his family had moved around quite a bit. Maybe that's the way he kept it straight.

He was staring down glumly at his juice box, and Abby was afraid the gaff over the Seminole house had upset him. She decided to ask him an open-ended question that would give him a chance to share. "Well, tell me, Dustin," she said, "what is your very favorite tribe?"

"Well," he said, considering, "I don't know if I'd say they're my favorite, but I really like the Nipmuc. Their name means fresh water people, and they were known for taking really good care of their land."

"That's very admirable, indeed," Abby said. "I know a little about the Nipmuc. Aren't they from around Massachusetts, Rhode Island, Connecticut, somewhere around there? Did you live there too?"

"No, ma'am," Dustin said, a little too quickly. "I just like studying them, but we never lived in Connecticut."

He seemed relieved when his phone rang, summoning him home. He thanked them politely for the invitation and the snack and said his good-byes.

Abby watched as he jumped on his bike and pedaled toward home. She thought he'd protested a little too quickly, a little too strongly and a little too specifically about never having lived in Connecticut. Why? What reason would the boy have to lie?

CHAPTER ❧ SEVEN

THE CHILDREN WERE UP early the next morning, their inner clocks having finally adjusted to the time zone. Abby heard some discussion coming from the den as she came down the stairs.

Emily was upset at having to have her bandages changed and feeling more than a little sorry for herself.

"And I didn't even get to see the kittens," she said, on the verge of tears.

"Me neither," Nicholas chimed in, imitating Emily's sorrowful tone.

"I'm sorry, Honey," Nancy began, "but—"

"I know, I know," Emily cut in. "It's my fault for disobeying."

"I wasn't going to say that, Emily," Nancy said, pulling Emily toward her on the small sofa and stroking her hair. "But I was going to say that sometimes things just don't work out the way we want them to. And when that happens, we just have to find a way to get over it and get on to the next thing life has to offer."

Abby saw that Nancy had gotten a faraway look in her eye, and she knew Mary had seen it too.

The phone rang and Mary answered. She talked for a couple of minutes as Nancy commiserated with Emily.

Abby tuned in to Mary's end of the conversation. "That sounds very nice. Just let me check please, okay? I'll call you right back. Yes, in just a couple of minutes."

She hung up the phone and asked, "Who's ready for breakfast. I have your very favorite cereals!"

"Me!" the kids both answered in unison.

Mary started to wheel toward the door, but Abby stopped her. "Let me get it for them."

She herded the children into the kitchen and got them set up with cereal and juice and went back into the den.

"So what do you want me to tell him?" Mary was asking Nancy. She looked up as Abby came in. "That was Dad on the phone," she said. "He'd like to show the kids around the farm today, including the kittens. He sounded nearly as excited as Emily. But I didn't want to tell him yes until I'd checked with Nancy and I didn't want to say anything in front of them. I'd hate for them to be disappointed if it doesn't work out."

"Well," Nancy said, nibbling at her lip, "I don't want to reward Emily for being disobedient, but it's not often they have a chance to be with Grandpa. Am I sending mixed signals if we go? I don't know. What do you think?"

"Oh, Nancy," Mary said, "I wasn't going to say a word unless you asked, but I think Emily's learned her lesson from this. And that, after all, is the point of discipline—not punishment."

Nancy smiled and turned to Abby, "Okay, we've heard from

the doting grandmother. Maybe she's a little soft. What do you think Aunt Abby?"

"Nancy!" Abby said. "You surely can't ask me to be objective. First of all, I feel guilty about my own responsibility in this. I used bad judgment in not having Emily come with me to get the camera, so I have to share some of the blame. And second, I'm the doting great-auntie. But I think Emily has beat herself up enough about this, and you're right that it would be a terrible shame to have them miss out on this time with Dad."

Nancy shook her head smiling. "Okay, okay. Maybe I am being too harsh. I just want to make sure Emily knows you don't always get what you want in life." Abby thought she detected a slight quiver in her words, but then Nancy recovered herself and said, "So today will be explore-the-farm day. Mom, are you coming with us?"

"I think I'll take a rain check," Mary said. "Mother's working at the Visitor's Center today, and my chair can't maneuver the places you all are going to want to explore. I have a few errands. I'll take this opportunity to do those while you're with Dad. Is that okay with you?"

"It's perfectly fine," Nancy said. "Except I promised you I'd help you with the errands. Do you want to wait until I get back?"

"I'm off today," Abby said. "I can go with her. Hugo's going to the mainland on Saturday to have lunch with a donor. I told him I'd cover for him then, so he insisted I take the whole day today. I'll do errands with Mary and you can use my car."

"Perfect," Nancy said. She got up and started for the kitchen, calling out, "Who wants to go to the farm to see Grandpa Stanton today?"

Mary and Abby looked at one another and grinned as the squeals from the kitchen echoed up the hallway.

"CLEARLY, SOMETHING'S WRONG," Mary said to Abby as she turned out of the driveway and headed for Green Harbor. "I'm very worried, Abby."

"Tell me why you're worried," Abby asked, more to see if Mary had noticed the same things she had than to try to convince her otherwise.

"Well, for one thing I've noticed that when Benjamin calls, the children each talk to him for a long time, but once Nancy gets on the phone with him, it seems all business, very short and, I must say, seemingly abrupt."

"Maybe you're reading too much into that, Mary," Abby said. "I mean, maybe it's something as simple as her being concerned about using up her cell phone minutes."

Mary shook her head. "She does it when she's on my phone, too, and she knows very well I have an unlimited calling plan. She's the one who urged me to get it so we could talk as long as we want without running up long distance bills. Don't gloss over this, Abby, I know you've noticed it too."

Abby sighed. "It's true," she said, "Nancy doesn't seem quite herself. But let's not get ahead of ourselves. It's obvious that she's overworked and stressed. Maybe this little getaway will be all she needs to get back to her old self." She wondered if she should mention to Mary that she'd seen Nancy looking very distraught the previous day—and that she'd been with John Parker at the time and failed to mention it later. But she decided there was no reason to cause Mary any more worry. There had to be a good explanation, Abby was sure of it.

"I'm hoping she'll open up and talk to me while she's here,"

Mary said. "But she continues to just pretend there's nothing
wrong. I know Nancy. The more I probe, the more tight-
lipped she'll become. There are some traits from her teen years
that she hasn't left behind."

Abby nodded. "Hard as it is, Mary, I'm afraid you're just
going to have to wait until Nancy's ready to talk," she said,
then immediately realized she needed to take her own advice.
She, too, had the urge to push Nancy into spilling what was
bothering her. She seemed fragile, brittle, not characteristics
Abby would normally attribute to her. As a scientist, Abby's
instinct was that once she'd identified a problem, the next step
was to move immediately toward fixing it. But that seldom
worked with human relationships.

She stared out the window at the passing landscape and said
a quick, on-the-go prayer, which were often her most fervent
and deeply felt ones. She prayed for Nancy and for all those
who loved her that they would all find the wisdom to discover
what needed to be done to help, and be shown the right way
and the right time to act.

"Well, of course you're right, Abby," Mary said. "Just say a
prayer for me. I need patience."

"Already done," Abby said.

"Do you think it's too early to pay a call on Mrs. Parker?"
Mary asked.

Abby looked at her watch. "I wouldn't think so, she said. "I
mean, she had to get Dustin off to school, so I'm sure she's up.
I feel a little strange about just popping in on her without at
least calling, though. I should have gotten their number from
Dustin, then I could have texted her, I suppose."

"I don't even know how to do that," Mary said.

"It's not that difficult," Abby said. "But I'm slow as

Christmas at it. I feel all thumbs on that little tiny keypad. I see these young kids like Dustin doing it, and their little thumbs are moving so fast I'm afraid they're going to snap right out of their saddle joints. It takes me forever to get one sentence, and I'm lost when it comes to some of the shortcut spelling and abbreviations."

"Well, anyway, I think we should risk a quick visit," Mary said. "We'll only stay a minute."

Abby gave in. There was no stopping Mary when it came to social engineering.

As it turned out, Elise Parker was not only up, but she was already outside, planting flowers along the front walk of the house when Mary and Abby pulled up. She jumped up when she saw the van approaching, frowning at the unfamiliar vehicle and looking like she might bolt for the house. Then she spotted Abby in the front seat and her expression relaxed, but only a little.

"The driveway's gravel," Mary said. "I may need Finnegan to help me a little. You go ahead and I'll be out in just a second."

Abby did as instructed and walked over to greet Ellie. She was polite, but not particularly warm, and again, Abby had the feeling she was enduring rather than enjoying the unexpected visit.

Mary wheeled over and introduced herself. Abby thought she detected a change in Ellie Parker's demeanor when Mary admired the flowers she was planting.

"This is a beautiful selection," Mary said. "You've chosen well. You'll have something blooming all summer long and into fall."

Mary was careful, Abby noted, to make sure she was looking at Ellie Parker when she spoke. But when she said, "You'll want to make sure the Red Columbine gets plenty of water; they're very thirsty little things," Ellie Parker only frowned.

Mary repeated herself, exaggerating her lip movements, but still Ellie looked blank and shrugged.

Mary held up a finger and dug in the pocket on the side of her chair and brought out a pad and pen and wrote.

Ellie Parker's face brightened. "Oh yes, I know," she said, "but thanks for the tip."

Mary continued to admire the plantings, asking about this one and that. They talked on about light, soil and drainage, and Abby saw that Ellie Parker had warmed up considerably.

"You certainly know your flowers," Ellie said to Mary.

"She should. She's a florist," Abby said. She told her about Island Blooms, writing down the name and drawing a rudimentary map of where it was located.

"Oh yes," Ellie said. "I've been by there. You have beautiful things in the window."

"Thank you. I'm glad you think so," Mary said.

"As you can probably tell, I really love flowers," Ellie said, gesturing at her plantings.

"Then we definitely have something in common," Mary said. "And I have another friend I'd love to introduce you to. Her name is Goldie Landon. She has a greenhouse here on the island filled with wonderful specimens, everything from exotic orchids to common field flowers."

Again Ellie seemed to draw back, but finally she said, "I'd love to see it sometime." She looked over at Finnegan, who had been sitting at alert by Mary's chair while all the flower talk was going on. "This must be the dog Dustin was telling me so much about. He's so well trained. Some of my deaf friends have companion dogs, so I know not to pet him, but he is a beautiful animal."

"He's a real blessing," Mary said. Abby noted that Mary was looking away and tapped her shoulder. Mary looked up and then seemed to realize she'd had her head turned, and therefore her words, directed at Finnegan. "A real blessing," she repeated, looking directly at Ellie.

Abby decided this was a good place to end the visit. She didn't want to overstay their welcome and lose the progress they'd made. "Well, we'll let you get back to your planting," she said and got a hard look from Mary.

Ellie Parker walked them back toward the van. She was clearly curious about the vehicle, and Mary opened the door and had her look inside.

"Dustin's told me about this too," Ellie said. "He is so impressed with it."

"So am I," Mary said. "I've never gotten over being impressed with it. I told Dustin I'd love to drive you two out to see the Sparrow Island Nature Museum one day. I don't know if he told you about that."

"Yes," Ellie Parker said. "Yes, he's told me about it, several times. And again, that's very kind of you to offer. But right now we need to just get settled in. It's not a good time. Perhaps later on."

Abby rummaged in her bag and gave her a business card with her phone numbers and also a brochure from the museum. Ellie glanced at it and said, "Yes, this is the kind of thing Dustin loves. Maybe we'll take you up on your invitation sometime soon."

"Why did you rush us?" Mary asked, as she backed down the driveway. "I thought things were going really well."

"They were," Abby said. "I didn't want to overstay our welcome. She's—well, as you can see—she's a bit skittish. I don't know, maybe it's the disability or maybe she's just naturally an introvert. And let's face it, Mary, you don't understand even the concept of being an introvert. I didn't want to overwhelm her."

"Okay, you're probably right," Mary said with a sigh. "I was just enjoying talking flowers with her. And I really want to get her out to visit Goldie's greenhouse. I think the two of them would really hit it off, don't you?"

"I suspect they would," Abby said, happy to see Mary had gotten her mind off Nancy for a while. "But let's take it slow and let Mrs. Parker warm up to us a little before we start trying to bring in the rest of Sparrow Island. I sense a reserve in her, in the whole Parker family in fact, even little Dustin."

"Really?" Mary said. "He seems like a very friendly little boy to me. And you and Nancy met John Parker on Sunday at the Medical Center. I thought you said he seemed very nice. Nancy said he was *very* helpful and understanding."

"He was—he is," Abby said, her mind again flashing to the image of Nancy sitting with John Parker at the picnic table at the marina. The more she tried to remember the scene, the more convinced she was that they were there together. She was sure Nancy had been crying, and she remembered that John Parker had leaned in closer to her. Had he reached across to touch her hand or had Abby's own concern for Nancy painted that part into her memory?

She thought back to Bernadette's comment about her new beau Lawrence: He really listens. That was certainly a very attractive quality in a man, especially to a woman who was feeling underappreciated.

Nancy was a woman of character; Abby had no doubts about that. She would never do anything to betray Benjamin. But if trouble was already brewing, it would certainly be unwise for Nancy to put herself into a vulnerable position.

"Abby?" Mary's sharp question jolted Abby out of her reverie. "Where'd you go? That's the third time I've said your name."

"Sorry," Abby said, only then noticing they were parked in front of the Green Grocer. "I was daydreaming, I guess. I was a thousand miles away."

"It looked like light-years," Mary said. "Is there something wrong?"

"No, no, I was just thinking about the Parkers, that's all," she said. Which was true enough. One Parker in particular. "Didn't you think it strange when Dustin was talking about all the places they've lived? It was as if he'd rehearsed the story. And then that quick denial about never living out East. What was that all about do you think? It was almost as if he thought I'd caught him at something. I don't know, Mary, there just seems to be something off about that family."

"Now, Abby," Mary warned, "let's not get off on one of your flights of imagination. I'll admit it's true that I don't understand introverts, but you, my dear sister, find mystery and intrigue everywhere you look." She reached over to pat Abby's shoulder.

"I don't find it so much as it seems to find me," Abby said, unbuckling her seat belt. "Besides, it's hard to go against years of training. What kind of researcher would I be if I weren't observant? I notice inconsistencies, that's all."

"Observation is all well and good, Abby," Mary said. "But

people aren't always consistent, nor are they always predictable. You can't know what goes on in people's hearts and minds just by observing them."

Abby smiled, thinking of the whole scenario she'd just imagined about what had surely been a totally innocent lunch. Nancy and John Parker sharing a table in the wide-open public area of the marina. Perhaps he saw Nancy crying and went over to say something to her, assuming as Abby herself had, that she was still upset over Emily's injury.

It was all perfectly proper.

INSIDE THE Green Grocer Abby observed a line had formed at the bakery counter.

"That can only mean one thing," Mary said. "Kari Dryson is making her Kari's Creams. Oh, Abby, get in line and let's pick up a few. Some for us and we'll take a couple by the Visitor's Center for Mom to take home. She and Dad both love them so."

It was worth the time Abby had to stand in line to see her mother's face when she opened the bakery box and peered inside a few minutes later.

"You almost didn't get them," Abby told her. "Mary's waiting in the van and I was rushing. I guess I didn't look where I was going, but that fellow out there ran into me as I was coming in and he was leaving. I nearly dropped the box."

Her mother looked to where Abby pointed out the large paned windows on the front of the center to where a man was pacing beside a car as he talked on a cell phone. He looked to be perhaps in his midfifties, with salt-and-pepper hair and a stout build. He was obviously stressed about something.

"Yes, I had sort of a strange conversation with him," her

mother said. "He brought in this chessboard. It was a beautiful thing, all inlaid wood in this extravagant pattern. He wanted to know who on the island made these. I told him the only one I knew who did any inlaid work like that was Rick, but I didn't think that was his. He got sort of snippy with me about it."

"Snippy?" Abby said.

"Well, that's not right," Ellen amended. "Just sort of curt. It seemed like he was really intent on knowing more about it, and he wasn't happy I couldn't help him."

"Did he get it at the craft co-op in Friday Harbor?" Abby asked.

"Well, yes. How did you know?"

"It's John Parker's," Abby answered. "I heard from Ana that the man who bought it was really interested in finding the artist."

Abby watched as the man talked, seeming more and more agitated as he paced.

"Shall I go out and tell him whose work it is?" Ellen asked.

"Let's not do that," Abby said. "He could be one of those art poachers—gallery owners looking for local artisans to exploit. In any case, I don't think John Parker's interested in any notoriety. He made that clear."

"Well, he's certainly entitled to his privacy then," Ellen said, carefully closing the lid on her precious pastries.

NANCY RETURNED with the children in early afternoon. They came tumbling in the door, each babbling away about everything they'd seen at the farm.

"And we saw *a-pac-kees*," Nicholas said, stretching himself up on his tiptoes to thrust the unfamiliar word out of his mouth.

"Alpacas, yes we did," Nancy said. "Grandpa took us out to one of the farms to see the alpacas," she said, enunciating carefully and looking at Nicholas.

"Uh-huh," he said, shaking his head in agreement so that his blond curls shook. "We saw big al-pa-cas," he said, speaking slowly to try to get his tongue around the word. "And baby ones. They're squishy." He held both hands up and made squeezing motions.

"Grandma," Emily said, "the farmer said they make yarn like you knit with out of the fur. Do you have that kind?"

"No, I don't believe I do right now, Emily," Mary said, "but I've used it before, and it's beautiful and soft and makes very cozy scarves and mittens. I'm so glad you all had fun today."

"We all had fun," Nancy said. "Including Grandpa. I think he'll be ready for a nap this afternoon. And you know what, Mom? This has gotten Emily excited about learning to knit. But it's been so long since I've tried it I'm not sure I'd even remember how. She's wondering if you'd teach her, and maybe give me a refresher course too?"

"Oh, I'd love to," Mary said. "That would be fun."

"Great," Nancy said. "I think I'll go into town to In Stitches and pick up some yarn and needles. Is it okay if the kids stay here with you? Nicholas will probably want to go down for a short nap, or at least some quiet time."

"Well, of course, Nancy," Mary said. "But you know I've got plenty of yarn and extra needles that Emily can have in my craft room."

"I know," Nancy said, shrugging on a jacket. She pulled her long hair out of her collar and checked herself in the mirror by the coat rack. "But I'd like to get alpaca yarn. The kids got such a kick out of seeing them. I'll knit each of them a small throw pillow for their bed since we don't have need of scarves and mittens in Tampa. It'll be a nice souvenir. Plus I'll get to see Ana."

"Okay then," Mary said. "The kids can help me make a salad for dinner. Sergeant Cobb is bringing over salmon steaks for the grill. How does that sound to everybody?"

"Great!" Emily said licking her lips. "I love salmon steaks. Daddy makes them at home for special occasions and he makes a yummy sauce to go on them."

"Yeah, I like salmon steaks," Nicholas said, imitating Emily and rubbing his belly.

Nancy, who was standing just behind him, shook her head slowly and scissored her hands in front of her, mouthing, *No, he doesn't.*

"Well, I'll tell you what," Mary said. "Sometimes I like salmon and sometimes I'd rather have nice crunchy fish sticks and baked french fries. I think we'll fix some of each and then we can have our choice of what we're in the mood for when we're ready to eat." She gave Nancy a wink.

"That sounds great," Nancy said, blowing her mother a kiss. "I'll be back in time to help."

"Nancy," Abby said, "I'm going into town in a few minutes to take something over to Rick DeBow. It's the repair list for the conservatory. I finally got around to doing the walk through and making the list of repairs for out there. It'll just take me a minute to go up, finish it and print it out. You want to wait and ride in with me?"

"Oh thanks, Aunt Abby, but I think I'll just take the bike. That way I can look around at my leisure and not feel like I'm holding you up. And since it looks like dinner's well in hand, I can dawdle a bit if I want. Plus, the ride will be good exercise."

"Okay then," Abby said, watching as Nancy kissed the kids and went out the door.

"I hope she gets a lot of yarn so I can make Daddy something," Emily said. "I miss Daddy."

"I miss Daddy too," Nicholas said.

"We do," Emily told him, "but I don't think Mommy does. I think she's mad at Daddy."

CHAPTER ✦ EIGHT

Wow, what are we doing, rebuilding the place?" Rick DeBow asked as Abby handed over the list of things that needed to be attended to in the conservatory.

"Not quite," Abby said, laughing. "It's not nearly as bad as it looks. I could do some of these things myself if I had the time, but I'm getting in tons of data from the annual bird counts that I have yet to finish logging in and analyzing. Plus, we have an exciting new development for the Native American multimedia booth."

"Another development?" Rick said, "We haven't even started building the thing yet."

"I know, but it's a good thing," Abby said. "We've been invited over to film at the Salish archaeological dig out near Cedar Grove Lake during their spring dig. One of Wilma Washburn's nephews is a documentary film student. He's going to film it for us to fulfill one of his class requirements, so it's all working out great. Except, of course, that while Hugo's overseeing that, I'll need to pick up some of his duties at the museum. Things are about to get very busy."

Rick leaned back against his workbench and looked over the list. Abby took that time to look around the workshop and enjoy the smell of the fresh-cut wood.

"You're right," Rick said, holding the paper up to her, "I can knock off half the list in one afternoon. Lots of little stuff."

Abby nodded. "And there's no real hurry on anything except the ones I've put an asterisk by. Those are safety issues. There's a step loose on the viewing platform, and one of the boards on the footbridge on the first loop of Trail A needs to be replaced. The rest you can do anytime you can work them into your schedule."

Rick looked up at the calendar he had tacked above his workbench. "I should be able to get to some of this early next week. I've got a few more things to do for Martin and Terza over at the Bird Nest. I think I can finish those up this week."

"That'll work fine," Abby said. She pointed to a plastic bag hanging on Rick's pegboard. It was filled with rolls of what appeared to her to be thick tape. "What in the world are these?"

"Wood veneers," Rick said, pulling the bag off the rack. He opened it up and handed her a roll. "I ordered them for John Parker for his chessboards."

Abby told him about the sensation the chessboard had caused at the co-op.

"That's great," Rick said, "I mean, not about the guy trying to steal his designs, but the fact that it sold for a good price. I know John can use the money. He's pinching pennies. I told him about this online place where I get most of my supplies for the boxes I make, and he had me order some for him. I told him he could do it direct, but he said he'd rather do it through me. I don't know why. I don't get a discount or anything, though I guess we did save a little on shipping by combining our orders."

Abby examined the tape and saw clearly now that it was very thin strips of different types of wood, so thin they could be rolled into a coil.

"Maybe his mother doesn't want to deal with the delivery people," she offered. "Mary and I were just over to their house this morning. She seems like a nice woman. And she and Mary are going to become fast friends. At least they will if Mary has anything to say about it. Mrs. Parker, Ellie, is a flower woman too."

"So, did you find someone on the island who signs then?" he asked.

"We did, but as it turns out, Ellie Parker reads lips quite well, and when we hit a snag we just used a little notepad," Abby said. "For casual conversation anyway, it worked out okay I think. Though of course you always wonder how much of the communication was lost."

"That's always true between humans, hearing loss or not, right?" Rick said.

"True," Abby said. "How'd you get so smart?"

"I hang around smart people," Rick said, smiling. "So, who on the island signs?"

"Bernadette Deasy," Abby answered.

"Bernadette from the book store? The dance teacher? She signs?" Rick asked.

"Yes, apparently she had an aunt who was deaf. She taught Bernadette," Abby said.

"Hey, I hear she's dating a hockey player," Rick said. "Do

you know who? Does he play for the Thunderbirds or the Chiefs?"

"I don't know," Abby said, laughing. "My, news does travel fast on this island, doesn't it?"

"Yep," said Rick. "I know you women get the rap about being chatterboxes and all, but believe me, when it comes to sports, we guys want to know every tiny tidbit—and every rumor too. So are you still going to try to hook up Bernadette with John's mother, even though you don't need her to translate?"

"Absolutely," Abby said. "I think it would probably be good for both of them."

"Yeah, I expect so," Rick said. "John doesn't talk much, not about personal stuff anyway. Though he'll talk about how he makes the chessboards all day long. But he did say he thought his mother was having a rough time adjusting to the move to the island."

Abby flinched. "Oh, I just hate to hear that anyone's unhappy here on Sparrow Island. We'll have to do everything we can to help smooth the way for her."

Rick looked at her, a smile playing around his lips.

"What?" Abby asked.

"I was just wondering how Sparrow Island got along all those years without you here as a booster," he said. "Even the language you use: 'We've got to smooth the way,'" he said, laughing as he put his hand flat on the workbench and moved it along. "I have this picture of you in a hard-hat, driving a big bulldozer along, plowing up any obstacle in the path to happiness on Sparrow Island."

"Oh dear heavens," Abby said. "And here I was this morning giving Mary a lecture about not being pushy. I need to take my advice and ease up."

"Don't do any such thing," Rick said. "You and Mary and folks like you, you're the heart of this island. You just keep right on smoothing the way!"

ABBY GLANCED AT HER WATCH, grateful to Henry Cobb for taking chef's duty tonight. It gave her time to run more errands. She drove to Holloway's Hardware for replacement latches for the sick-bird cages in her laboratory.

One of the birds she was taking care of at the moment was a gray jay with a broken wing. This corvid wasn't a common visitor to the San Juans, and Abby had soon found he was unusual in other ways as well. All the corvids are crafty birds, but this one had proved to be particularly talented. He'd somehow found a way to pick the hook-and-eye latch on his cage, which was loose from having been opened and closed so many times.

She and one of the volunteers had found him flying in a wobbly circle in the laboratory, his weak, half-healed wing putting him into a canted flight pattern. Along with that, he was also gaining and dropping altitude like a trick kite. It had taken them a half hour to catch him without hurting him again and get him back into the cage.

On Aaron Holloway's recommendation she purchased slider bolts to replace the old latches and checked that errand off her list. She'd just stepped out onto the sidewalk, headed for Willoughby Pharmacy, when she met up with Margaret Blackstock.

"Just so you know," Margaret said, her Brooklyn accent still much in evidence even after all the years she'd lived on Sparrow Island, "Bobby and his cohort are in there." She jerked her head toward the pharmacy. "He's a good kid, but he does talk a blue streak."

Abby smiled. "His cohort? Would that be Dustin Parker?"

"The same," Margaret said.

"Glad to hear it. I guess Dustin's being given a little more freedom. Maybe his grandmother has come around. I thought for a while I was going to have to line up character witnesses for Bobby before she'd let the boys be buddies."

"Well, my testimony would have done no good at all, I can tell you that," Margaret said. "Mrs. Parker and I got off on the wrong foot I'm afraid."

"How so?" Abby asked.

"I don't know," Margaret said, shaking her head. "When she came in to register Dustin for school she was telling me how no one—*absolutely no one*—was authorized to pick him up at school other than her or his father. I said okay, but I didn't write it on his chart. She got very annoyed until I wrote it in big black letters and underlined it. She got upset with the paperwork too. A lot of Dustin's records are missing, and she said if it was going to be this much trouble, she might just homeschool him again in the fall."

"I know they've moved a lot. It's probably difficult to keep up with everything," Abby mused.

"Yes, I expect so," Margaret said. "But then, I was trying to be extra friendly to smooth things over, and I made a comment about her being from back East and that I was too—like anybody couldn't tell. Anyhow, that really got her upset with me. It was like I'd insulted her or something. She said she wasn't from back East, that she was from the Midwest, someplace in Michigan. Maybe her accent has changed because of the hearing thing, but she sure sounds to me like she's from back East. Anyway, I felt bad about how it all went."

"I'm sure you didn't do anything wrong, Margaret. I think maybe she's just having a hard time settling in."

"Yeah, I figured as much. Or maybe she's just naturally the nervous type. In any case, I hope she lets the boys have their friendship. They're busy, inquisitive boys, those two. Peas in a pod."

"That they are," Abby said, glancing at her watch. "Good to see you, Margaret. I'd better get a move on."

As she went in the door, she mulled over what Margaret had said. Why was Elise so protective? Had Dustin been ill? The boy didn't look frail. Was she, as Margaret had offered, just the nervous type? Was she paranoid or did she have legitimate reason to be concerned?

"Hey, Abby," she heard and turned to see Bobby sitting at the soda fountain, waving furiously, Dustin beside on him the next stool.

"Well, hey, yourself," Abby said, noting the tall glasses sitting in front of each boy, "and what are you boys enjoying there?"

"Malts!" Bobby announced. "Really, really good ones. Mr. Willoughby mixed them himself."

"Indeed I did," said Ed Willoughby from behind the counter. "These boys are budding entrepreneurs. They offered to sweep my sidewalks and pick up the trash in the parking area for these malts. I'd say we got a win-win."

"I'd say so," Abby said.

"Yes," Ed said, his eyes sparkling. "I think these two young men have the job for the summer. What do you say boys, once a week?"

"Cool!" Bobby said.

"Yeah, cool," Dustin added.

"Good for all of you," Abby said. She lifted her basket. "I need to get on with my shopping."

"And I have to go in the back for supplies," Ed said, "Boys, could you give me a shout if a customer comes in?"

"Sure thing, Mr. Willoughby," Bobby said, then immediately took another long drag at his straw.

Abby went around to the next aisle and began looking over the shampoo and conditioner selections. They'd gone through a lot more than usual with the house now full. She was studying the labels, looking for some no-tear variety for the children, when she overheard Bobby say, "I can't believe school will be out tomorrow. I can't wait in one way, but I'll sort of miss it too. We were just getting to the good part in science."

"Yeah," said Dustin. "But we can study on our own. And my grandmother's going to keep up my lessons this summer. I like that better anyway because she lets me pick what I want to learn about."

"Yeah, that's way more fun," Bobby said. "You know there's a really cool science program on the PBS channel tonight, and I really, *really* want to see it—every minute of it. But I'll only get to see half. I can't believe it, but my mom's making me keep my regular school bedtime even though tomorrow's only a half day. It's not fair."

"Just be glad you have a mother," Dustin said. "I love my grandmother, but it's not the same. Trust me, just thank your lucky stars."

"What happened to your mother?" Bobby asked.

"She's gone," Dustin said, his voice flat.

"You mean gone away or do you mean she, like, died?" Bobby asked, and Abby cringed at his bluntness.

Dustin didn't reply right away, and Abby wondered if he was upset, but then he said, "Dad says I'm not supposed to talk about my mother."

"Okay," Bobby said. Abby recognized the tone and knew there was probably a shrug that went along with it. They returned to the conversation about what they intended to do with their free time all summer.

As Abby went on through the store filling her basket, she had Dustin's words rolling around in her head. Dustin had said he wasn't *supposed* to talk about his mother. That seemed an odd way to put it—not that he didn't want to talk about her. And not even that talking about her was a choice. Abby couldn't imagine what would cause a father to impose that kind of rule, especially a father who seemed as kind and understanding as John Parker.

Abby was still thinking about Dustin and wondering about the situation with his mother as she walked back to her car. As she got closer to Island Blooms, she noticed a commotion down near the marina. She put her purchases into her car and hurried down to see what was going on.

Just as she got there she saw Duncan Grady, the harbormaster, being loaded into the back of the ambulance. John Parker, in street clothes, was climbing into the back along with the EMTs.

Abby looked over and saw Nancy standing in the crowd, wringing her hands. Abby made her way over to her. "Nancy," she said, reaching out to take hold of her niece's arm, "what's going on? What happened to Duncan?"

"I'm . . . I'm not sure," Nancy said, her voice unsteady. "He came out of his office over there," she gestured vaguely. "His eyes were bulging and he was gasping," she went on, her own hands fluttering to her throat, "I was sitting up there," she pointed in the direction of the sundry shop. "I was talking to John Parker and the next thing I know, he's running down here and Mr. Grady's on the ground and John is doing something to his throat. I don't know. It was all so quick and scary."

Just then Joe Blackstock walked over. As Abby was talking to him, Nancy went over to the picnic table to sit.

"Duncan had some kind of allergic reaction. Pretty severe one by the look of it. He couldn't get any air at all," Joe said. "That new fella there,"—he nodded toward the ambulance as the EMT closed the door and they began to move away—"he did an emergency trach on him, right here on the spot. He told the EMTs he was in anaphylactic shock and to give him epinephrine. He was giving out orders like he was a doctor himself. Duncan's lucky that particular fella happened to be here at that very minute."

"I'd say so," Abby said, as a million questions whirled in her mind.

"Somebody over there," Joe continued, nodding his head toward the cluster of people who were now dispersing, "said he was a new physician's assistant over at the Medical Center." Joe shook his head. "That was some pretty fancy work for a physician's assistant, or else I don't understand what their duties are. It was like the man came prepared for it. He had a razor blade, a little section of tape and a piece of flattened drinking straw all in a little credit-card-sized pouch in his wallet. I held Duncan still for him. He had the whole thing done in no time flat. I saw this a couple of times back when I was in Korea. This guy's obviously done this before. He's good."

Abby turned to check on Nancy and was surprised to see that she'd grabbed her bags and was wrestling her bike from the rack. Abby hurried over, "Nancy, are you okay?"

"Yes," Nancy said. "Just a little shaken up is all. I hope Mr. Grady will be okay. I'll...I'll see you back at home." And with that she jumped on to the bike and started to pedal away.

Abby started to call after her, but decided better of it. Maybe she needed to be alone to calm down.

But, Abby resolved, there would be a conversation about this, and sooner rather than later.

CHAPTER ❧ NINE

Wʜᴇɴ ᴀʙʙʏ ɢᴏᴛ ʙᴀᴄᴋ ᴛᴏ her car, she pulled out her cell phone and called Rev. Hale. He'd want to know immediately about Duncan, though she suspected he'd already heard, or seen for himself if he was at home or at the church.

Sure enough, when Patricia came on the line she said he was already on his way to the Medical Center.

Abby sat still for a few minutes and prayed for Duncan and for all those who had been distressed by witnessing what had happened. She also said a prayer of thanksgiving that John Parker had been there to help.

As she began the drive home, she wondered what Nancy had been doing there talking to John Parker—again, but she refused to let herself speculate about it.

She was more curious about what Joe had said about John Parker's expertise in handling the situation. How many people went around with tracheotomy kits in their wallets? Like Joe, she was a little fuzzy about what a physician's assistant's duties included. But she did know their training was different from that of emergency medical technicians. It seemed odd that he would be giving orders to the guys accustomed to dealing with emergencies.

When she arrived home she found Mary setting the dining room table, with the somewhat inconvenient help of the children, who each seemed to hold a different view about how best to arrange the flatware. Mary quickly headed off an argument by having Nicholas fit napkin rings onto the linen napkins.

"Hi Abby, you're back," she said. "We were going to eat outside, but I was afraid it 'd get too chilly out there, especially for my little tenderfoot Floridians."

"What's a tenderfoot, Grandma?" Emily asked, pushing blonde strands of hair away from her face.

"It's someone who's new at something or who's sensitive," Mary said. "It's not a bad thing, Emily. I just meant that you all are not used to the cold."

"No," Emily agreed. "I don't like it cold, unless it snows. That's fun, but I wouldn't like it to be like that every day. Mommy doesn't like the cold either. I know. I heard her tell Dad. She likes Florida. Me, too, I like it warm like at our house."

"I like Florida," Nicholas repeated, looking up as if just tuning in to the conversation.

"Is your mommy back yet?" Abby asked.

"Not yet," Emily reported, continuing to line up the handles of the spoons and forks with precision.

Mary looked up and frowned and Abby jerked her head toward the kitchen.

"Okay, you two are doing a good job," Mary said. "I'll be right back. Just let me show Aunt Abby where the platter for the salmon is."

"What is it?" Mary asked when they were out of earshot of the children.

Abby told her about what had happened to Duncan Grady.

"Oh good heavens," Mary said, careful to keep her voice low. "Is he going to be okay?" She pressed her hand to her lips.

"I hope so," Abby said. "He looked like he was conscious when they put him in the ambulance. And Joe seemed to think John Parker got to him just in time."

"Thank God," Mary said. "How was it that John Parker happened to be there?"

"I'm not sure," Abby said, "But he seemed to know instantly what was happening with Duncan and he performed an emergency tracheotomy right there on the spot. Nancy was there in the crowd and, naturally, it upset her."

"Well, yes, I'm sure it did," Mary said. "It's upset me and I wasn't there watching. So it's John Parker to the rescue again. You say he did a tracheotomy on Duncan? The EMTs didn't do it?"

"It was already done by the time the ambulance got there," Abby said. "And, according to Joe, done expertly."

Nancy came in at that moment, her face flushed, whether from the exertion of the bike ride or because she was still upset, Abby couldn't tell. "Did you tell Mom what happened?" she asked.

"Yes, she was just telling me," Mary said, putting her finger to her lips, then pointing toward the dining room. "We don't want to upset the children."

"Poor Mr. Grady," Nancy said, not seeming to take notice of Mary's warning. "He just couldn't get a breath and he looked terrified. It was awful."

Mary looked toward the dining room where the children's

discussion about where the spoons should go started up again. "Nancy!" she said, "Honey, why don't you go upstairs and splash some water on your face."

Nancy bit her lip, then nodded and made for the stairs.

Abby went outside where Henry was constructing an elaborately built mound of fire materials in the grill consisting of small twigs, charcoal and either mesquite or hickory chips. Abby couldn't remember which Henry preferred for salmon.

"You certainly like to make a ceremony out of this, don't you?" she asked.

"I, as you well know," Henry said, "am king of the grill. I must protect my crown. Besides which, I have to do justice to the salmon I caught my very own self."

Abby told him about what had happened to Duncan.

Henry stood up straight and a series of lines stitched across his tanned forehead. "I've never heard of Duncan having any problems like that. An allergy that severe? I don't like the sound of that."

"Well, it was definitely serious," Abby said. "I'm not positive it was an allergic reaction. That was just the speculation floating around."

Henry pulled out his phone. "Mike Bennett's on patrol tonight. If he's not tied up, I think I'll have him go over to the Medical Center and find out a little more."

"I don't think there was a crime involved, Henry," Abby said.

"All the same," Henry said. "It can't hurt to find out what's what. You say this happened when?"

"Less than a half hour ago," Abby said.

She left him to his phone call and his grill preparation and went back inside. She heard Mary in the dining room still talking to the children and went upstairs to Nancy's room.

She rapped lightly on the half-open door and peeked in to find Nancy sitting in the chair in the corner of the room with her knees drawn up to her chest. She was crying.

She raised her head and saw Abby and her face crumbled. She got up and headed across to Abby, who gathered her up in a hug. Nancy began to sob.

Abby let her cry for a minute then sat her down on the end of the bed and knelt beside her. "Nancy, what's wrong? Is this about Duncan? I know it was scary, but I think he's going to be okay."

"That was upsetting," Nancy said, nodding in agreement. "Very upsetting, but it's more than that. Oh, Aunt Abby. I just ... I don't know what I'm going to do. Ben and me. I just don't know if we're going to make it." She dissolved into sobs again, and Abby had to clamp her lips together to keep from gasping.

She got up and went across to close the bedroom door, then came back to sit beside Nancy, gently rubbing her back. "What's happened, Nancy?" she asked.

"Nothing's happened exactly," Nancy said, sniffling. She leaned over to pluck a couple of tissues from the box on the nightstand. "We just, well, we can't seem to agree on anything these days. We hardly ever even see each other and when we do, we're always talking about the kids and the house and logistical things," she said, swiping at her eyes with the tissue. "It's never about us anymore—the two of us. I can barely remember what that was like."

"Oh, Nancy," Abby said, pulling her niece toward her and resting her head next to Nancy's, "I'm in no position to give marital advice, but from what I'm told this sounds like a very common problem in a marriage at your stage of life. Maybe it's like you said when you arrived; maybe you just need a few days away to get some perspective."

"It's been a few days, Aunt Abby," Nancy sniffed. "And the only perspective I have is that I've been happier here for the last few days—away from Ben—than I have been in months. What does that tell you?"

Abby chose her words carefully. "I'd say it tells me that when you're here, you're free of your normal responsibilities and you're more relaxed," she said slowly, trying to figure out how to approach the question she had to ask. "Plus, this is your home. It's natural you'd find comfort here. Nancy, tell me, how did you happen to be with John Parker when the incident with Duncan happened?"

"I saw him at the marina and we were just talking," Nancy said, pulling away from Abby. It was a slight movement, but Abby felt it.

"And yesterday?" Abby asked, careful to keep her voice soft. "I saw you yesterday, and it looked like you were having lunch together."

Nancy looked stricken. She turned to face Abby. "Please, Aunt Abby, you can't tell Mom any of this," she said, the words coming out muffled as if her throat wouldn't quite open to let them through.

"Any of what?" Abby asked, now truly concerned.

"About John Parker, or my problems with Ben, any of it. She'll be so disappointed in me."

"Oh, Nancy," Abby said soothingly. "I'm sure you haven't done anything to be ashamed of. Still you are in a vulnerable state right now, and I'm not sure it's wise for you to be seeing John Parker, even at an innocent lunch."

"Wait!" Nancy said. "You think it was like, a social thing? Aunt Abby, I was seeing John Parker for counseling. When I was talking to him at the hospital after Emily's accident, he was so helpful and he told me he's a licensed counselor. He said if I'd like to talk with him while I was here, he could maybe help me sort some things out. And he has—or at least he's given me a place to start. What did you think was going on?" Nancy demanded. "If you saw me, why didn't you just ask me about it?"

"Maybe for the same reason you didn't volunteer it," Abby said softly. "Why didn't you say where you were going?"

"I told you, Aunt Abby," Nancy said. "I don't want Mom to know. She won't understand. She and Dad had a perfect marriage. Ben and I don't. Right now it's anything *but* perfect. You can't tell her any of this. You have to promise!"

"I won't tell her anything, Nancy," Abby said. "You have my word. But I certainly would urge you to confide in your mother. She's a very understanding woman. She's not going to sit in judgment of you—"

"Yes, she will, and Ben too," Nancy cut in. "I don't want her to think less of him. He's a good man. It's not that, it's just . . ." her voice trailed off and her hands fell limply into her lap. "Well, I guess if I knew what the problem was, I wouldn't be such an emotional mess now, would I?"

"And you say John Parker's helping you?" Abby asked.

"Yes," Nancy said, frowning thoughtfully. "He's helping me sort out everything. I've been so angry with Ben—unreasonably angry, I can see now. We're never able to really talk about anything without interruption, and that just makes it worse. John helped me look at things a little more clearly just in our two brief conversations. He's really a sympathetic person, but he didn't let me get away with any excuses either. He held my feet to the fire. I have the feeling he's suffered some in his own life. But of course, he's a professional, so he's not going to talk about himself."

"Are you paying him for these sessions?" Abby asked.

"Aunt Abby," Nancy said, giving her a hard look, "please give me credit for having a little sense. We hashed all that out when he made the offer at the hospital that day. I asked him how much he charges, because we truly don't have any room in our budget for much discretionary spending. He said he wouldn't take payment because he isn't licensed in Washington State. I offered to pay something nominal—far less than what he'd ordinarily make, I'm sure—but he insisted he just wanted to help. And before you ask, since you obviously think I'm totally gullible, no, there has been nothing untoward or inappropriate. He's been nothing but professional. In fact, it was his idea to talk at the marina out at the picnic tables in a public area."

"Well, that's good," Abby said. "Strange though, that he's a licensed counselor and he's working as a physician's assistant."

"Not all that strange," Nancy said. "He was a social worker, and he burned out and decided to go back to school."

"I see," Abby said.

"It's a loss, I can tell you," Nancy said. "It's ironic, in a sad sort of way, that money's one of the big issues with Ben and me, and we can't afford to go to a counselor to work on the problem."

"Could your pastor help?" Abby asked, thinking of how often she had turned to Rev. Hale for solace.

"Yes, some," Nancy said. "I mean, we've talked to him a couple of times, but in a church the size of ours, he doesn't really have the time to do a lot of personal counseling. Not the kind Ben and I need."

The door opened suddenly and Emily burst in. Nancy quickly wiped her eyes and put on her game face.

"Grandma says to tell you Mr. Henry's putting the fish on the grill and that dinner will be in fifteen minutes. She says you two should freshen up and come on down. What does that mean—freshen up?"

"Well," Nancy said. "It means you should wash your face, pinch your cheeks to make them rosy, check to make sure your clothes are presentable and put a nice, bright smile on your face. Nancy looked over at Abby, her smile anything but bright.

When they'd all gathered downstairs, Henry came in the door carrying a platter, and the mingled aromas of the fish, spices and wood smoke quickly filled the dining room.

"I have good news and better news," he announced. "First off, the fish turned out just right, and second, Duncan's going to be fine."

Abby, Nancy and Mary all gave a sigh of relief.

"What does that mean, Mommy?" Emily asked, pulling on Nancy's sweater sleeve.

"A friend got sick," Nancy told her. "But now he's better."

"Do they know what it was, Henry?" Mary asked.

"The report I got said the doc thinks it was, indeed, a reaction to either an insect bite or a food allergy. They strongly suspect the latter. Duncan's niece sent him a big box of fancy chocolates for his birthday, and he'd been indulging in those in the minutes before this happened. Some of them have different varieties of exotic nuts in them. Doc says one of those is the likely culprit. They're going to do some more tests so Duncan will know what to stay clear of from here on out."

"So he'll have to stay at the Medical Center?" Abby asked.

"For a day or two anyway," Henry said. "They want to keep an eye on him. One thing everybody seems to agree on is that if Parker hadn't been there, Duncan might've—" He stopped abruptly and looked down to see four small eyes fixed on him. "Well, things might have turned out a different way," he said at last. "It was a lucky thing."

Abby looked across at Nancy who had gone pale. "Well, you know how I feel about this kind of thing, Henry," Abby said. "I believe John Parker was meant to be there at just that moment. Sometimes things happen according to a larger plan we can't see."

The dinner was wonderful, and the pleasant conversation was a respite from the emotional turmoil of the day.

Nicholas stubbornly refused to go back on his claim that he loved salmon. He ate a couple of small bites, making such a terrible face, it was all the adults could do to keep from laughing.

"I think I'd enjoy a fish stick," Mary said, picking up the platter and serving one onto her plate.

"Could I have one of those, Mary?" Henry asked, giving her a conspiratorial wink. "I just love fish sticks."

"Me too," said Nicholas. "May I have one, Grandma? Two, I mean," he said, holding up three fingers.

At the end of the meal Nancy gathered up the children to take them upstairs to get ready for bed. Abby brought in the decaf Mary had brewed and poured them each a cup.

"You didn't really have to eat that fish stick, Henry," Mary said, showing him she'd hidden hers under a leftover bit of salad greenery.

"What do you mean? I really do like fish sticks," Henry said with a laugh. "You forget, Mary. I'm accustomed to fixing bachelor meals, or I was before you and your angel of a mother started feeding me regularly. Fish sticks were always a staple in my freezer."

"I'm so relieved Duncan's going to be okay," Abby said.

"Oh, so am I," Mary said. "It sounds like that was a very close call."

Henry nodded. "They don't get much closer from the sound of it. It's uncommon enough for there to be someone around who knows CPR when something like this happens, but to have someone sitting ten feet away who knows how to perform an emergency tracheotomy—and very efficiently from what I hear. It's nearly a miracle."

"No nearly about it," Mary said.

Abby recounted what Joe Blackstock had said. "Maybe John Parker has a background in the military, as a medical corpsman or something like that. Or as an EMT?"

"I don't know," Henry said. "That wouldn't seem to track, would it? Why would he be working as a physician's assistant then? Wouldn't that be below his pay grade?"

"I don't know," Abby said, tapping her finger on her chin as she mulled things over. John Parker, it seemed, wore many hats. She made a mental note to do a little checking around about John Parker, especially since Nancy was now confiding personal information to him.

After a little more conversation, Abby excused herself to let Henry and Mary have some time alone to visit before Henry had to go home.

She went upstairs to find the children crawling into their beds, each fresh from a bath and smelling of soap.

"So, tomorrow's your day to come and visit me at the museum, right?" she asked them, rubbing her hands together.

"Right!" Emily said. "I can't wait!"

"Right!" Nicholas said. He looked up at his mother as if asking for confirmation, and when she nodded he rubbed his own pudgy hands together.

As Abby looked at his sweet face she felt a deep sadness. Except for his blue eyes, he was the image of his father. A montage of images of Ben and Nicholas together flooded her mind. She had always thought Benjamin to be a loving and attentive father, and she'd always believed that he and Nancy had a solid marriage. Mary would, indeed, be devastated if it failed, not to mention the pain and heartache it would cause the children.

Surely their troubles could not be as serious as Nancy believed them to be. It was unthinkable to Abby that this family could be broken apart.

She kissed the children goodnight, then went to her own room and knelt by her bed, where she stayed for a good long while, praying ardently for Nancy, for Ben and for the children.

She had sat in the front row at Nancy's wedding. It had been obvious to everyone present that she and Ben were deeply in love. The ceremony that sanctified their union was so moving and beautiful she and Mary had gone through half a box of tissues before the service was over.

It was late when Abby finally got up and went in to take her shower and get ready for bed, but even then she was still thinking of Nancy. She felt guilty about not telling Mary about this. She hoped Nancy would change her mind and talk to her mother. After all, Mary was the one with the perfect marriage, just as Nancy had said. She was certainly more qualified than Abby to offer advice.

Abby thought, too, of what Nancy had said about John Parker, that she suspected he'd had some pain in his own life.

Was that related to why Dustin was not allowed to talk about his mother? Did that have something to do with the "price they had to pay?" A bitter divorce perhaps? But even if that was the case, wouldn't Parker know it was harmful to forbid his son to even talk about his mother, particularly if he really was a licensed counselor? Of course, even those who are otherwise reasonable, amicable people could go a bit nuts when a marriage dissolved. She'd seen it happen with friends and colleagues.

It made Abby shudder to even think about that right now. She hoped what she'd said to Henry turned out to be true for Nancy too. That John Parker was sent to be in the right place at the right time to help Nancy as well. To save her marriage just like he'd saved Duncan Grady.

CHAPTER ✤ TEN

ABBY'S MIND WAS SPINNING as she walked down the gravel road behind the museum toward the conservatory the next morning. She had just gotten off a call, with Cecily Denning at the craft co-op in Friday Harbor. She'd called her to ask about the man who had purchased Parker's chessboard.

Cecily, too, had conjectured the man might have been a scout, there to search out native crafts to resell at double or triple markup in a fancy urban gallery.

"He was middle-aged, right?" Abby had asked. "Salt-and-pepper hair, sort of burly?"

"No, no, Abby," Cecily replied. "This guy was young. Midthirties maybe. Slender, with dark hair and eyes. Very handsome, really, if not very mannerly."

"I understand he used a credit card," Abby said. "Would it be unethical for me to ask you the name on the card?"

There had been a silence on the other end of the line for a long moment. "Well, Abby, I'd say it was unusual, but I don't see anything unethical about it. Could I ask why you want to know?"

"Cecily," Abby said, "I know this is a little weird, but I do have a good reason. If you'll just bear with me, I can tell you everything later."

"Since it's you, that's good enough for me, Abby," Cecily had said. "I've got it right here. It's a corporate card: SES, Ltd. Does that help?"

"I don't know yet," Abby had told her, "but thanks."

Now, as she mulled all this over, she was even more puzzled. So there were two men asking around about the chessboard? And what was SES, Ltd.? Could be a company that supplied art galleries, she supposed. She'd immediately checked the Internet, but there was no Web presence for an SES that dealt with art. Just another oddity attached to the Parker family.

Abby carried a canvas bag filled with placards she'd had made up in Friday Harbor at the sign shop. She'd spent an hour earlier in the morning checking all the weather-resistant placards for spelling and accuracy, then mounting them all on wooden stakes, with the exception of the one that said Western Red Cedar. That one would have to go back for a do-over. The western red cedar wasn't a true cedar, but a member of the cypress family, so punctuation and spacing mattered.

She was happy to be outdoors. The sun, just up over the tree line, was shining with the promise of a full fair day, as it did nearly 250 days a year on Sparrow Island, thanks to the rain shadow effect created by the Olympic Mountains.

But despite the pleasant surroundings, dozens of thoughts floating around in Abby's head kept her from enjoying her time outdoors to the fullest. In addition to her concerns about the Parker family, she was worried about Nancy. Those things, coupled with the workaday challenges at the museum, had her mind racing.

She checked her clipboard as she went off on the first loop of Trail A. She put down her bag and flipped through the placards until she found the one for the Pacific madrone that stood just in from the turnoff on the trail, clinging tenaciously from a rocky outcrop. People who weren't familiar with this species sometimes asked whether the peeling rust-colored bark was a sign of disease. Abby had gotten the question so many times she'd had the answer printed on the placard. This tree was a healthy specimen and the peeling bark that exposed the smooth skin underneath was simply a characteristic of the tree, as were its leathery evergreen leaves and the way it could defy gravity, leaning out over the water on the dry, rocky bluffs, spreading its roots wide to find purchase in scant soil.

Abby took the rubber mallet and hammered the placard into place, being sure to choose a spot that was unlikely to damage the root system. She stepped gingerly. Madrones were notoriously messy trees, dropping bark and leaves and berries. It all composted and enriched the soil, but it made a mess that was an invitation to slip and fall.

She wiped her hands on her jeans and began writing on her clipboard. Her notes would be added to the self-guided tour sheet available in the museum's lobby.

Birding groups had been asking that information to aid them in spotting different species be added to the plethora of information that was provided on trees, flora and fauna.

Abby scribbled furiously: "Watch for insect-eating birds such as the chestnut-backed chickadee, the Hutton's vireo and the orange-crowned warbler in or near the madrone. Beginning in later summer when the tree is berrying, be on the lookout for the spotted towhee and the varied thrush."

This tree was relatively young, so the cavity nesters and woodpeckers hadn't found a home here yet, but she added a note to look for those in the older madrones.

She took her small digital camera out of her vest pocket and took a picture. She had a plan in mind to come back to photograph this tree again in each season for a year. And each of the other sites on her list as well. If she found something of particular note had changed she would post the photos side-by-side on the museum's Web site or perhaps use the collection for a display in the museum.

She worked her way around the trail, repeating the procedure at each of the sites she had marked on her clipboard. Soon a fine sheen of perspiration had formed on her forehead, and she regretted the heavy sweater she'd selected in the morning when it was still cool.

She drove her last stake into the ground near a nurse log that had nurtured a thriving western hemlock tree. She backed up to take a picture, getting as much of the decaying log in the picture as she could. It was then that she heard Hugo's voice. She frowned and reached for her vest pocket, only to realize she'd forgotten to bring the walkie-talkie with her.

"Yes, you forgot it," Hugo said, smiling as she turned to see him appear in person. "But for that I thank you. I needed to get out from behind my desk."

"I'm so sorry, Hugo," Abby said. "I got it out of my desk drawer, but I remember now I left it by the jay's cage when I checked on him."

"And how is our Houdini bird today?" Hugo asked.

"I think he may have set his healing time back a little in that escape attempt," Abby said, "but he's going to be ready for release in another week—ten days maybe."

"I'm not so sure he was trying to escape," Hugo said, laughing. "I think he may have been practicing his stunt flying, or else just taunting you. It was a pretty funny sight, you two trying to corral that little prankster."

"Yes, I'm sure we must have looked like a Laurel and Hardy skit," Abby said. "Was there something you needed, or are you truly out here for sunshine and fresh air?"

"Both!" Hugo said. "But mainly I came to tell you that Mary called to say she and Nancy and the children will be out at one instead of noon as you'd originally planned. And that she will be bringing a slightly larger entourage. She'll bring Bobby, Dustin and Elise Parker along as well."

"Oh my," Abby said, wondering how in the world Mary had managed that. "It's nothing short of amazing how Mary can draw people out."

"Who needed drawing?" Hugo asked.

"Elise Parker," Abby said. "She seems uncomfortable with letting things move beyond the level of trifling pleasantries, and I had the distinct impression she was relieved when our last visit ended."

Hugo reached down to pick up the canvas bag and tossed the mallet inside. "I imagine it would create some barriers in regular social discourse to lose one's hearing," he said as he and Abby fell into step and headed back to the museum.

"Yes, of course," Abby said. "But Ellie Parker's a good lipreader. We didn't have much trouble at all with understanding one another."

"Yes," Hugo said, "but nuances are lost—the tone of voice,

the loudness or softness, the hesitations and rushes of words. That all goes by the wayside."

Abby nodded. "Yes, I suppose that's true. But there was something more with her. She seems very, well, I guess guarded is the best way I can say it."

"If that's the case, I guess her son shares the family trait," Hugo said.

"John?" Abby said. "What do you mean?"

"I ran into William Jansen this morning," Hugo said, "and he was hopping mad. He wants to do a story on Duncan and about how John Parker saved him, but Parker won't grant him an interview or cooperate for a profile or anything. He says he doesn't want a big deal made about it."

"So, we add modesty to his growing list of attributes," Abby said. *Was* he being modest, she wondered, or were there other reasons he wanted to avoid publicity?

"That's not all," Hugo said. "He's requested that Duncan not grant an interview about it either, and Duncan says seeing as how the guy saved his life, the least he can do is honor his wishes about it. So poor old William is left with interviewing bystanders."

Abby glanced at her watch. She wouldn't have long before Mary and the crew arrived, but after she got cleaned up maybe she'd have a few minutes to try to unearth some information about the wonderful-and-modest John Parker.

It troubled Abby to be suspicious of people. As she and Hugo walked on in companionable silence, she did some soul searching about whether she was doing the right thing in prying into the Parkers' lives.

She believed very strongly in giving everyone the benefit of the doubt, but she was also disinclined to be blindly trusting.

She knew in this case she was probably more sensitive to the little things that didn't seem to add up because of Nancy's involvement with John Parker. She was grateful that he seemed to be helping Nancy, but she wanted to make sure it was support that helped to mend her marriage. She had no idea what John Parker saw as the end goal.

She wiped perspiration from her forehead with the sleeve of her sweater. "Hugo, do you think it's wrong to pry into people's lives if your motive is to *maybe* protect other people from harm?"

"That's quite a hypothetical," Hugo said. "Would you care to be more specific?"

Abby looked at him and sighed. "I can't," she said.

"Well, Abby," Hugo said, "I'd say you should trust your instincts. You're a principled person, and I'm sure you'll know the right way to handle it."

"I hope you're right."

MARY'S VAN PULLED into the museum parking lot precisely on the stroke of one. Abby went out to greet her special tour group and walked them back into the museum.

"I'm so happy you came," she told Dustin and Ellie.

"Mary can be very persuasive," Ellie said, but she was smiling, so Abby took that as a good sign.

"I'm sure glad of it," Bobby said. "Dustin, you're not going to believe all the stuff we've got in here," he said, swinging the door wide and holding it for the others like a doorman at a fine hotel. Abby was amused, and pleased, by his use of the word *we*. It was obvious he felt a sense of ownership about the place, and Abby hoped other Sparrow Islanders did too. The museum was a celebration of the history and the spirit of the island, as well as its natural bounty and beauty. Its success, though, depended on the help and support of many community volunteers.

Abby's tour-guiding skills turned out to be redundant with Bobby along. And Dustin was clearly having the time of his life. For the first time Abby saw the boy looking truly happy, carefree and animated. At each exhibit he would turn to sign something lightning fast to his grandmother.

Abby had been studying her ASL book, but it was slow going, and with their hands moving so fast, she couldn't pick up much. It amused Abby to realize that Dustin preferred signing to speech because then he could go right on looking at the exhibit and didn't need to tear his eyes away to turn completely toward her.

Abby noticed that while Elise appeared to be totally engaged, she looked around every few minutes, scanning the museum.

Dustin's enthusiasm jumped to a whole new level when they came to the Native American exhibit. Following Bobby's instructions, he pressed the button to start the film presentation that played on a small screen set in the faux forest on the right side of the exhibit.

Both Dustin and his grandmother watched the film with rapt attention, but soon Abby noticed that during significant portions of the film there was only voice-over description of footage showing artifacts or reenactments. Dustin continued to watch the film, but signed to his grandmother at the same time. She, in turn, was trying to watch both the film and Dustin. It was clearly not the satisfying experience it could have been for either of them. Why had neither she nor Hugo thought to take this into consideration? Abby made a mental note to check into having the presentation subtitled.

The only time Elise left Dustin's side was when she stepped over to look at the flora and fauna exhibit. It was just at that time that Hugo came out of his office and wandered over to say hello to Bobby. Bobby was introducing him to Dustin when Elise turned and saw them. She blanched and moved with lightning speed, coming back to Dustin's side and putting herself between the boy and Hugo. Dustin quickly stepped to her side and signed an introduction. She shook hands with Hugo, but she did not look happy.

Emily and Nicholas, for whom the museum was not new, each wanted to visit their favorite exhibit, so Mary and Nancy had split up, Mary to take Emily to the butterfly exhibit and Nancy to take Nicholas to the one on the orcas.

When Bobby had shown Dustin and Ellie every exhibit—some of them twice—Mary announced that she'd brought a snack along and asked Abby if she had time to join them at the picnic tables outside.

"Oh, I'd love to," Abby said, glancing at her watch, "but I can't stay too long. I've still got quite a lot to do before I can head home."

The others went on out and Abby told them she'd be along in a few moments. She went to her desk, wrote herself a note about looking into closed captioning on the Native American exhibit, then headed for the front desk to let Wilma—the receptionist, ticket seller and general go-to gal—know she'd be outside.

As Abby approached the desk, she saw that Wilma was talking to someone and decided she would just wave and point to indicate where she'd be, but at that moment the man turned and went out the door of the museum. He was a young, dark featured man and he carried a rather large bag. He walked toward his car as if in a big hurry.

"What was that all about?" Abby asked Wilma.

"That's the fella Ana told me about. He's nosing around trying to find out something about a guy new to the island who makes these chessboards."

"Yes, I know about that," Abby said.

"Sure was wanting all the nitty-gritty," Wilma said. "And he didn't even stay to look at the museum, even after he'd paid admission. I'd say he's not really much interested in native crafts."

"What did you tell him?" Abby asked.

"The truth," Wilma said, "that I don't know the person who made the chessboard. I haven't met John Parker yet." She gave Abby a slow smile.

As Abby went out to join the others, she wondered if she should say anything to Ellie about the man. But the poor woman was already a bundle of nerves about Dustin. She decided to wait until she could find out more about what was going on. And she *would* find out more. Why was this man snooping around? He sure seemed persistent, and Abby was determined to get some answers.

With Nancy's help, Mary spread a tablecloth on the picnic table and started to unload the cooler bag she'd brought along.

Ellie admired the flowers growing in the beds that lined the museum and the front edge of the parking lot.

"Mary helped us with those," Abby said. "She wanted to make certain we didn't accidentally introduce any invasive species. She did all the research."

"What are the bluish-purple ones with the twisted stems?" Ellie asked.

"American vetch," Mary replied.

Ellie frowned and started to dig in her bag, as did Mary.

They each came out with an identical notepad and started to laugh.

Mary wrote out the name for the flower. "It's even edible," she said, pantomiming taking a bite. "Oh, and Ellie, down in the conservatory there's a colony of Calypso orchids." She scribbled down the name. "Have you seen those?"

"I don't believe I ever have," Ellie said.

"Oh, you have to see them. They're absolutely gorgeous," Mary said. "They're very delicate with little nodding heads. They look almost like porcelain someone's hand-painted rosy-purple and with a deep red streak at the throat."

"Sounds beautiful," Ellie said.

"Normally my chair will make that loop, but with the recent rains I'd be afraid to try it. Perhaps Abby could take you down."

Abby was relieved when Ellie said she'd love to see them, but that it would have to be another day. Abby felt pressed for time and wanted to make sure she got home early in order to spend time with Nancy.

When the snacks had all been put out onto the table, Nancy called to the children who were playing in the grass. As they sat down at the table, Dustin spotted the thin ginger cookies Mary had brought. He picked up one and nudged his grandmother. He signed to her, and Abby thought she saw the word *mother* in his gestures, but then she thought maybe it was the word *remember*. Both involved touching the face, she knew, but she couldn't recall the handshape.

Dustin held the cookie up toward his grandmother with a wide grin. She frowned and shook her head and his smile faded. She signed something to him, but she did it so rapidly Abby couldn't pick out a thing. Dustin literally slumped. As the other children chattered on, Dustin sat glumly eating his cookie.

Abby saw Ellie Parker put her arm around him and squeeze him to her, but Dustin hardly seemed to notice.

Abby invited the children each to name their favorite thing about the museum. When it came to Dustin, it was no surprise that he picked the Native American exhibit.

"Hey, Dustin, the gift shop has a DVD," said Bobby. "It's a longer version of the one they play in the exhibit. It's really cool."

Dustin's eyes lit up and he turned to sign to his grand-mother, bouncing up and down on the bench.

She shook her head and said maybe for his birthday.

Dustin got a scowl on his face, and for the first time, Abby saw not sadness but anger in his eyes. He signed something to his grandmother. This time Abby was sure she picked up the word *mother*.

Ellie signed something back to him. She was smiling, but Abby sensed there was conflict in the exchange. Ellie turned to the group. "I'm sorry," she said, "sometimes children don't understand about keeping to a budget."

"I sure know what you mean," Nancy said, spreading peanut butter into the valley of a celery stick. "It's such a chal-lenge to make the dollars stretch over the necessities and to try to save toward college. There never seems to be much left over for anything else. So you have a birthday coming up?" she said, turning to Dustin. "That's great. When is it?"

"Next month," Dustin said. "It's June ten—"

"June the seventeenth," Ellie cut in. "On June seventeenth he'll be eleven years old. I can hardly believe it, they grow up so fast," she said, pushing Dustin's juice toward him and tidy-ing up a few crumbs on the tablecloth.

Abby saw a brief scowl flit across Dustin's face as he twisted the oversized watch on his wrist. Abby was surprised. She knew he was a grade behind Bobby. She had assumed he would be turning ten. He was certainly bright enough for eleven, but quite small for his age.

As the others moved on to other topics of conversation, Abby saw Bobby lean over toward Dustin. "I thought you said you were going to be ten," he whispered.

Dustin looked at him and shrugged.

The alarm Abby had set on her watch chimed and she rose. "Oops, there's my signal. I've really got to get back to work," she said. "Thank you all for coming."

The kids cheered and clapped, prompting Abby to bow. She turned to Ellie. "I look forward to showing you those orchids out in the conservatory. Anytime."

MARY AND THE CHILDREN were in the living room when Abby got home, watching a movie about a dog that looked remarkably like Finnegan. Finnegan, too, seemed to be watching with rapt attention. Abby understood that dogs weren't supposed to be able to see in two dimensions, but Finnegan had his head up, alert, his eyes glued to the screen.

Blossom, on the other hand, was in her special chair and had positioned herself with her hindquarters to the screen, perhaps expressing her opinion of the film's hero.

Abby went upstairs to take a shower and change clothes. She had mud spatters on the legs of her jeans from her morning's work in the conservatory and the warm day had left her feeling wilted and grubby.

As she went by the open door to Nancy's room, she saw her sitting at her old high school desk, checkbook and calculator in front of her. She was chewing on her pencil.

"Hey, Nancy," she called, and as Nancy turned toward her, Abby saw that she had been crying again.

"Would you like to talk?" Abby asked.

Nancy nodded and Abby went in and sat down on the end of the bed.

"Oh, Aunt Abby, you must think I'm such a wimp," Nancy said, choking back tears. "Every time you come up here I'm falling apart."

"I don't think any such thing," Abby said firmly. "Nancy, you're much too hard on yourself. You're going through a rough time right now. Is there anything I can do to help?" She nodded toward the checkbook, remembering Nancy's comments earlier in the day about the difficulty of making ends meet. "Are you and Benjamin having money trouble?"

"Isn't nearly everybody?" Nancy asked with a mirthless laugh.

"Nancy, I'm far from rich, but if you need some help getting over a bump I could—"

"No!" Nancy interrupted. "No, Aunt Abby," she said, her voice softening. "It's dear of you to offer, but this is not that kind of problem. It's more of a differing philosophy, I guess. Just another symptom of how Ben and I don't seem to be on the same page anymore."

"Have you talked about it?"

"We do nothing *but* talk about it. Or that's the way it seems," Nancy said. "The trouble is, it's always on-the-fly in little bits and snatches. That's how we talk about everything these days. We never seem to find the time to have a civilized or meaningful conversation anymore. What with work, the kids' activities, meetings, our volunteer obligations, keeping up with the house and the yard. Honestly, I don't know how Mom and Dad did it!"

"With a lot of patience and prayer I suspect," Abby said.

Nancy smiled. "They were always so in harmony with one another. I never ever heard them fight—not once. And no matter how busy they were, they always made time for one another and were supportive of one another's dreams and goals. I don't think I'll ever get to realize..."

Her voice trailed off and she looked up at Abby, then squeezed her eyes shut.

"Realize what, Nancy?" Abby asked. "What were you going to say?"

"It's silly," Nancy said, shaking her head.

"I'm sure it's not," Abby said. "It's obviously something important to you."

"Well, I'm afraid I won't get a chance to realize my dream. I want to write a children's book. Or more to the point, I want to illustrate one," Nancy said. She took a deep breath and blew it out. "There, I've said it out loud. I've been thinking about this for a while now."

"Oh Nancy, that's wonderful. So this explains why you've been sketching so furiously."

"It's a pie-in-the-sky notion, but I have an idea for a children's book about Mom and Finnegan. I sent an old friend of Dad's an outline of the idea and some of the sketches. Of course, he's long retired from the publishing house now, so he's not in any position to help me, but he was encouraging. Still, I know I could put in a lot of work on this, only to have it come to nothing."

Despite how Nancy was trying to downplay it, Abby could see the excitement in her eyes. "Nancy, your father would be so proud."

"Oh, let's not get ahead of ourselves, Aunt Abby," Nancy

said with a sigh. "It's a long way from a reality. I can't possibly do it with things the way they are now. I can barely find time to brush my teeth when I'm at home. I'd have to cut back on my hours at work to make the time for it. And with this," she said, pointing to the checkbook, "posing such a challenge, I don't see how I can do that."

"What does Benjamin say about it?"

"He doesn't say anything at all."

"What do you mean, nothing at all?" Abby asked. "I'm sure if you put your heads together, you could find a way to make this work out."

"He doesn't know about any of this," Nancy said. "I haven't even told him about the idea. I just can't think of how to tell him I want to put us in worse financial shape than we're already in. It would be such a gamble. He wouldn't be for it. I'm sure of that. And it would just be one more thing coming between us."

"Nancy, you don't know that. It's not fair to Benjamin to be angry with him about something you think he'd say or do."

"You're right. It's because I think if I were in his shoes, I'd probably think it was a dumb idea. I probably have no chance at all of getting it published."

"Well," said Abby, "I'm certainly glad your father didn't feel that way. Otherwise you'd have been in a real pickle. No food or clothes—or that college education."

That got a smile from Nancy. "Thanks, Aunt Abby. You make me feel much better. John's right, it does feel good to talk about things." She looked up and held Abby's gaze, going somber again. "But I'm still holding you to your promise. Not a word to Mom. I don't want her worrying about any of this."

Abby pinched her lips shut. "But, Nancy," she said, "I'm

urging you—strongly urging you—to talk to your mother. You just said it yourself: you feel better talking it out. And your mother already senses there's something wrong. I know she does. You probably have her thinking all sorts of terrible things."

Nancy turned away. "I'll think about it," she said. "But right now this does feel like a terrible thing."

Abby patted her on the knee. "Yes, you think about it, but don't forget to pray about it too."

CHAPTER ❦ ELEVEN

THAT EVENING, AFTER THE children were in bed, Abby went to her room to work on entering the data from the annual bird counts. She was hoping if she made herself scarce and gave Mary and Nancy an opportunity to have some time alone, maybe Nancy would open up to her mother.

She worked steadily for a half hour, but then her mind turned back to Nancy and her situation and to John Parker, who was counseling her.

She found her fingers tapping across the keyboard, entering John Parker's name in the search engine before she'd even fully realized she was doing it. There was something about that family's situation that made her feel uneasy. John didn't seem to be exactly what he purported to be professionally; Ellie was protective of Dustin to the point of being obsessed; the men asking about the chessboard artist seemed to be going to extremes; and there was that troublesome phrase that had been echoing in Abby's mind since the beginning: "It's the price we have to pay for what we've done."

Hundreds of entries popped up on the screen. She sighed. Of course, John Parker was a common name.

She switched to the image search and tried again. Same result. Hundreds of entries, but as she scrolled quickly through the first ten pages or so, none looked anything like this John Parker.

She tapped her fingers on her chin. She entered John Parker along with "physician's assistant" and got two hits. But one was twenty-three years old according to the resume posted on a job search site, and the other reference was an obituary from a small-town Kansas newspaper.

She thought of searching through licensing agencies for counselors, but then realized she'd have to know the state he was licensed in. She tried Florida, but got no hits.

She tried Elise Parker, but even with her more unusual first name, there were still too many to sort out. She tried coupling her name with services for the deaf but found no useful information.

She stared at the screen and again twiddled her fingers on her chin. She thought of trying Dustin Parker, but he was so young, how could he have made it onto the Internet? She needed more specific information.

Suddenly she remembered she knew Dustin's birthday.

She and Mary had an account on a genealogy site where they had been researching the Stanton family history. She logged in and typed Dustin's name, plus his date of birth. There he was: Dustin R. Parker.

She tried it with John Parker, but without his date of birth, there was a ridiculously long list and it didn't really tell her anything anyway.

But when she typed in Elise Parker, she got only seven hits. She looked over the birthdates, but the women all seemed too young to be this Elise, or they were deceased. Then she noticed that many of the entries had only an initial for the middle name. Perhaps Elise was a middle name. She sighed and signed off the site. This was a pointless exercise. She didn't have enough information.

She started to sign off the Internet and get back to her data entry, but then she had one last thought. She entered the terms *tracheotomy*, *razor blade*, *drinking straw* and *duct tape* into the search engine. She was surprised to see the screen again flooded with selections.

She started to scan through the entries and soon detected a common thread. Several of the articles either mentioned or were linked to an emergency aid class taught at St. Mary's Hospital near New Britain, Connecticut.

Abby tried to think why that rang a bell with her. Then she remembered that Diane Marsh, one of her old friends from her undergraduate days at Cornell was a hospital administrator at St. Mary's.

She went to the hospital's Web site and found the information on the emergency aid class and pictures of the disassembled trach kit. The pieces, including the razor blade, sheathed in a hard plastic guard that covered the cutting edge, all fit neatly into a plastic photo sleeve about the size of a credit card.

It had, the article explained, been the brainchild of an emergency room doctor on staff at St. Mary's after he'd seen three deaths within a two-month period due to severe allergic reactions, all of which, he believed, could have been prevented with earlier intervention to clear a breathing passage. His view was that with the right preparation and quick access to the right materials, many people could be trained to perform this lifesaving procedure just as so many citizens had learned to do CPR. He had designed the kit and included the procedure in the advanced emergency aid class he taught at the hospital.

Abby glanced at her watch. It was getting late, too late to make a social call. She jotted a reminder on her notepad and went back to work on her data.

ABBY FOUND MARY ALONE in the kitchen the next morning. She was getting breakfast on the table.

"Where are Nancy and the kids?" Abby asked. "Both their doors were open. I assumed they were up already."

"Yes," Mary said, lining up boxes of cereal on the table. "They are up and full of vim and vigor. They're outside in the yard giving Finnegan a romp. Or at least Nicholas is. If I know Emily, she's likely curled up in one of the patio chairs with Blossom on her lap. "My heavens, but those children are animal lovers."

"I know," Abby said. "What will Finnegan and Blossom do when they leave? They're going to be so let down to be left here with just you and me again. The children are spoiling them with all that attention."

"Finnegan's impossible to spoil," Mary said. "He's far too responsible and levelheaded a dog. And, as for Blossom, well, I'm afraid Blossom was incurably spoiled long ago. Cats seem to expect to be pampered."

"Where's Nancy?" Abby asked, getting juice glasses from the cupboard and setting them at each place.

"She's outside keeping an eye on the kids. I think she's on the phone with Benjamin. Abby, something is just not right. Has she said anything to you?"

"Tell me why you think there's something wrong." Abby said, sidestepping Mary's question.

"I can tell," Mary said flatly. "There's something in her tone when she's on the phone with him. She's just not herself. I know her. I'm telling you, something's going on and it's not good."

Abby didn't reply immediately. She was trying to think of something to say that was safe.

Mary cocked her head and looked at her. "And, Abby, don't think I didn't notice that you dodged my question."

"Mary—" Abby began, feeling terrible.

Mary held up a hand. "It's okay. Really. I'm glad she's confiding in someone, and I'm happy it's you. I don't want to put you on the spot. Keeping confidences is a high trust and I know you'd never violate that, nor would I want you to. I just wish Nancy would talk to me. I can't deny that doesn't hurt a little."

"Mary," Abby said, stopping behind Mary's chair to hug her shoulders, "Nancy loves you so very much and she respects you. I think," she said, continuing on to the fridge for the orange juice, "she just wants you to believe she can handle anything that comes along."

"And can she?" Mary blurted. "Can she handle whatever this is?" She drew in a breath and held it for a moment before letting it out in a gush. "Please, just forget I asked that," she said.

Abby put the carton of juice on the table and sat down next to Mary's chair. "Mary, Nancy will talk to you . . . when she's ready. I know she will. I think you, and Jacob too, just set the bar so high, well, Nancy expects perfection of herself in every single facet of her life."

"I certainly don't hold myself up as perfect, and neither did Jacob," Mary said.

"No, I know you don't," Abby said. "But I'm in a unique position to tell you this: You are a hard act to follow! I know we've talked about a lot of these issues since I came back to Sparrow Island, and through the grace of God and a lot of love between us, we've worked it all out, but it wasn't easy growing up as your sister. You were—and are—so beautiful. And you're artistic, talented, outgoing—all of it. Then you married a wonderful man and you had a perfect marriage and two beautiful children."

"Stop right there," Mary said. "I don't want to dredge up all that stuff again, Abby. We had enough trouble getting it all worked out in the first place!" Abby thought she heard irritation in Mary's voice, but when she looked over she saw a mischievous smile playing around her lips.

"Oh, Abby," Mary said, going serious again. "I don't know what gave you the idea that Jacob and I had a perfect marriage. A wonderful, rich marriage, yes, but not perfect. We loved one another deeply, but we certainly had our ups and downs just like any other couple."

"Well, they must have been pretty small ups and downs. I never saw you two when you didn't seem to be completely in sync."

Mary rolled her eyes. "Oh, I could tell you stories—"

She was interrupted by Nancy, the children and the animals all coming in from outside in a clamor. Abby grabbed a towel from the hook by the back door and bent down to wipe off

Finnegan's paws, which were wet from the dew. She laughed when she saw that Nicholas was still wearing his pajama bottoms. The legs were wet from the knees down. "Looks like you need a wipe-down too," she told him.

Nancy looked down. "He couldn't even wait to get dressed before he came down to play with Finnegan," she said. She reached down to take off his sneakers, each hook-and-loop closure making a *rrrrrippp* sound that seemed to puzzle Finnegan. "Okay Nicholas," she said, "let's go up and get some real pants on, okay?"

Nicholas nodded, but the wet pajamas didn't seem to be bothering him at all and he looked lustfully at the boxes of cereal lined up on the table.

Ten minutes later, after they'd all settled down at the table and said grace, Abby asked, "So what do you all have on the docket today?"

"Mr. Henry is taking us fishing," Emily said.

"Yeah," Nicholas said. "I'm going to catch a big fish." He held his arms out wide.

"And we're going to have a picnic too," Emily said. "Can you come, Aunt Abby?"

"Maybe," Abby said. "I have to go to work this morning, but maybe I can come for the picnic part." She sent a questioning look at Mary.

"I'm going to skip the fishing part myself," Mary said. "Nancy and Dad are going to have that privilege. I'll bring the picnic lunch out to Cedar Grove Lake when they call. That way, I can go to my crafters' group while these kids are catching our dinner, and we can all have the afternoon to relax and recover."

"Sounds good to me," Abby said. "I need to check on my

bird patients, and Rick's supposed to come today to check our wiring to see if we're going to need an upgrade for the new media booth. Bobby's going to do his junior docent duties today, so he'll help me clean up the workroom."

"What will Dustin do without his sidekick?" Mary said.

"Maybe Dustin could be a junior docent too," Nancy said. "He sure seems like a bright kid and full of curiosity. Though, come to think of it, would you want one more boy shadowing you and peppering you with questions?"

Abby chuckled. "Bobby does have an unusually high level of need-to-know, doesn't he? But I love it. He's going to do great things in the world someday. And I'd like to have Dustin come out too. There are actually a few things I could use him for out in the conservatory today. But I doubt his grandmother will let him."

Nancy shrugged. "I don't blame her for being protective. I wouldn't let my kids go with anyone I didn't know either. But maybe she'd let him, now that she knows you."

Abby tilted her head. "Maybe you're right. I shouldn't assume. I think I'll at least ask."

She started for the phone, then stopped in her tracks. "Oh, that's right, I have to text." She pulled her cell phone from her pocket and started to enter the invitation on the tiny keypad. She was frustrated with how long it took her. "I need a teenager to do this for me," she said.

"Doesn't take a teenager these days," Nancy said. She nodded her head in Emily's direction. "She already knows how to text and she's only in first grade."

"I text Daddy," Emily said proudly. "I text I LOVE YOU, every morning so he'll see it when he gets up."

"It's free on our plan," Nancy said with a shrug. Abby saw her bite her lip as she busied herself with stacking dirty dishes and tidying up the table.

Abby's phone signaled she'd received a message. She examined her screen for a reply and laughed. "Well, it looks like I'm going to get Dustin *and* Ellie. Either you did a great sales job on those Calypso orchids yesterday, Mary, or she really doesn't want to let Dustin out of her sight."

"Either way, I'm glad she's going with you," Mary said. "Is that okay with you? If it doesn't work with your schedule, I can come out and pick her up midmorning."

"We'll see," Abby said. "I think it'll be okay. I got four more placards in yesterday. I can go ahead and install those when I walk that loop with her. I won't be as good a guide to the wildflowers as you would be, Mary, but I'll give it my best."

"No one's as good as Mom with San Juan wildflowers," Nancy said, dropping a kiss on her mother's head. "She's perfect."

CHAPTER ❧ TWELVE

TALK IN THE CAR ON THE way to the museum came mostly from the backseat. Abby appreciated immediately that a conversation with Ellie while driving was problematic. She couldn't look at the road and Ellie at the same time, and Dustin was in the backseat and couldn't sign for her.

Abby turned on the radio to a classical station and turned the speaker knob to the front. The boys seemed to think this meant she couldn't hear them and started up a conversation of their own.

"Are you going to get that DVD for your birthday?" Bobby asked Dustin.

"I don't know," Dustin said. "I think maybe, but I'm not sure. My dad says he already got my birthday present, but maybe my grandmother will get it for me. Who knows? My dad's always saying we have to watch our money. He doesn't get paid much."

"Really?" Bobby said. "I thought he was like a doctor or something."

"No, not here," Dustin said. "He's more like a doctor's helper. And it's not like before..."

Abby glanced into the rearview mirror and saw Dustin looking at his grandmother. Ellie was looking out her window. She appeared to be admiring the scenery.

"Like before what?" Bobby asked.

"Before we started moving around," Dustin said. He lowered his voice so that Abby could barely hear. "I'll tell you something," Dustin said, "but you have to promise not to tell."

"I won't tell," Bobby said. "What is it?"

"We used to be rich," Dustin said.

"Wow."

"Well, not really rich," Dustin amended. Abby saw Dustin cast another furtive glance in his grandmother's direction. He slumped in the seat and continued. "But we didn't have to worry about money because my dad made a lot more. And you know what else?" he asked.

"What?" Bobby asked.

"My grandfather is really, *really* rich," Dustin said.

"Wait, you have a grandfather?" Bobby asked. "Then why isn't he here too, with you and your grandmother?"

"Not that one," Dustin said. "This grandmother is my dad's mother. That grandfather died before I was even born. It's my mom's father who's rich."

"How rich?" Bobby asked.

"Filthy rich," Dustin said. "That's what my dad says, and he says there's a good reason people call it that. They fight—a lot."

"What about?" Bobby asked.

"About me," Dustin said. "If my grandfather was here, he'd buy me a dozen DVDs if I wanted them. He used to buy me anything I wanted, but my dad got upset about it and made him stop. Or tried to."

"Well, maybe you could call him up and get him to buy you the DVD for your birthday. Not a dozen. That's crazy. But one."

"I can't, Dustin said.

"Why not?" Bobby asked.

"I can't talk about it," Dustin said. "I'll get in deep trouble. You've got to promise you won't tell anybody what I told you."

"Okay, I won't," Bobby said, obviously perplexed. "Can you talk about your mom now? I mean, I don't want to make you sad, but if you want to tell me—"

"It does make me sad," Dustin cut in. "It makes me very sad. I'd like to tell you, but I just can't."

"Well, okay then," Bobby said. There was silence for a time and Abby glanced in her rearview to see Bobby fidgeting.

"Hey," he said, finally, "do you want me to tell you about the Salish archaeological dig out by Cedar Grove Lake?"

"Yeah," Dustin said, perking up. "I want to know everything about that. Have you been there?"

"Yeah, my dad took me last season," Bobby said. "It was cool, even though you really can't see too much. They have it roped off so people don't disturb things. But my dad talked to one of the archeologists, and he let me go down into one of the trenches. One of his students showed me how you have to uncover the artifacts using just a little paintbrush. And they take tons of pictures at like different stages when they're uncovering things."

Abby wanted to tell them about the film the museum had gotten permission to do, but she didn't want the boys to know she'd been freely eavesdropping on their conversation.

"That's so cool," Dustin said, envy dripping from every word. "Man, I wish I could do that."

"Maybe you can," Bobby said. "Maybe your dad will take you."

"He's working. He's always working," Dustin said, dejectedly.

"Well, maybe my dad will take us out," Bobby offered.

"They wouldn't let me go," Dustin said with a sigh. "Tell me about what they've found."

"I didn't get to go near this discovery, but they've found a part of a cedar-plank longhouse. The site's on a shell midden between the lake and ocean. Do you know what a midden is?" Bobby asked.

"Um, I'm not sure," Dustin said.

"Well, a midden is what the archeologists call it when they find a place where there's lots of people's stuff around where they lived. The stuff they used everyday, you know, like tools and dishes and stuff. And a lot of the stuff the Coast Salish used was made from shells, so they call it a shell midden."

Abby was impressed. Bobby's description may have been a little rough around the edges, but it was informed.

"Oh, okay, a midden," Dustin said, repeating the new word as if savoring it.

"Yeah, and anyway," Bobby rushed on, "there was a mudslide sometime way back years and years ago, and it rolled in and like sealed up part of the village and preserved it, so they're finding lots of stuff 'cause they figure the Coast Salish have been here for seven hundred years or something—about three hundred generations. Can you imagine that?"

"No," Dustin said. "I can't imagine being anyplace for more than a few months."

"Well, I hope you'll be here for longer!" Bobby said. "Hey, guess what? Next year Sparrow Island's going to host the Intertribal Canoe Journey. That'll be cool!"

"We'll probably be gone before then," Dustin said miserably.

Ellie Parker turned to the backseat. "What are you boys talking about?" she asked Dustin.

"The Salish tribe, Grandma," Dustin said, signing and speaking, without much enthusiasm.

"Good," Ellie said, reaching back to pat his knee.

Abby was mulling over all that she'd heard as she parked in the museum's parking lot. Was that why Ellie Parker was holding back? Did she know they'd be gone again in a few months? And if that was the case, why was she putting so much work into the little house? And why all the moving around in the first place?

Abby gave Dustin and Ellie a quick tour of her workroom and then they headed out for the conservatory.

"How are things going with the house?" Abby asked.

"Oh, don't ask," Ellie said. "It's been let go quite a long time, I'm afraid. The owners have given us an allotment for fix-up. John and I are trying to stretch it by doing most of the work ourselves."

"Well, don't forget my offer," Abby said. "I think you'll find there's always a helping hand available on Sparrow Island."

"Yes, I can see that," Ellie said. "I'll keep it in mind."

"Have you moved a lot?" Abby asked.

Ellie didn't answer right away and Abby wondered at first if she'd understood her. But finally she shrugged. "Oh, you know, it's a mobile society these days."

Abby didn't want Ellie to get the impression the conversation was turning into an interrogation so she shared how she'd left the island for college and ended up living in New York for many years. "I came back here to take care of Mary after her accident," she said. "Then when Mary was stronger, I found I didn't want to leave again."

Ellie smiled. "We all have a place that's home to us," she said.

"And what's yours?" Abby asked.

Ellie's smile faded. "Wherever my son and grandson are," she said at last.

Abby could see her questions were clearly making Ellie uncomfortable, so she started telling her more about how the museum and conservatory had come into being.

As they walked, the boys ran ahead, with Bobby giving Dustin a running account of every point of interest and every experience he'd ever had in the conservatory.

When Abby saw the look on Ellie Parker's face as they came upon the colony of orchids, she knew that however much this detour had upset her schedule for the day, it had been well worth it.

Ellie gazed at the orchids with what could only be called reverence. Then she said, almost in a whisper, "They are *so* beautiful." Unconsciously she signed the words as she spoke and somehow the gestures enhanced the words and the image. Abby looked out at the Calypsos, which she'd seen so many times, and found she had a new appreciation for them. She remembered Ellie's gestures—a ballet to honor the flowers. Flowers that seemed to nod to their admirers, accepting their admiration.

Abby thought she heard her name being called and it snapped her out of the moment. She looked up to see

Bernadette Deasy and a tall, barrel-chested man approaching along the trail.

"Hi, Abby," Bernadette said as they approached. "I'm so glad I found you out here. We were wondering what those are," she said, pointing to the orchids. She turned to Ellie with a questioning look.

Abby introduced them and the conversation was now accompanied by quick, deft hand movements from each woman, making it seem much more lively.

Bernadette introduced her companion. "Abby, Mrs. Parker, this is Lawrence Griffin. I told you about him, Abby."

"Indeed you did," Abby said. "It's nice to meet you."

"Lawrence has been wanting to see the museum since I've talked it up so much," Bernadette went on breathlessly, her hands moving almost automatically it seemed. "The dance studio's opening up again next week and I'll be back to work, so we grabbed this chance. We thought we'd get in a little hike first. It's such a beautiful day."

She asked again about the flowers and Abby said, "Well, I can tell you what they are, but I suspect Ellie knows more than I do, so I'll let her tell you about them while I put this in." She brought a placard out of the canvas bag and turned it so that they could see the information it contained about the colony. "You aren't the first to ask."

"Could I help you with that?" Lawrence asked, as he saw Abby pull out the mallet.

"Thank you," Abby said. "I'd appreciate it."

The two women talked while Abby chatted with Lawrence as they hammered the placard's stake well in front of the closest specimen in the colony. The orchids couldn't stand much disruption, and as they walked, Abby looked for a place to put a separate placard advising visitors of that fact. Too many people had already been tempted into going off the path to get a closer look.

Lawrence hammered in the stake for Abby, then they fell into easy conversation. Abby confessed she didn't know very much about hockey to which Lawrence responded, "That's okay, I don't know much about birds. Maybe we can enlighten one another."

Abby liked the man. He seemed like a very genuine person and Abby could see he was very taken with Bernadette.

As they returned to Ellie and Bernadette, Abby saw they were laughing and talking like old friends already. All of Ellie's reserve seemed to have evaporated with Bernadette.

But then Ellie looked at Abby as if suddenly remembering something. She looked around, craning her neck. "Can you still hear the boys?" she asked.

Abby looked down the trail and scanned the woods to see if she could see them on the next loop. She called out for them, but there was no answer. She frowned and called louder. Still nothing.

"Dustin!" Ellie called, her eyes gone wide. She grabbed at Abby's hand. "We have to find them," she said, starting off down the trail at a run without waiting for an answer.

Abby reached Ellie and tried to calm her down. She told her the conservatory was a safe place and that there was no need for worry, but the woman seemed to be getting more frantic by the moment. Abby thought maybe she hadn't understood her and had Bernadette give it a try, but Ellie signed something to her rapidly, even as she was still scanning the surroundings anxiously.

They moved on, shouting out the boys' names until finally

Abby heard Bobby call back. She shouted for him to come back to where they were.

Bernadette signed to Ellie, assuring her that the boys were nearby, but Ellie didn't look as if she trusted the news. When Bobby and Dustin finally rounded the bend at a sprint she looked as if she might faint with relief.

As Dustin approached she signed something to him, but didn't speak. The gestures cut through the air and Abby saw that Ellie's face had gone from pale to flushed.

Dustin hung his head, then looked up as his grandmother as if he might cry. "Sorry I worried you, Grandma," he said, his voice choking.

"Gosh, I'm sorry," Bobby said to Abby. "We were just exploring. I didn't realize we'd gotten so far away from you. I thought you were going to hike on behind us. I didn't know you'd stopped."

"It's okay now," Abby said. "Mrs. Parker just got worried. Why didn't you answer?"

"I didn't hear you," Bobby said. "We were down at that sandstone bed looking at the fossils. I'm really sorry."

Bobby looked perplexed and Abby couldn't say she really blamed him. She reached out and put her arm around his shoulders to reassure him. She was a little in the dark about what had just happened herself.

Ellie Parker pulled Dustin to her and squeezed. It seemed she couldn't get him close enough. "I'm sorry," she said, smiling weakly. "I didn't mean to make a fuss."

Dustin looked down at his tennis shoes and Abby saw a fat tear spatter onto the blue canvas.

CHAPTER ❦ THIRTEEN

Aunt abby, you missed the picnic!" Emily said. "It was so much fun and you missed it all."

"I know, Emily. I was disappointed," Abby said. "Did you catch any fish?"

"I caught two and Nicholas caught three," she said, skipping along beside Abby as she made her way from the garage into the kitchen. "We're having them for supper."

"Did you clean them yourself?" Abby asked. "That used to be the rule with Grandpa Stanton. If you caught it, you had to clean it."

"No, he cleaned mine for me," Emily said. "It was yucky," she wrinkled her nose.

"Typical, isn't it?" Mary asked, nodding hello. "Different rules apply for grandchildren and great-grands!"

"So I see," Abby said. "Where's Nicholas?"

"He's upstairs taking a nap," Emily said. "Mom says he was

tuckered *out*," Emily said, swiping her small hand through the air.

"That he was," Mary said. "We missed you, Abby. You said something came up and you'd tell me later. What was it?"

Abby reached into her bag and brought out a DVD she'd brought from her office for the children to watch. "Emily, would you like to watch this? It's about butterflies."

"You bet," Emily said. "Did you bring one for Nicholas too?"

"Yes, on the orcas, of course. But you can watch yours now if you'd like while I help your grandmother get dinner ready. Do you know how to work the player?"

"Better than I do," Mary said.

"I didn't want to say anything in front of Emily," Abby said once she'd gone into the living room. "But we had a little incident this morning that may have undone all your goodwill with Ellie Parker."

Abby related what had happened. "So, of course, I had to bring them home after that. Then I dropped Bobby off and felt I had to go in and explain to Sandy what had happened since Bobby was upset too. He kept asking me if he'd done something wrong."

"It sounds like she overreacted," Mary said. "Why, do you suppose?"

"I have no idea," Abby said. "I mean, she doesn't know the conservatory, so perhaps she imagined them wandering off cliffs or into quicksand or something. Then again, maybe it has to do with her not being able to hear. I'd imagine that makes her feel more vulnerable.

"The upside is, she loved the Calypso colony—in a big way. And by sheer happenstance she got to meet Bernadette.

Though I'm not sure those things outweighed the five minutes of sheer terror she seemed to experience when we couldn't find Dustin."

"I'm sure now that she's had a chance to reflect on it she realizes she needn't have been so alarmed."

"Maybe," Abby said. "I hope so. I felt awful that it upset her, but honestly, I didn't think it was a problem at the time. I still don't get why she reacted so strongly."

"Well, we have the advantage of the home turf. We know the place, and we know Bobby and his never-ending curiosity," Mary said.

"True," Abby said. "But, Mary, this seems to be part of a pattern. I know you think I see intrigue around every corner, but there are some things that are troublesome about that family." She shared with Mary some of the things she had observed about the Parkers, including the man who asked Wilma questions about John Parker.

"You don't suppose they're in one of those witness protection programs or something, do you?" Mary asked.

"I think that's pretty unlikely," Abby said, smiling at Mary. "But something doesn't add up and I certainly would love to know what's going on. But I guess all in good time. Anyway, I hear Emily and Nicholas had a good haul. We're having fish for dinner?"

Mary laughed. "I'm afraid that would require another miracle of the loaves and the fishes if everyone's to be fed off their catch. None of the fish was as big as your hand. Henry's raiding his freezer for more. But don't dare let on to them, they're so proud to be supplying supper."

"Not a word," Abby said. "You know, I think Mom and Dad may have pulled that trick on us a few times."

"I know they did!" Mary said. "I caught Mom getting fish out of the freezer once."

The phone rang and Abby picked up the receiver. It was Bernadette inquiring about Ellie Parker. "Is she okay? That was terrible for her and for Dustin too. I felt like it was my fault for distracting her."

"Don't be silly, Bernadette," Abby said. "It wasn't anyone's fault. I don't know what that was about, but she seemed okay by the time I dropped them off. Dustin was very unhappy, but I think he may have been more embarrassed about being scolded in front of us than anything else."

"What did Mrs. Parker mean when she told him 'They're still after us.'?" Bernadette asked.

"They're still after us?" Abby repeated.

"That's what she signed to Dustin when they came back. She said, 'You know better than that. You always have to be where I can see you. They're still after us.'"

"I have no earthly idea," Abby said. "Who would be after them? That sounds ominous."

"Hold on," Bernadette said. "I don't want to start rumors. That's what I thought she signed to him, but maybe I misinterpreted. I may be rusty, or maybe I just fleshed it out wrong because Mrs. Parker was so upset."

"I'm sure there's some reasonable explanation," Abby assured Bernadette, wondering herself what such an explanation could possibly be. "Ellie's still getting her sea legs here. She probably imagined all sorts of hazards. You were good to call and check on her though."

After Abby hung up, she turned back to Mary, who was mixing her special breading for the fish.

"What in the world was that all about?" Mary asked.

Abby filled her in on the exchange.

"Who is still after them?" Mary asked.

"Who's still after who?" asked a bass voice. They turned to see Henry coming into the kitchen. "Emily saw me pull up and greeted me at the door," he said, reaching under his jacket to pull out a paper bag. "I stuffed these in here so she wouldn't see them. Now I think two of my ribs are frozen together." He passed the supplementary fish off to Mary. "Now what's that you were saying? This sounds like police business. Who is still after who?"

Abby hesitated. Like Bernadette, she didn't want to spread rumors, but she trusted Henry to know how much weight to give what she was about to tell him.

Henry listened and after a bit, the smile faded from his face. He reached up to rub his balding pate, a gesture Abby knew well.

"May be a tempest in a teapot," he said at last. "But I believe I'll do some discrete checking on the Parkers, especially if there's someone here on the island asking questions."

LATER THAT EVENING Mary took advantage of the quiet time to sort out her thoughts and to pray for the right words to come to her at the right time.

Henry had gone and Abby had excused herself to go up and work on her data entry, making a point about how far behind she was. Mary saw right through it. She had no doubt Abby had work to do, she always did, but she knew her sister was also trying to allow her time alone with Nancy.

She could hear Nancy's voice, faintly. It was coming from the baby monitor receiver in the kitchen. The monitor was in the kids' room since Nicholas was still given to waking up in the night occasionally. When it happened here in unfamiliar surroundings, it disoriented and frightened him.

Nancy was saying night prayers with Nicholas, who was winding down his long list of God-bless petitions.

Mary smiled as Nicholas asked Nancy, "Did you send Daddy the picture of me and my fish? What'd he say?"

"Not yet, Nicholas, but I will. Remember, I've told you, it's a different time back at our house."

"But you could do it now," Nicholas said, "isn't it now everywhere?"

Mary smiled and listened for Nancy's reply.

"Yes, it is, but—" Mary heard her let out a long sigh. Her voice sounded very tired. "Never mind. I'll send the picture to Daddy, I promise. Now snuggle in and go to sleep, okay?"

"Okay," Nicholas said. "But say, "Good night, don't let the bed bugs bite!'"

Nancy repeated the words, but to Mary's ear they sounded mechanical. Not at all like Nancy's usual demeanor with the children.

Something was definitely wrong. She wondered if Nancy was ill. She was chronically tired and had lost weight since Mary had seen her last. But surely Benjamin wouldn't have let her make this trip alone if that was it. Taking care of two children was physically and mentally taxing.

Mary knew better than to push Nancy too hard. She could be a stubborn woman. Like her mother, Mary had to admit. The fact that they were so much alike had been at the heart of many of their squabbles when Nancy was going through her teen angst.

Mary thought back to when Nancy had been in high school. She'd started dating a young man from Shaw Island who had no ambition at all. *He was what the kids today would call a slacker,* she thought. Not only that, Mary had sensed something duplicitous in the boy. When she'd voiced her concerns to Nancy, the girl reacted by digging in her heels. She kept right on dating the slacker long after she could barely stand the sight of him, just so she wouldn't have to admit her mother had been right.

Nancy came in and plopped down on the sofa. "You want to watch some TV?" she asked Mary.

"You could see what's on," Mary said, pointing to the guide on the coffee table. "Nancy, is everything okay? You look pale. Are you ill?"

"No, Mom," Nancy said, thumbing through the guide. "I'm fine. Just tired."

"Are you *sure*?" Mary said.

Nancy looked up. "Mom, yes, I'm sure. I'm fine. I had a checkup two months ago. Do I look that bad?"

"You just look exhausted, honey," Mary said. "And you've lost weight. I worry about you."

"I'm fit as a fiddle," Nancy said. "Just run ragged, like practically everyone else in the world. Please, Mom, don't worry so much."

"Is everything okay with you and Benjamin?" Mary blurted before she could stop herself. She grimaced. So much for patience.

"Did Aunt Abby—" Nancy began, her lips pinched.

Mary held up a hand. "Abby didn't say a word. You know she wouldn't. But Nancy, you're my daughter. I know you. Something's wrong. What's going on?"

"I think—" Nancy began, then fell silent. Mary thought she was going to clam up, but then she went on, speaking in a low, sorrowful voice. "Mom, I'm worried that my marriage is in trouble."

Mary willed herself to stay calm. "What's wrong, Nancy?" she asked softly.

"I don't know," Nancy said. "We just seem to be growing apart. Ben works so many hours and I'm either working or looking after the kids or—" she stopped and shook her head. "This all sounds so lame," she said at last. "It sounds silly when you say it, but when you're living it, there's nothing funny about it at all."

"Why didn't you say something before now?" Mary asked.

"I didn't want you to worry," Nancy said. "I don't want you to worry. I don't want you to think I'm a failure, and most of all, I don't want you to think badly of Ben."

"Nancy, you know I love you both," Mary said. "When you brought Benjamin into our family I made a vow, too, that I would love him as my own. And since that time I've come to respect and admire him as well. As a man, as a husband and as a father."

Nancy nodded, biting at her lip.

"Have I been wrong about Benjamin?" Mary asked gently. "Has he treated you unkindly, or is—is there someone else?"

Nancy looked over at her, a stricken look on her face. "Mom, no! It's nothing like that. No—" she stopped short and let out a groan. "Oh," she said miserably, "this is why I didn't want to talk to you about this. You don't understand. Ben's a good man and there's no betrayal or big blowup or anything dramatic like that. I just feel like we're pulling away from one another."

Mary's heart twisted. She knew Nancy was in pain. "Oh,

honey," she said. "All marriages go through difficult periods. You're just going through a rough spot."

Nancy got up from the couch. "You and Dad didn't have *rough spots*," she said, putting the words in fingertip quotations. "Look, Mom, I'm sorry. I don't want to talk about this anymore with you. You'll never understand it. You and Dad always had your act together. Not everyone's that lucky. You know, sometimes I think maybe you two didn't do me or Zack any favors. We expect perfection and it's just not that way in our world."

Mary reached out to grab Nancy's hand. "Don't be angry, Nancy," she said softly. "I want to help if I can."

"You can't," Nancy said. "Just try not to worry about us, Mom. We'll be okay. I'm really tired. That fishing really took it out of me too," she said, trying for a light tone and falling way short of the mark.

She kissed Mary goodnight, and as she clamored up the stairs Mary could hear her sniffling.

Mary felt helpless and impatient, much as she had during her rehabilitation. She took a deep breath and began to pray.

ABBY HEARD NANCY come up the stairs and go into her room. She glanced at her watch. It had only been half an hour. This probably was not a good sign. Abby had gone down as far as the landing a few minutes earlier, thinking if there'd been no breakthrough, she'd go on in and watch a movie with Mary and Nancy. But she'd overheard them talking and crept quietly back up the stairs.

She'd been pleased but now felt her optimism had been premature. She sighed, closed down her computer and started to neaten her desk. There would be no more work tonight, not with this on her mind.

She was thinking, too, of what Bernadette thought she'd heard—or rather seen—at the conservatory between Dustin and his grandmother. Could it have been just a misinterpretation? Abby doubted that. The whole episode had been unsettling. There had been so much raw emotion in Elise's panic. Why did she insist on keeping such a close watch on Dustin? Abby certainly didn't expect Elise to give him as much latitude as Bobby had; Bobby had grown up on the island. He knew the land, the rules of island life and most important of all, the people.

But it seemed Ellie hovered over Dustin. It had to be smothering for the boy. Now another phrase kept running through Abby's brain: *They're still after us.* What in the world could that be about? Who would be chasing a deaf woman and a boy? Should she be worried about the men asking questions about the chessboard artist?

She thought of Dustin and how anxious and unhappy he seemed a good deal of the time. And what was to be made of the conversations she'd heard between the boys? *What's the deal with Dustin's mother?* she wondered.

There were other things. She'd noticed the boy still didn't respond when he was spoken to. He often had to be nudged or prompted, but she was pretty sure his hearing was fine. Also, it was strange how he always responded so stiffly to questions about the places he'd lived. Then there was that denial of having lived in Connecticut that had come so quickly and adamantly.

Connecticut! Abby grabbed her address book out of the drawer. The call she'd planned to make to Diane today had gotten scuttled along with the rest of her to-do list after the incident in the conservatory.

She glanced at the clock. It was chancy, but she picked up the phone anyway, hoping Diane was still a night owl, as she had been back in their college days. Sure enough, she picked up on the second ring. After Abby identified herself, they had a nice catch-up chat for a few minutes, trading their latest news and exchanging information about mutual friends. Then Abby told her why she was calling. "What can you tell me about your emergency aid course? It looks awfully impressive online. I think it's possible one of your course graduates saved a friend's life right here on Sparrow Island this week."

"Really?" Diane said, "Well, isn't that wonderful to hear! You know, it's strange. You're the second person to ask me about that course in the last few days. I had a man in my office yesterday asking all about it. He said they wanted to start one at his hospital in Toledo."

"I'm not surprised," Abby said. "It looks like a very effective course."

"Oh, it is. It definitely is," Diane said. "But I was leery of this guy."

"Why?"

"I don't think he was so much interested in the design of the course as he was in my personnel. I think he was looking to steal my doctors. That happens now more than you'd believe. Some places are just blatant about it; others are sneaky."

"What made you think that's what was going on in this case?" Abby asked.

"Because that's all he wanted to know about, the people involved. Particularly the emergency room doctor who designed the course."

"Did he talk to him?" Abby asked.

"No, I'm sorry to say he couldn't have," Diane answered. "Not here anyway. He moved on to greener pastures more than a year ago. I was sorry to lose him, but apparently he got a better offer. We're not a teaching hospital and we're not particularly well endowed, so we can't offer the big salaries larger hospitals can. I hated to lose Dr. Donovan. He was a fantastic doctor and a good human being. He taught this class in addition to an already grueling schedule in the ER. He had probably a hundred people certified by the time he left."

"Do you have a list of those people?" Abby asked. "I'd like to know if the man who saved my friend here on the island is one of them."

"Well…" Diane said, hesitating.

"I'm sorry," Abby said immediately. "I didn't mean to put you on the spot, Diane. Confidentiality and all that, I understand. Let me tell you his name and you can tell me if you remember him. It's John Parker. He's a physician's assistant here at our local Medical Center."

"That name doesn't sound familiar," Diane said, "but of course, I wouldn't have the actual registrant lists. Tell you what, Abby. I'll look when I get back to work. Why is it that you're so curious about this?"

"Well, John's being modest. He doesn't want any publicity about it, but he deserves recognition."

"Why don't you just ask him directly?"

"I'll be honest with you. He's new here and he's a little prickly about his privacy."

"I see," Diane said. "That's not true. I really don't see, but I trust you have your reasons, Abby. You always did."

They chatted a few more minutes, then Abby put the phone back in the cradle. She got ready for bed, her mind still on both the Parker family and Nancy. So much seemed to be in shadows in both cases.

Nancy had built up resentment against Benjamin for— among other things—not supporting her dream of writing a children's book when she hadn't even told him about it.

With the Parkers, there was obviously something very serious —and possibly dangerous—going on, but they chose to keep it hidden.

Abby pulled out her Bible. As was her habit from time to time, she fanned the pages and stuck her finger in to choose a random passage. Except, of course, they never seemed truly random.

She read: "But whoever lives by the truth comes into the light, so that it may be seen plainly that what he has done has been done through God" (John 3:21).

Abby prayed that if there was anything she could do to help bring light and truth to both Nancy and poor, sad Dustin Parker that she would be shown the way and given the strength and the courage to act.

CHAPTER ❦ FOURTEEN

Mary glanced in the rearview mirror at Bobby before she pulled out onto Ocean Boulevard. He was stroking Finnegan's head and was uncharacteristically subdued.

It had taken a flurry of e-mails to convince Ellie Parker to come out to Goldie Landon's place on this fine Saturday morning to see the greenhouse and Goldie's collections of rare and exotic specimens.

Mary had been afraid that if they didn't do something quickly to erase the unpleasantness of the incident at the conservatory, Ellie might slip right back into her shell. She had tried enticing her with details about the flowers. When that didn't work she had played shamelessly on how upset Bobby had been about yesterday, which was certainly true. He still didn't understand what he'd done wrong, or why Ellie had gotten so upset, and he wasn't the only one.

Mary's troubled conversation with Nancy the night before was still with her too. It broke her heart to see her daughter in distress. Nancy had come down the stairs all cheerful and upbeat, but Mary saw through it in an instant. Her daughter was putting up a front again.

It made Mary deeply sad to think that Nancy would work this hard to keep things hidden from her. But she didn't know what to do to get through to her, especially since Nancy was pretending that their conversation had never happened.

Nancy had chattered on about trivial things as she got the children dressed up to go visiting with Grandma Stanton. Nancy and the children were to be Ellen's show-and-tell today as they made the rounds visiting friends. There were so many people on the list that Mary had opted out. She explained that it took a while for her to get in and out of the van, so they'd make better time and be able to see more people without her. And, though she was loathe to admit it, Mary was exhausted. She loved her grandchildren fiercely, but their energy was boundless, and quiet time had been in short supply during the last week.

She wondered at how Ellie managed the full-time care of Dustin. She guessed Elise Parker to be about the same age as she—closing in on sixty. Not old certainly, but an age when one's energy did flag on any given day. Given that, by her own choice, Ellie seemed to keep Dustin with her practically every hour of every day now that school was out, she had to be tired.

"Bobby, are you okay?" Mary asked.

"I guess," Bobby said. "I just, well, I don't know if Mrs. Parker is mad at me or what."

"Nobody's mad at you, Bobby," Mary said gently. "You don't need to worry. Everything's fine."

"Dustin may be mad at me too," he said. "I guess I got him in trouble. But I sure didn't mean to."

As prearranged, Mary pulled up into the Parkers' driveway and waited. Ellie and Dustin came out almost immediately. Dustin trudged along beside his grandmother until they reached the van, but when he saw Bobby and Finnegan in the back he perked up.

"Now remember, Dustin," Mary said. "You may sit in the back and pet Finnegan all you want right now. He loves it. But once we get to Goldie's, he'll be working, okay?"

"Yes, ma'am," Dustin said, "I remember, I have a good memory." As he climbed into the van, Mary could just make out his mumbling under his breath, "I *have* to have a good memory." He settled into the seat and buckled up, grinning over at Bobby, who seemed as if he'd just had the weight of the world lifted off his small shoulders.

ELLIE AND GOLDIE, as Mary had expected, hit it off famously. When they started the tour of her greenhouse Goldie gave Bobby and Dustin a few small jobs to do for her. They happily busied themselves with moving bags of soil and plant food from one place to another with the wheelbarrow as she'd instructed.

As Goldie showed off the first orchid specimen, she told Ellie where she'd gotten it. Ellie frowned and rummaged in her bag. Mary did the same. Just as on the day at the museum, they each came out with a notepad.

"You two come prepared, don't you?" Goldie said, pushing a strand of gray hair back into her braid.

Ellie scribbled and handed hers to Goldie, who quickly wrote the name of the plant as she repeated it aloud. "Ellie may want to keep her notes about the flowers, and you already know about all my collections," she told Mary.

As they moved on, Goldie wrote as she talked and seemed not at all uncomfortable about Ellie's deafness. "This one's an Abyssinian banana plant," she said, "or some folks say Ethiopian banana. I'm not even sure you can bring these into the country anymore," she told Ellie, who nodded, admiring the plant. "Though I don't believe there's any danger they'd become invasive here. They're used to the tropics so I don't think they'd last long in our climate."

"And what is this one? I've never seen this before," Ellie asked, pointing to the next pot over.

"That's cardamom," Goldie said and scribbled again.

"It's—" Goldie stopped as Ellie turned her head to check to make sure she could still see Dustin, but she picked right back up when Ellie turned back to her. "It's used as a spice, as I'm sure you know. But the Chinese used it as a medicinal herb. It's also used in perfumes and even to make a sort of cardamom coffee over in the Middle East."

"Will it flower?" Ellie asked, holding an imaginary flower to her nose.

"I hope so," Goldie said. "They don't flower until the second season, but even the leaves smell good."

She bent to smell it, and both Mary and Ellie did the same. Ellie breathed in deep. "That's a wonderful scent," she said. "I feel like I should be cooking!"

And so it went for almost an hour. Ellie seemed to be enjoying herself. She seemed comfortable, all the stiff reserve set aside, though she kept a close eye on Dustin.

Mary wondered if perhaps Ellie and Goldie sensed something in one another. Goldie had been almost a total recluse when Mary had first become acquainted with her on a chance meeting aboard the ferry from the mainland. Goldie had been carrying a bundle of cuttings and Mary had struck up a conversation.

It had taken some doing to coax Goldie out of her shell, but slowly Mary had persuaded her to take part in community life once again.

Though she was still content with her own company and was happiest when tending her flowers, she'd made room for other people in her life again. She now attended Little Flock regularly and took part in many of the island celebrations and activities. And she'd renewed old friendships she'd let slide as she'd started keeping more and more to herself.

"I've got a really nice chicken salad made," Goldie said when they'd looked at everything in the greenhouse. "I hope I can talk you into staying for lunch. We can eat out at the patio table where we usually have coffee, Mary."

Mary thought for sure Ellie would balk, but to her surprise, she said she'd love to if Mary had the time.

"Well, good then," Goldie said. "I'll go inside and get things fixed. Mary, you can show Ellie some of the things out in the beds and the yard."

"Do you need help?" Ellie asked.

"No, it's all made," Goldie said. "I'll just fix up some hot dogs for the boys. I'd much rather you spend your time admiring my flowers than my kitchen. I can tell you, my flowers get a lot more attention."

When they were back outside, Mary took Finnegan's harness off. "Off the clock," she told him, and the boys ran to play with him in the yard. Ellie caught Dustin's arm as he ran by and turned him around to face her. "You stay where I can see you," she said. When he continued to look at Finnegan, she took his chin and turned his face toward her and said, "Do you understand me?"

"Yes, ma'am," Dustin said, signing and speaking aloud. "I understand. It won't happen again, Grandma."

Mary was a little taken aback by the stern tone Ellie had used with Dustin. She wondered if she'd meant it or if her hearing impairment might interfere with how she perceived the modulation in her voice.

Mary reached over to touch her arm. "It's okay," she said, "they'll stay right here in the yard."

Ellie nodded. "I'm sure you think I'm being hard on him," Ellie said with a baleful look in Dustin's direction. "But I'm responsible for him and I have to keep him safe."

"You can relax. He'll be safe here," Mary assured her.

They continued on across the yard to Goldie's raised beds and Mary told her as much as she could remember about what Goldie had planted there.

"Flowers have become very important to me," Ellie said. "I've always loved them, but since I've lost my hearing, they've become much more than a passing interest." She got a faraway look in her eyes as she continued, unconsciously beginning to sign as she spoke. "There are so many things I miss from the hearing world. Music, of course, but little sounds too. Good sounds. Beautiful sounds. The crackle of a leaf skittering across the ground, the howl of the wind, birdsongs, church bells, water lapping against a stone. Those are lost to me now. But flowers—those I can still enjoy completely!"

Mary nodded. She shared with Ellie that after her accident she'd spent a lot of time cataloging the things she couldn't do anymore. "Then one day when I was working on an arrangement at my shop, it occurred to me that this thing that I held so dear was practically unchanged. I had to have a new worktable built, but our dear friend Rick DeBow had that done for me in no time at all."

Mary always appreciated it when people who were clearly curious about her chair simply came out and asked her about her accident. And since Ellie had opened the door a little, Mary plunged in, "Tell me about how you lost your hearing. You sign and lip-read so well, it must have been a while ago."

"Not so long," Ellie said. "It was gradual, a degenerative disease. In a way that was terrible—that daily reminder of what was slipping away. But in another way it was a blessing. It gave me time to learn and it made me appreciate sounds and store them up in my memory for a time when the silence would overtake me. I've been profoundly deaf for about five years now. How about you?" she asked, nodding at Mary's chair. "How long for you?"

"Long enough to stop feeling sorry for myself," Mary said. Then she smiled and amended, "Well, most of the time anyway. I still get frustrated at my limitations sometimes. But mostly I'm just grateful to be alive. The accident took place right down there," she said, pointing toward the access road to Goldie's. "I was foolish enough to take my eyes off the road when my purse slid off the seat. It all seemed to happen in the blink of an eye."

"That must have been difficult to have everything in your life change so suddenly."

"Yes, it was," Mary said. "But I had so much help from family and friends, and I truly believe my faith became deeper and stronger."

Ellie nodded. "Speaking of family, you have beautiful grandchildren. And Nancy is lovely. She looks like you."

"Yes, so people tell us. I know we're a lot alike in temperament," Mary said. "Most times that's a good thing, but not always. I have a son too, Zack. He's very much like his father. Do you have other children?"

Ellie frowned, but said nothing. At first Mary thought she hadn't heard the question, but then she saw the frown twist into a more anguished expression.

Mary wondered if Ellie had perhaps lost a child. She tried to think of something to say to release Ellie from the obligation to answer, but Goldie did it for her, coming out at that moment and motioning them over to the table.

The lunch was a delight and Mary congratulated herself on her instincts about introducing Ellie and Goldie.

"Mary and I have had a lot of very pleasant conversations out here at this table in recent times," Goldie told Ellie, reaching over to pat Mary's hand. "And now she's brought me a new friend to talk flowers with," she said, being sure to face Ellie. "I'll bet she wouldn't leave you alone about it, right?"

Ellie smiled. "She was pretty persistent," she said.

"Pushy, you mean," Goldie said, laughing. "But, I'm glad of it. My life's a lot richer now than it was before I met Mary. And I know the same will be true for you."

Ellie nodded, but again Mary saw something troubled in her eyes. It was the same fretful look she'd seen in Nancy last night.

The boys finished eating quickly, thanked Goldie politely, and went back to playing with Finnegan in the yard. Mary noticed that Ellie looked over every few minutes to seek Dustin out. It was even tiring to watch.

When they were finished eating Ellie insisted on helping Goldie carry the dishes back into the kitchen. She rose and called Dustin over. Her eyes scanned the yard and turned to look down Goldie's long driveway. She told Dustin where she was going and that she'd be right back and warned him, quite sternly again, to stay where Mary could see him.

Now Mary fully understood what Abby had been trying to describe to her about the incident in the conservatory the day before. This all seemed excessively diligent.

Finnegan had apparently had about as much fun as he could take and flopped down in the grass, panting. The boys sat down beside him, then sprawled on the grass for a round of the time-honored game of looking for images in the cloud formations.

They seemed to forget Mary was sitting behind them, or perhaps they didn't realize the wind was carrying their voices in her direction.

"Boy, your grandmother really likes you to stay close, huh?" Bobby said.

"Yeah," Dustin answered glumly. "It's kind of hard to explain. There's like, trouble in my family."

"You mean like between your parents? Is that why you can't talk about your mom?"

"Sort of," Dustin said.

"Are they getting a divorce or something?"

"I don't know," Dustin said. He sat up and started to pull blades of grass from the yard and examine them. "Maybe they will," he continued. "Nobody tells me anything. I can't even talk to my mom right now."

"Why not?" Bobby asked.

"I just can't," Dustin said. "It's dangerous."

"Dangerous?" Bobby repeated. "How can it be dangerous to talk to your own mother?"

"I better not talk about this anymore," Dustin said. "My dad would freak out if he knew I'd told you anything about my mom. I'm supposed to say I don't have a mother if anyone asks. But I can't do that. That's like saying she's dead or something and she's not. Just don't say anything about this to anybody, okay?"

"I won't," Bobby said, marking an X across his heart.

Mary's heart ached for the child. What did he mean when he said it was dangerous for him to talk to his mother? Was he the prize in an ugly custody battle?

She thought again of Nancy and Benjamin and the children. She could never imagine Benjamin keeping the children from their mother, or Nancy forbidding them to talk about Benjamin. She couldn't picture them ever getting to the point where they would do anything to hurt the children. But until a few days ago, she could never have imagined anything seriously wrong in their marriage either.

ABBY AND RICK had been working steadily all morning. Rick had called early to tell her that some parts he needed for a job at the Chois' weren't coming in until the afternoon, so he was available if she wanted him to knock off a few of the jobs at the conservatory. This had seemed to Abby a much more appealing prospect than the stack of paperwork on her desk, so she'd gone out to finish the tasks that had been cut short by yesterday's incident with Ellie and Dustin.

"That's everything I can do today," Rick said, wiping his forehead with the sleeve of his flannel shirt. "I'll order a new timber for that footbridge. I put a brace under it for now. And you're going to need a new latch for that display case on the viewing platform. I think the wind sprung it open and bent the old one. It probably wasn't big enough in the first place."

"That's not worth your coming back out for. I can pick up a latch at Holloway's and put it on myself on Monday or Tuesday when those corrected placards come in."

As they walked back to the museum, Abby asked, "So, what have you got for the rest of the afternoon?"

"Pretty light for a Saturday," Rick said. "A few things at the Bird Nest this afternoon, then John Parker's coming by to pick up that veneer and to show me a little trick he's come up with to cut the pieces. He's devised a jig that lets him do cuts with a lot more precision than I can get with a steel ruler."

"How do you think John's adjusting to life on the island?" Abby asked.

Rick shrugged. "Hard to say. We're not pals or anything. It's the wood projects we talk about mostly. Why?"

"I'm worried about his mother and his son," Abby said. "She seems to have a lot of anxiety, and Dustin just seems sad much of the time."

She thought of telling Rick about what had happened at the conservatory yesterday, but relating what had happened didn't really convey the emotional weight it had carried. In fact, saying that Dustin wandered off and Ellie Parker got upset sounded perfectly reasonable.

"John's a pretty serious guy," Rick said. "I mean, he doesn't kid around. Seems like he always has a lot on his mind. I'm not as astute as you are about things, Abby, but there's one thing I've noticed that seems weird."

"What's that?" Abby asked.

"Well, he's lives really simply from what I can tell, and he was all about saving a little money by ordering these veneers from this place at a good price, but he's got a very expensive carving set. Nicest I've ever seen. Fine German steel." Rick made a whistling sound. "It's primo, and very, very pricey."

"Maybe it was a gift," Abby ventured.

"Maybe," Rick allowed, "or maybe that's just his one big splurge. Who knows?"

"Does he ever mention his wife?" Abby asked.

"No, but he has one, or did until recently anyway. I noticed when he was showing me the chessboard that he's got a faint white band on the ring finger of his left hand. Guess with all the hours he works, he hasn't been out in the sun enough for it to tan."

"Do you think he's recently divorced?" Abby asked. "I suppose that would explain a lot."

"I don't know," Rick said, shaking his head. "Let me put it to you this way, Abby. I can't define it exactly, but there's something about John Parker that I recognize. And identify with. You know, when I came here I was trying to start over, to turn my back on an empty life and to try to find something more authentic and worthwhile. I think the same may be true for John. I think he's trying to leave something behind. I like the guy, Abby. I hope whatever he's looking for . . . I hope he gets as lucky as I've been and he finds it here."

"I know you're wrong about one thing," Abby said.

"What?" Rick said, stopping in his tracks.

Abby turned to him. "Despite what you say, you are, in fact, very astute!"

CHAPTER ❦ FIFTEEN

ABBY DROPPED BY Holloway's Hardware on the way home to special order a heavy-duty latch for the platform display case. She was eager to have every item checked off the conservatory list by the middle of next week. She got out of her car, and just as she was about to take the first step up onto the broad porch, she met John Parker coming out. He was wearing paint-spattered clothes and was carrying a bucket of paint.

"Hi there," Abby said. "Looks like you're working hard on your day off."

"Yes, thanks to your sister," Parker answered with a smile. "She took Mom and Dustin out to introduce her to your flower friend, so I thought I'd try to get some of the painting done while they're gone. Surprise her."

"I know she'll appreciate that," Abby said. "And she'll love seeing Goldie's place, I'm sure. That woman has the greenest thumb of anyone I know, except Mary, of course."

"Listen, I appreciate everything you ladies have done to make my mother feel welcome. I hope you won't be offended if she doesn't always accept your invitations. She wasn't ever a very social person. And since she's lost her hearing that's become even more pronounced."

Abby had the distinct impression he was trying to warn her off. "I see," she said. "Well, we'll keep inviting her to things—that's just the Sparrow Island way—but we won't take it personally if she declines. It's the Sparrow Island way to respect privacy too."

Parker nodded. "How's Emily?" he asked.

"She seems to be mending fine," Abby said. "She doesn't complain about the cut at all except when the dressing's changed. It's hardly slowed her down."

"Good, good," Parker said then hefted the paint can. "Guess I'd better get back to it," he said.

ABBY LEFT HER CAR and set out for the Springhouse Café where she was to meet Janet for lunch. Her phone rang. She stopped, fished it out of her pocket and heard Henry's recognizable bass voice. "How do you always pick 'em?" he asked.

"Pardon?" Abby said, pressing a finger in her other ear as she passed by the park where children were running and playing.

"I've been checking up on the Parkers," he said. "Quietly, of course. "If John Parker lived in Florida, he never had a driver's license there. Not unless he's lost about a hundred pounds, or dyed his hair or changed ethnicities. There were a number of John Parkers licensed there, but none who look anything like our John Parker."

"Maybe he never got a license there. I think they only lived there a short time. Dustin said his grandmother homeschooled him. Maybe she did that because they knew they weren't going to be there long. Maybe he didn't own a car. He doesn't have one here. Probably lived near his work or took public transportation."

"Maybe, but I'd think that unlikely in Florida. Where else did the boy say they lived?"

Abby thought of Dustin reciting the town names in that stiff, formal way. "Mount Pleasant," she said, "That was one, Mount Pleasant, Michigan. They have the Ojibway there."

"What's that?" Henry asked.

"Oh, nothing" Abby said. "Dustin said they lived there, but not for how long. I don't know anything about the place."

"Me either," Henry said. "But I'm curious now. I believe I'll find out a little more about Mount Pleasant."

"Henry," she said, "I'm feeling pretty conflicted about this. We don't really know that anything's wrong here, do we? They're entitled to their privacy."

"Yes, they are," Henry said. "But I'm obligated to do my job. If someone's after the boy like the grandmother said, I need to know about that. Maybe he's been snatched in a custody dispute. If that's the case, I need to know that too."

Abby grimaced. Of course, that would make sense. But still, it was only speculation.

"Abby, you still there?"

"Yes, Henry," she said. She drew in a breath and let it out slowly. "Listen, Henry, about that possibility—" She told him what she'd overheard Dustin say about his mother. "Let me make it clear, I don't know anything about what's actually going on here, but it does seem strange that he can't talk about her." She reminded him about the men who'd been asking around about the chessboard. "Something just seems off. That's the only way I can explain it."

"Your instincts are usually good, Abby," Henry said. "That's why I say this warrants looking into. I'll let you know if I turn up anything. You let me know if you learn anything else."

Abby entered the café and looked around, letting her eyes adjust to the change in light. She spotted Janet waving to her from a corner table.

"Well, finally we get to squeeze in a lunch," Janet said as Abby threaded her way to the table. "We've missed the last two weeks. I was beginning to think you were avoiding me."

"You know very well that's not true," Abby said. "In fact, if I recall, it was you who cancelled last Friday."

"Yes, yes it was," Janet said. "I was afraid I'd get overexcited and spill the beans about Nancy and the children coming. I didn't trust myself around you. You know Abby, sometimes you pick up on things I don't even know I'm saying, and I didn't want to flat out lie if you caught on somehow."

"Well, you certainly kept this secret held tightly," Abby said. "I was truly floored when you all pulled up. I didn't have a clue Nancy had this planned."

"Is Nancy doing okay?" Janet asked, worry lines appearing between her brows. "She seems a little down in the dumps."

Abby was saved from having to answer by Ida Tolliver who suddenly appeared beside the table, her order pad at the ready. "Do you know what you'd like today?" she asked.

Abby and Janet glanced over the menu, then placed their orders.

"Coming right up," Ida said, smiling as she walked away.

As Abby looked up, she saw Dr. Dana Randolph squinting

and scanning the place, just as Abby had done minutes earlier. She caught sight of Abby and Janet and waved, then came over.

"Hi," Abby said. "Would you like to join us?"

"Thanks, but no, I'm meeting one of the board members, but I don't think he's here yet," she surveyed the place again from her new vantage point. "Nope, not here."

"I just saw your new physician's assistant at the hardware store," Abby said.

"John?" Dr. Randolph said. "Yes, he has a well-deserved day off today. I tell you, I don't know what I ever did without him. He is without a doubt the best physician's assistant I have ever encountered."

"You're lucky to have him then. The whole island's lucky to have him," Abby said.

"Yes, very lucky," Dr. Randolph answered. "It's almost like having another doctor on staff. In fact, I got a call from someone back East a couple of days ago asking if we had a new doctor on staff. He said he'd met someone at a medical convention who said they were taking a job at Sparrow Island Medical Center and he'd forgotten the name. He wanted to reach this doctor to return a rather expensive fountain pen he'd borrowed. I was trying to tell the guy he had the wrong place and that we didn't have any new doctors, but he just barreled right on and wouldn't let me get a word in edgewise. He rattled off a physical description of the doctor he was trying to locate and it fit John to a tee."

"Did you tell John about it?" Abby asked. This seemed entirely too coincidental. Too many people were trying to get information on Parker, and from too many angles, for it to be pure happenstance.

"Not yet," Dr. Randolph said. "I was going to tease him

about being a dead-ringer for a doctor and tell him he needed to demand a raise, but I don't know John well enough yet to start kidding around with him. He's sort of a private person, always very professional."

"So what did you tell the guy who was looking for the doctor?" Janet asked.

"Well, I was going to tell him he might try the Medical Center over in Friday Harbor," Dr. Randolph said, "I know they have a new doctor on staff, but as soon as I said we didn't have any new doctors, the guy hung up on me. Very rude! People these days." She looked up and saw her lunch date come in the door. She said a quick good-bye and went off to join him.

Ida came toward them, balancing a laden tray. She lowered it deftly until it rested on the edge of the table. "Did I tell you two," she asked as she placed their orders in front of them, "that I'm going to be working on the archaeological dig this season? Volunteer—but still!"

"No, when did this happen?" Abby asked.

"Well, you know I've been taking these classes," Ida said. "Writing classes mostly. I'm really interested in what they're finding on the dig, so I want to write a story about it. I mean, of course there will be lots of academic papers written about it, but—no offense, Abby—those can be sort of dry. I want to write something more about how what they're finding out can help us imagine the real lives of all those generations that lived on this island before us. I was thinking maybe a book for middle-schoolers, or even a children's book if I could find an illustrator."

"Maybe you will," Abby said, thinking of Nancy's secret dream. "I think that's a wonderful idea."

"You go for it, girl," Janet said.

"You'll have to tell Bobby about this," Abby said. "He has a new friend, Dustin, who's really into learning about the dig."

"Don't I know it," Ida said. "I saw them at the marina a couple of days back and I told Bobby about being let in to work on it. Both of them had about a million questions." She laughed. "I was almost late for work because they followed me halfway here, talking nonstop. I didn't think there was another kid in the world who could ask as many questions as Bobby McDonald, but I think his new friend's right up there with him."

After Ida had returned to her work, Janet told Abby that Ellen, Nancy and the kids had come by to visit her mother that morning. "Doug said it really brightened Mother's day." Janet stirred a packet of sweetener into her coffee. "Those kids are growing so fast. I'll bet Ben's really missing them."

"Yes, I'm sure he is," Abby said, feeling a heaviness in her heart. She hadn't had a moment alone with Mary to find out how things had gone with Nancy.

She tried hard to tune in to her friend's cheerful ramblings about island happenings, but she couldn't concentrate very well.

They were just finishing up their meal when Janet looked up and said, "Uh-oh, here comes the boss' wife and she's brought reinforcements."

Abby turned to see Patricia Hale approaching, followed by Sister Maeve, an Irish nun who'd been helping out at St. Christopher's for the past year.

"Don't worry," Patricia said, putting a finger to her lips. "I won't rat you out for taking a long lunch. You can just take it off the thousand or so hours of comp time you have coming to you, Janet."

"And what are you two doing?" Abby asked, "Is this luncheon work or pleasure?"

"Both!" they answered together.

"We're working on some programs Patricia and I dreamt up over the long winter," Sister Maeve said. "We're going to have some community-building events for the summer people and the tourists to try to make them feel more a part of our community and particularly, we hope, our faith communities."

"That sounds wonderful," Abby said.

"I'm glad you think so, dear," Sister Maeve said, "'cause we're going to be calling upon you to help us out with some things, especially with your bird-lovers."

"Anything I can do to make people feel welcome on the island, I'll certainly do if I'm able," Abby said.

"I know that to be true," Sister Maeve said, "And on that note, I'd like to thank you and dear Mary, too, for befriending Elise Parker. I've been a little worried about her. I think her adjustment to the island has been a bit of rough sleddin'. I wish I could do more for her, but our communication's hindered I fear because of my brogue."

"I'm glad Ellie has been getting out a little more," said Abby. "She and Mary have discovered a shared love of flowers, so they've had a lot to talk about. When they have trouble, they just use a little notepad."

"Ah," Sister Maeve said, "I wish that would work with Father's sermons. She can't follow very well from even the distance of the first row, and he doesn't write them out, he only makes notes. He and God are the only ones could translate them, I can tell you for sure."

"Would it help to get someone to sign?" Janet asked.

"Yes, it would, indeed," Sister Maeve said. "You know, it was strange. About a week before Elise and John came in to join the parish, someone called the church office and asked if we were in need of a signing interpreter. 'Twas a new service being offered through an agency over on San Juan Island, the man said. I thanked him and told him we didn't have any need of the service, which we didn't at the time. But after Ellie came I went looking for the number and discovered I hadn't jotted it down, which means he didn't offer me a number. In fact, I can't find any service of that kind in all of San Juan County, and I've searched far and wide. Such a lovely opportunity missed."

"Yes," Abby said, her mind spinning. Maybe Elise Parker wasn't paranoid after all. Someone was trying to get to them. Why? And did it have anything to do with what Bobby had overheard about their isolation being the price they had to pay for what they'd done? Abby forced her attention back to the conversation, telling the nun about Bernadette Deasy and the fact that she signed.

"Does she now?" Sister Maeve said. "Well, perhaps I'll be asking her if she's up for some community service once in a while. You know, it's not just the hearing impaired who bene-fit. It's just lovely to watch someone sign the scriptures. It's almost like watching a beautiful dance. I love to watch it myself. I'll call Bernadette later today." She turned slightly. "Patricia here says I'm shameless about putting the touch on people to help out with things. And let's face it," she said with a twinkle in her eye, "it's hard to say no to a nun, now isn't it?"

Patricia laughed. "Sister Maeve has a remarkable talent for getting people to volunteer. She's already gotten businesses to come forward and donate supplies and financial assistance for some of the summer events."

"And Patricia's so well-organized and creative and likes to

look after all the details in a way that would drive me to utter distraction. So we make a good team!"

After Patricia and Sister Maeve had taken their leave, Janet looked at her watch and said she really had to get going. "That's really funny that the call from the translator service would come right when they get a new member who's deaf, isn't it?" she said as she dug in her bag for her wallet. "Too bad the timing was off."

"Yes, it's too bad," Abby said slowly. But her mind was racing. Two more inquiries within the last few weeks that seemed to target the Parker family. Something was definitely wrong with this picture.

WHEN ABBY GOT HOME later that afternoon she found Mary and Nancy at the kitchen table with lists spread all around.

"What's going on here?" she asked.

"Mom's gotten it into her head to have a Sunday afternoon cookout here tomorrow," Nancy said. "There's no dissuading her."

"I think it's high time to give our poor mother a break from Sunday dinner duty," Mary said. "It's spring and I'm in the mood for a get-together here. Can't you two work up some enthusiasm, or at least not rain on my parade...or my cookout?"

"I'm not raining," Abby protested, throwing up her hands. "I'm all sunshine. It sounds like fun. Who are we inviting?"

Nancy cleared her throat and passed across a sheet of paper. "Here's the guest list." Abby widened her eyes at Nancy as she looked at the list that marched down the page.

"Wow, that's quite a list," Abby said, reading the names off: "Mom and Dad, Henry, Rick, Bernadette and her new beau, the Parkers, Goldie Landon, Hugo, the McDonalds, the Hales, the Heinzes and the Blackstocks. Let's hope it doesn't rain. We can't fit all these people in the house."

"The forecast is for a clear, sunny day," Mary said. "And should it rain, we'll just back the cars out of the garage and set up tables in there."

"It was all I could do to rein her in to this number," Nancy told Abby in a stage whisper. "She'd have invited the whole island." She pointed to the multiple lists littering the table as proof.

"I wish I could," Mary said. "But even my whole backyard's not big enough for that. Now, for the menu." She looked around the table for a clean notepad. Abby was writing down phone numbers next to the people's names on the guest list. Mary pulled her notepad from the bag on the side of her wheelchair, but then saw that Nancy had already labeled a sheet of paper MENU.

"Use this," Nancy said. "We can put it on the refrigerator."

Mary set the notepad on the other side of the table, out of the way. "Okay, what shall we serve?" she asked.

Abby half listened as the suggestions flew. "I'll ask Janet if she could bring her potato salad," Mary said. "That's always a hit."

"Brats, hamburgers and hot dogs for the grill?" Nancy asked.

Abby noticed the light from the window slanting in on Mary's notepad and began to study it. Something had been written using a lot of pressure on a page that had been torn off already. It had made an indentation on the clean page below. Abby could make out what looked like the word WARN near the bottom of the page.

She slid the notepad toward her and picked up a pencil. She began to rub the side of the lead lightly across the paper.

She frowned as the words began to distinguish themselves from the gray surface area.

"Mary, where did you get this notepad?" she asked.

Mary glanced at it. "Over in Friday Harbor at that little office supply place. I get them in a package of six. It's the kind I always use."

"No," Abby said. "I mean, where did you get this particular one?"

Now it was Mary's turn to look perplexed. "Ah . . . oh yes, I think Ellie and I accidentally swapped at Goldie's today. But they're just the same kind, so it doesn't matter, why?"

Abby turned the pad toward them.

Mary squinted. "What does it say? I can't make it out."

Nancy leaned over and put her face closer and began to read aloud. "He's getting—something, something—Bobby. He may not hold—then there's something else I can't make out—doesn't understand the danger of—another unreadable word—you have to talk to him again. Warn him."

Nancy looked up. "What does that mean? Who wrote it? Warn who about what? Is Bobby in some kind of danger?"

"All good questions," Abby said. "But I don't have any real answers. I suspect Ellie Parker wrote it, probably for John. And, no, I don't think Bobby's in any danger—not directly anyway. At least I hope not."

"Oh dear," Mary said.

"What?" Nancy asked, "What is it, Mom?"

"I overheard the boys talking today out at Goldie's. Dustin was sharing some things with Bobby that his father—and I'm assuming his grandmother also—had told him not to talk about."

Abby nodded. "His mother," she said.

"Yes, how did you know?" Mary asked.

"I overheard what I suspect was a similar conversation at the drug store. I didn't hear much, but enough to know that Dustin's not supposed to talk about his mother."

"I would guess that means this is a custody dispute, wouldn't you think?" Mary said. "That would explain a lot. Oh, I feel so sorry for that child. It's always the children who get hurt in a divorce."

"Speaking of children," Nancy said, getting up from the table quickly, "I should go check on mine."

Her voice was level, but Abby saw she'd gone pale.

When she was out the door Mary turned to Abby, "I shouldn't have said that, of all things. I wasn't thinking."

Abby reached over to pat her sister's hand. "You didn't say anything that wasn't true," she said. How did your talk go last night?"

"Not particularly well, I'm afraid," Mary answered. "She told me what's troubling her—about feeling her marriage is on shaky ground—so you don't have to worry about betraying that confidence. But, I pushed too hard and she shut down. I don't know if she'll open up again. I think I blew it." She pointed to the lists spread across the table. "That's one reason I wanted to do this, as a reminder to Nancy of how precious family and friends are. She used to love these get-togethers when she was young."

"That was a good thought," Abby said. "I think it'll do us all good."

"I can't decide," Mary said, "if telling Nancy about the struggles Jacob and I had in our marriage would be a help or make things worse. She seems to have such an idealized view of our marriage. Maybe shattering that would be traumatic for her. But, on the other hand, if she knew how hard we worked at it, maybe that would be helpful. I don't know. What do you think, Abby?"

"I think the reality is far preferable to the fantasy in most cases," Abby said. "Nancy is a perfectionist, Mary. I can't imagine where she gets it." She smiled, and Mary rolled her eyes.

"Being a perfectionist is good," Abby continued, "in that she always strives for excellence, but it's bad in that she gets frustrated when things aren't perfect all the time. Nancy's willing and able to work hard at whatever she does, but it might not have occurred to her that her marriage is one of those things. Young girls get so much exposure to the happily-ever-after myth, but we know that's not the way it is with human relationships. We're dynamic beings. We grow and we change and so do our relationships. If we're not careful, we can grow apart because we don't make the effort to stay connected."

"I wonder if that's what happened with poor little Dustin's parents. What could have happened that was so bad that they won't even let the boy talk about his mother?"

"I can't imagine," Abby said. She glanced at her watch, trying to remember what Henry had said about his schedule. In truth, she could imagine numerous scenarios where a marriage could plummet into spitefulness and discord. And she had a terrible sinking feeling about a theory that might fit many of the oddities that she'd observed in the Parker family. Maybe it wasn't a custody dispute. Maybe John had taken Dustin. Simply taken him, in violation of a custody arrangement, or to preempt one. Custodial kidnapping cases make the news every day. Sometimes the victimized parent searched for years to find children who'd been taken, only to end up meeting half-grown kids who had no recollection of them and oftentimes had been subjected to years of indoctrination against them.

"I'm going to make these calls," Abby said, noting to herself that Henry should now be first on her list after what's she'd learned today.

"Thanks, Abby," Mary said. "We're having a clean-out-the-fridge night for dinner. We have so many leftovers. Plus, we'll need the room. I'm going to make a couple of pies tonight, and we could put together that seven-layer, Tex-Mex dip everyone loved so much at the last Little Flock newcomer's dinner."

"Sounds great," Abby said. "Do you need me to pick up anything?"

"I don't think so," Mary said. "I'll check the pantry, but I think we have everything we need." She glanced toward the back door. "When Nancy comes back in she can help me get dinner. You go ahead and make your calls."

Abby went upstairs to change clothes and to make sure no one overheard her calls. She put the list on her desk, took off her hiking boots and put on sneakers.

She turned on her laptop and let it boot up while she went into the bathroom and washed her face.

She had an e-mail from Diane. She clicked it open and read: "No luck on John Parker, Abby. He wasn't on any of the lists of registrants. Course, your guy could have taken one of the classes that our class spawned across the country—not to mention the recycled content. Some places sent people here for the course, then had them turn around and teach the basics to their own people in-house. As an administrator, this makes me very frustrated because we could certainly use the revenue. But as a human being, it makes me immensely proud and grateful that something that was designed at my hospital has been credited with saving lives. Stay in touch, please, and next time you're back East please, please come see me."

Abby stared at the screen. Maybe there was no connection here. Maybe John Parker had picked the trach kit idea up from somewhere else, at another hospital or training course. Could have been anywhere.

She went over what she'd learned recently. Someone had called Dr. Randolph to inquire about a doctor who happened to fit John Parker's description; a timely call to St. Christopher's from an apparently nonexistent company offering services for the deaf; two guys were skulking around the island inquiring about the chessboard. She thought of Ellie's hyperalertness when it came to Dustin. What was that old saying? It's not paranoia if they really are out to get you?

She dialed Henry's number. Once she'd gotten the social niceties of inviting him for tomorrow's cookout out of the way, she tried her theory out on him.

"That's a thought," Henry said. "Actually one that had crossed my mind as well. Family child-snatching cases are rampant these days. I've been running a check on custodial interferences reported from both Florida and from Michigan. Nothing matches our Parker family. You know, that's always a problem with these things. There's no national registry just yet, so everything's piecemeal."

"Surely it would have been reported if that's what happened, if it was a custody thing, right?"

"Maybe, maybe not," Henry said. "I mean, it could be they aren't legally separated. Those things happen all the time too. There's a fight and one parent runs off with the kid. That's a legal gray area."

"What a mess."

"Look, Abby, I agree with you that something smells a little on the fishy side here, but there's just not enough hard evidence yet. I guess all we can do is watch and wait."

"I guess so," Abby said. "But one more thing—" she told him about the inquiry to Dr. Randolph and the one Sister Maeve had fielded. "Does that seem a little too coincidental to you?" she asked.

"Does sound awfully convenient, doesn't it?" Henry said. "But you say neither of these things got any payoff, so to speak. Dr. Dana told them no such person was here and Sister Maeve the same?"

"Yes," Abby said. "Course, that doesn't mean whoever this is—assuming they're connected and it really is someone trolling for information on the Parkers—wouldn't try again, right?"

"That's a lot of ifs, maybes and assumptions, but I'll keep my ears open and you do the same. Let me know if you hear anything further. I don't feel I can approach Parker directly, not just yet anyway. I'd run the risk of everything from making a fool of myself if we're wrong, to causing him to bolt if we're right."

"In any case, I hope for Dustin's sake I'm just making a mountain from a molehill," Abby said. "I like Ellie Parker and John too. They both seem like good people. Kind, caring people. It's hard for me to imagine they'd do anything that would be hurtful to Dustin. I hope there's a reasonable explanation for all of this."

"I'd like that too, Abby," Henry said. "But in my experience, your instincts are rarely wrong. Though you do sometimes get a little offtrack interpreting the particulars." Abby could hear in his voice that he was grinning. "I'll see you tomorrow," he went on. "Tell Mary I'll do my grillmaster magic in the afternoon, but I do have duty tomorrow evening."

"I'll tell her," Abby said.

"And will you," Henry said, "for pity's sake, just lock her and Nancy in a room and get them to talk to one another? Mary's worrying herself sick, and Nancy's obviously got something she needs help with. I don't understand those two sometimes."

"They're working on it, Henry," Abby said. "We just have to be patient and let them find their way."

"I know," Henry said with a sigh. Abby could picture him rubbing his balding head with his palm. "I've got patience by the bucket when it comes to something that affects just me, but I just hate like the dickens to see Mary upset."

"You're a good man, Henry Cobb," Abby said. "I'll see you tomorrow."

CHAPTER ❧ SIXTEEN

MARY DABBED AT HER EYES as she sat in her customary place at the end of the pew at Little Flock. Rev. Hale's sermon on this bright spring Sunday was on love and trust. As she often did, Mary felt as if it could have been just the two of them talking over a cup of coffee. His words seemed to be meant specifically for her and her current situation. But the beauty of it was that Mary was certain there were many others in the congregation who felt the very same way. Such was the gift and the grace of Rev. Hale's sermons.

He ended with a verse from Psalms: "But I will sing your strength, in the morning I will sing of your love, for you are my fortress, my refuge in times of trouble" (Psalms 59:16).

Mary reached over to take Nancy's hand and squeezed it. Nancy, too, had tears in her eyes.

Back at the house Mary went in to change her clothes. She was eager to get everything ready for the afternoon cookout. Nancy came in to ask whether she should go ahead and put the large pot of baked beans they'd prepared last night into the oven.

"Oh yes," Mary said, glancing at the clock. "Thanks for remembering that."

Nancy turned to leave the room, but Mary called her back. "Listen Nancy," she said. "Things will be hectic for a few hours here with the party and all, but tonight I'd like us to set aside some time—just the two of us. I have some things I'd like to share with you."

"Is everything okay?" Nancy asked. "With your health and all?"

"Everything's fine, Nancy," Mary said. "I'm getting along great on that score."

"Okay," Nancy said with a sigh, "but if this is about what we talked about the other night, you don't need to worry," she said, forcing a smile. "I was just being ridiculous. Everything's going to be fine with Ben and me."

"Let's just make sure we set aside the time to talk," Mary said. "This isn't about you and Ben. I have some things I want to share with you."

"Okay," Nancy said, looking doubtful. "We'll talk later then."

Mary watched her as she left the room. Her beautiful, wonderful daughter, her *adult* daughter. It was sometimes difficult for Mary to remember that her children were no longer under her wing. They were strong, independent people. She felt relieved having made the decision to share with Nancy the struggles she and Jacob had endured in their marriage. Perhaps she would shatter an illusion, but it would be worth it if she could get through to Nancy that those struggles only made her parents' marriage stronger in the end.

She wasn't sure yet what she'd say, or how she'd put it, but she trusted she'd be given the right words when the time came if she put her trust in the right place. And she would, in part thanks to the timely reminder in Rev. Hale's sermon that morning.

She wouldn't try to push Nancy or preach to her. She would share with a mother's open heart and simply trust.

ABBY WENT OUT TO MEET her parents as they pulled up in the driveway. Ellen was smiling brightly and Abby realized it truly was a gift to give their mother a break from the responsibility of Sunday dinner once in a while. Though she loved cooking for the family, and both her parents treasured having the family around the table at Stanton Farm, it took a lot of planning, even if everyone pitched in with the actual work.

But if Mary had thought their mother would take full advantage of the opportunity to be relieved of cooking duties, she was sorely mistaken. Abby watched, amused, as her mother handed her father a cake carrier, then a pie carrier. She handed off a big bowl of fruit salad to Abby, then reached in for a bag. "I brought a couple of loaves of homemade bread and a few rolls," she said.

"So I see. A few!" Abby said as she took the oversized grocery bag.

"I do love an impromptu party," Ellen said. "There's no time to fret over the plans. Things just seem to come together and get done. Or they don't, but it doesn't matter. How many from your list were able to make it on such short notice?"

"Miraculously, every single one, at least for a little while. Some will arrive late and others will have to leave early, but everyone's planning to come for a little while anyway."

"Excellent," George said. "I suppose Henry's out minding the grill."

"Yes, he's out there, but I'm sure he could use some help. We borrowed grills from the Heinzes and the McDonalds, too, so even Henry will have to call in reinforcements."

Abby didn't mention the fact that it had taken all of her persuasive powers to get John Parker to agree to come to the gathering. Abby had driven over to their house late the previous afternoon to issue the invitation. She wasn't sure they'd see e-mail in time, but she also reasoned it would be harder to say no in person.

John had declined at first, but when Ellie learned Goldie would be there she put her hand on John's arm. "Would you like to go?" he asked her.

"Yes," Ellie said, shaking her head. "I'd love to see Goldie again, and Mary and Abby have been so good to me. I think I would like to go if you think it would be okay."

John had turned back to Abby. "We'd love to come, thank you for inviting us. But we won't be able to stay too long. I hope Mary won't take offense if we leave early. My mother finds social gatherings taxing."

The Parkers hadn't arrived yet, but Abby had a hunch she'd know the minute they did. Bobby was keeping vigil in Mary's driveway.

Abby had offered to drive over and pick them up, but John had insisted they would bike over. "We try to bike together on my weekend off anyway," he said. "This time we'll just have a destination."

Abby had congratulated him on the contribution they were making to the environment by not having a car.

"We're doing a sort of experiment," he'd said. "We've been car free for more than a year now, and while there have been times when we've needed to bum a ride, we've generally managed fine."

Okay, Abby thought, *no car, no driver's license needed. No wonder Henry hit a dead end.*

The weather, as forecasted, was slightly overcast and balmy. Perfect for a backyard get-together. Abby had asked those who could easily manage it to bring their own lawn chairs and the children were spreading blankets so they could eat picnic style.

She and Henry had talked earlier and while both agreed there were still things that seemed peculiar in the Parkers' lives, they would settle right now for trying to get to know them better and keep an eye out for any dangers—real or perceived—to Dustin.

Almost everyone else had arrived by the time the Parkers got there. Abby was delighted to see that Ellie seemed relaxed and was soon enjoying herself. She sat at a table on the patio with Bernadette and Goldie.

People were all pitching in to help get things set up for the meal. Just as Abby was coming out the door with a plate of hot-dogs bound for Henry's just-right charcoals, she heard Bobby ask his mother if there was anything he and Dustin could do to help.

"Well, as a matter of fact, I do have a job for you two," Sandy said. "Thank you for offering. Bobby, I brought over the card table from our house; it's propped up against the back of the garage over there. And there's a tablecloth in that bag on the ground right next to it. Would you two set the table up right over there at the end of the patio and put the tablecloth on it, please? That will be our dessert table. And this way you two will get a preview of all the yummy desserts so you'll know how much room to save, right?"

The breeze had shifted and Henry had moved the grill back away from where people were sitting to keep them from getting choked by the smoke.

As the boys ran by to get the table Abby heard Dustin say, "Boy, your mom's so nice. You're lucky."

"Yeah," Bobby said. "I love my mom. She's cool. Well, most of the time anyway. What's your mom like? I mean, can you say that much at least?" Bobby asked.

"She's really beautiful," Dustin said, "but she doesn't smile a lot like your mom. She seems sad most of the time. She didn't used to be like that. When we lived in—" He stopped for a second, then continued. "When we lived away from my grandfather, she was happy. But when he's around, she gets sad and upset."

"Why?" Bobby asked. "I mean that's her dad, right?"

"Yeah," Dustin said. "It's hard to explain. I mean I know grandfathers are supposed to be like jolly and nice and all that, but my grandfather's not like that. He's sort of mean. He yells at my mom a lot, and he's really, really mean to my dad. He's always telling my mom she married beneath her, whatever that means, then there's a big fight, and it gets my mom and dad both upset."

Abby looked over and saw Dustin's face go pale. She turned to see what he was looking at and saw John Parker walking in their direction with an iced tea glass in hand.

"I'm not supposed to be talking to you by myself," Dustin hissed. "I'm supposed to stay in a crowd. Let's go get Nicholas and Emily to help us, quick."

Henry caught Abby's eye and raised an eyebrow.

"Hey, John," Henry called, putting out a hand as John grew closer to waylay him. "Henry Cobb. Don't know if you remember me or not. We met when I was over visiting Duncan Grady."

"Yes, I remember," John said. "Sergeant Cobb, isn't it?"

"That's right, but it's Grillmaster Cobb today. How are things at the Medical Center?"

"Busy, but mostly with routine things, thank goodness," John answered. "Do you need any help here?"

"No thanks," Henry said, "I've got things under control."

John wandered away from the grills and joined a cluster of men talking sports: Rick, Bernadette's boyfriend Lawrence, Joe Blackstock and Doug Heinz. Abby stopped on her way back to the kitchen to say hello. She'd been so busy she hadn't even seen some of them when they came in.

Bobby, Dustin, Emily, Nicholas and Toby all came up and stood silently by Abby. "Is there something you all need?" she asked, when they continued to stand there.

Bobby crooked a finger at her and she bent to let him whisper in her ear.

"Let's ask," she said. She stood back up and said to Lawrence, "You have some fans here who would really love an autograph."

"Oh? Cool! Absolutely," Lawrence said, grinning at Abby. "Makes me feel like a real celebrity." He took the paper and pen Bobby offered. "You know, if you guys ever want to come over and watch us practice, I could arrange it. Only a few special people get to do that. Or if you want to come to a game, I could hook you up with some good seats."

Bobby and Dustin were practically jumping up and down. Emily, Nicholas and Toby were grinning too, but Abby felt sure none of them had a clue about minor league hockey.

Dustin looked at his father, his eyes pleading.

"Maybe, sometime," John said, putting his hand on Dustin's shoulder.

Dustin immediately went quiet and still. "Sometime means never," he muttered to Bobby.

"Thank you," Bobby said to Lawrence. "For the autograph, I mean. And maybe we *can* come see you sometime."

"Offer stands," Lawrence said, spreading his hands.

The food was wonderful and the good fellowship continued. Abby saw John go over to check on his mother twice and each time she signed something to him and shook her head no. Abby had the impression he was asking her if she was ready to leave.

At last the kids were called and allowed to go through the dessert line first. Dustin chose a nice big chunk of Ellen Stanton's double fudge chocolate cake.

A little while later, while the last adult stragglers, including Abby, were milling around the dessert table, Dustin was back again.

John Parker, who was standing nearby with Rick called over to him. "Dustin, you've already had dessert. That's enough, buddy."

"No, I didn't," Dustin said, despite the chocolate evidence on his face.

"Dustin, I saw you take cake earlier," John said. "You know better than to lie."

Dustin looked at him, his face going red. He threw down his paper plate and signed something to John.

Ellie Parker had noticed everyone turning to look and she turned too. Abby saw her smile fade as she watched Dustin continuing to sign. He was crying now.

John drew in a breath. "I'm very sorry," he said to those standing nearby. "I think maybe we've overdone it today. Dustin needs a little time alone to remember his manners." He turned to Abby. "Please accept my apologies and thank you very much for inviting us."

Ellie was already on her feet, and they made a hasty departure, with Dustin looking defiant, but crying nonstop.

Abby walked them out and tried to assure them that they needn't be embarrassed. "None of us are at our best a hundred percent of the time," she said.

"Thanks," John said. Abby thought he seemed more sad than angry with Dustin. She knew that was true of Ellie because she'd seen tears in her eyes.

Abby watched them as they rode away, Dustin's bicycle between those of the two adults. He pedaled with his head downcast, not looking at either of them.

Abby tried to piece together what had happened. Why had Dustin been so angry? Was it really just a tantrum over a dessert denied? Abby didn't think so. It seemed to have been building up.

Abby returned to the backyard and went over to sit with Bernadette and Goldie.

"I'm sorry your visit was cut short," she said. "I think Ellie was enjoying herself, that's too bad."

"Lawrence feels terrible," Bernadette said. "He thinks maybe he set this off by inviting the kids to come watch a practice. He was only trying to be nice."

"It *was* nice," Goldie said. "A very generous offer. Say, see if you can get him to invite me. I dearly love ice hockey."

"I'll see what I can do," Bernadette said with a smile.

"Clearly little Dustin is one unhappy boy," Goldie said. "And it's also clear that Ellie's having a hard time with him. It's not a healthy life for either of them."

"I know," Abby said. "I think he was signing that—something maybe about being unhappy with his life."

"Not *life*," Bernadette said, "*lie*." She demonstrated the two words, both done with a gesture across the mouth. *Life* she showed as a gesture with one finger extended. "And *lie*," she said, "is with the flat of the hand. He told his father, 'You lie, you lie all the time, and you make me lie too.' What do you suppose that's all about?"

"I have no idea," Abby said. "Kids sometimes say mean things to strike out at their parents when they know they've been caught at something. The old ploy the-best-defense-is-an-aggressive-offense. I hope they get it worked out and he's not in too much trouble." Inside, Abby was quite worried by Bernadette's interpretation of Dustin's signing, but she tried to enjoy the rest of the party.

Only a few people had been close enough to observe the scene between Dustin and his father, and guests continued laughing and talking for another hour or so. The first to leave was Henry, who had to go on duty. Then Bernadette and Lawrence made ready to leave and since they'd offered to drive Goldie home, she gathered up her things as well. Abby walked them to the door. When she opened it, she was surprised to find John Parker standing there with his finger poised over the doorbell. Ellie stood just behind him, wringing her hands. Abby looked around and didn't see Dustin.

"I'm really sorry to bother you," John said, "but is Dustin here?"

"No," Abby said, stepping outside along with the others. "I haven't seen him. Why, what's happened?"

"I think he *is* here," John insisted.

"No, John, he isn't," Abby said, taken aback by the anger in his voice. She looked around at the others who were also frowning and shaking their heads.

"This says he is," John said, showing her a small, black

electronic device he was holding in his hand. "He has a tracking chip in his watch."

Abby squinted at the device. "What? Well, you're welcome to come in and see for yourself, John. If Dustin is here, he's hiding somewhere; we haven't seen him since you left."

She opened the door and John brushed past her, Ellie following close behind. He went into the backyard, holding the device up and walking steadily toward the children. Abby followed along.

When they got to the blanket where the children were sitting they looked down to see Nicholas playing with the watch Dustin always wore.

"Nicholas, where'd you get that?" Abby asked, trying to keep her voice neutral.

"Dustin gived it to me," Nicholas said, holding it up proudly. "He said he didn't want it anymore."

"Oh no," John said, running his hand through his hair.

"Let's talk over here," Abby said, moving him away from the wide-eyed children.

After they'd moved up on the patio, John said, "He was upset and angry with me. I sent him to his room to calm down so we could talk, and when my mom went in to check on him, he was gone. I'm sure he's just somewhere sulking. But we'd really like to find him just the same."

Ellie Parker was not nearly so sanguine. She had a distressed look on her face. Her breathing was coming in shallow, jerky drafts.

"We could drive around and look for him," Lawrence offered.

"Thanks," said John, "we'd appreciate that. It would be a lot faster since we're on our bikes."

"Yes, it would," Abby said, "but let's wait just a minute to make sure we get things coordinated. "I'm sure others will want to help out as well. The more people we have looking, the sooner you'll find him."

Ellen Stanton came out of the kitchen and asked what was going on. Abby explained.

"George and I can help look too," she said. "I'm sure there's nothing to be worried about," she said, placing her hand on Ellie's arm. She turned to John, "By the way, did your friend find you?"

"Pardon?" John asked.

"Your friend. I'm sorry I didn't get his name. He came into the Visitor's Center yesterday looking for you. He said he'd lost your address and phone number and that you were expecting him and he was late."

John had gone pale and Ellie looked from one to the other, puzzled. Abby thought Ellie hadn't heard all of what her mother said, since she was turned toward John. Bernadette had the same thought apparently, because she signed something quickly to Ellie.

Ellie's eyes got very wide and dark and she clutched John's arm. But he just gave a shaky smile and patted her hand. "I'm sure there was some mistake, I wasn't expecting anyone."

"But he asked for—" her mother began, but then she stopped short. "Oh good heavens, that's not important now. Abby, did you have in mind to divide us up to look for Dustin?" she asked.

"Yes," Abby said, now feeling a sense of dread. She turned to John, "I really think we need to call Henry," she said.

"Oh, I don't think that's necessary," he said, trying to comfort his mother, who seemed to be growing more distraught by the moment.

Others were beginning to gather round to see what was going on. "John, I don't want to alarm you," Abby said, "and I'm sure Dustin is just fine, but we don't want him wandering around the island after dark. Especially since he doesn't know the terrain well. Let me just call Henry and give him a heads-up. If we find him right away, there's no loss. If we don't, he can have men in place to help us."

John nodded and Abby started to gather everyone around the patio table to explain what was going on and get other volunteers to help find Dustin. As she was walking away, she saw Ellie grab hold of John's arm, pulling at it as if she were a drowning woman. "Greg, you have to tell them!" she said, her voice low and hoarse.

John signed something to her and shook his head.

Greg? Abby wondered if she'd heard that right. *Tell who what?* She shook her head as if to clear it. Right now she didn't have time to deal with that. Her only concern was finding Dustin. Sparrow Island, as beautiful as it was, was no place for a young boy alone at night. Especially one with no experience with the waters, tides, mud flats or any of the other dozens of hazards cloaked in the night. And if someone was stalking this family, perhaps they'd found their mark. Abby could only hope Dustin had chosen to do his sulking somewhere away from their clutches.

CHAPTER ❧ SEVENTEEN

I'M SURE WHEN WE FIND Dustin he'll be embarrassed and in big trouble with his dad and grandmother for all this worry and fuss," Abby said to the assembled, sounding far calmer than she felt. "I'm sure he'll be fine. As I've told John and Ellie, people on Sparrow Island look after one another. But we do want to find him before dark."

She glanced over at Ellie, who had just texted Dustin for about the tenth time in the last fifteen minutes. She shook her head at Abby. No answer.

Everyone put their cell phone numbers on a list and chose a route to drive in search of the boy.

"Okay," Abby said. "Mary and Nancy will stay here and be the call center. If you spot Dustin, obviously call his father or text his grandmother first, then call Mary and they'll call everyone on the list so you'll know he's okay and you can go about your business."

"One thing," John said, "I've sort of drilled it into Dustin's head that he's not to go with strangers—I mean, like every parent these days. He's not going to get into the car with you. At least I hope he won't, or else all my warnings haven't sunk in. Anyway, if you can just call me and let me know where he is, I'll come right away."

It was decided that Ellie would go back to their house to wait, in case Dustin came home on his own. Bernadette and Goldie volunteered to wait there with her.

John Parker would go with Lawrence and Rick to drive the streets in and around Green Harbor.

Abby found a moment to take her mother aside and asked about the man who'd said he was John's friend. Her mother described to a tee the younger man who'd been asking around about the chessboard.

"Did I do something wrong?" her mother asked. "I mean, I know you said he wanted his privacy about the chessboard, but this was a friend of his. He asked for him by name. All I told him was where he lived."

"No, Mom, it's fine, I'm sure," Abby said. "I'm just trying to cover all bases."

Abby called Henry and he said he'd have his officers on the lookout, but that if they hadn't found the boy in an hour, she was to report in again and they'd begin a more intensified search. She stepped out of hearing range of the others and told Henry what her mother had said about someone dropping in to the Visitor's Center asking for Parker's address.

"I don't like the sound of that one bit," Henry said.

"Nor do I," Abby replied.

Abby took Bobby with her. She thought perhaps he'd have a better idea of where Dustin may have gone since they'd been out riding their bikes together.

Once they were under way, Abby could see that Bobby was uncharacteristically quiet, and he seemed confused. "Are you okay, Bobby?" she asked. "It's going to be okay, you know. We'll find him."

"Yeah," Bobby said, squirming in the seat. "But it's like you said, he doesn't know the island, and he's sure ticked off at his dad—even at his grandma."

"They'll work it out," Abby said reassuringly. "Was there any place you two have been together that Dustin especially liked?"

"I guess he liked all of it. We went down to the marina to watch the boats a couple of times."

"Well, then, let's try that first," Abby said.

But they found no sign of him at the marina. Abby talked to the clerk at the sundry shop. She told her what Dustin looked like and asked her to call Mary's house if she spotted him.

Then they tried the park and all the lookout points along Randolph Bay. No sign of Dustin. Abby looked toward the horizon and put her fingers up to measure the time left before darkness fell. She was not comforted by the result of her calculation.

"Is there anyplace else you can think of, Bobby?" she asked.

When she turned to look at him he was on the verge of tears. "I don't know what to do," he said, his face twisting.

"What is it, Bobby?" Abby asked softly.

Bobby didn't reply, he bit at his lip and made a couple of murmuring noises.

"Bobby, listen," Abby said. "It's good to be a loyal and trustworthy friend, but if you know something that can help us find Dustin, you have to tell—for his own safety."

"I don't know where he is, honest," Bobby said. "And I didn't know he was going to run away, but I wouldn't blame him."

"Why do you say that?" Abby asked.

"There's something weird going on with his family."

"That may be true," Abby said. "But right now we just need to find him."

"He's been getting madder and madder at his dad and his grandmother because they won't let him do anything and for some other stuff that's been happening a long time, I guess. I mean, let's say I was a boy the same age and everything as Dustin," Bobby said, switching to a hypothetical, Abby noted, to maintain his promises to Dustin. "And if my dad or my grandmother wouldn't even let me talk to my own mother or see her ever, I'd sure be mad."

"Me, too, Bobby" said Abby. "Me too."

WITH THE SUN RAPIDLY DROPPING down to meet the sea, Henry took over and the search became official.

Abby went home to get flashlights, a heavy jacket and her hiking boots.

"Bobby," she told him, "I think you'd better stay here."

"But, I want to help find Dustin," he protested. Abby could see that he was getting increasingly worried.

"I know you do," Abby said. "But we need someone here to help with the communications part of the search," she told him.

"There hasn't been much communication to monitor," Nancy whispered as Bobby trudged off to the kitchen.

"I know, but we don't need two boys lost," Abby said. And he's so upset and afraid for Dustin, I'm afraid he'd go too far afield himself if we get farther out from town to search. Could you two please try to reassure him and keep a close eye on him? He's pretty emotional."

"Sure," Nancy said. "We'll look after him. Don't worry."

"Mary," Abby called, "I'm going to take Finnegan, okay?"

"Yes, of course," Mary called, wheeling out into the hall, "if you think he can help. He's not trained in search and rescue though, you know."

"I know, but he has a good nose," Abby said. "And when we find Dustin he'll likely be upset. Finnegan might calm him down."

As she opened the door to leave, Bobby came running from the kitchen. "I think I may know where he is," he said, breathing hard.

"Where?" Abby asked.

"He's been talking for days about how mad he is that his dad and grandma won't take him out to the archeological dig at Cedar Grove Lake. He said he wanted to go real bad. We talked to Ida the other day. She told us all about what they were going to be working on this season. After that Dustin got really steamed and he said if they weren't going to take him, he'd just go on his own one of these days. This afternoon when his dad put him off about going to see the hockey team practice, he said something like he couldn't do that by himself, but he could ride his bike as far as Cedar Grove Lake. I didn't think he meant now; I thought he meant like, sometime this summer. But he was so mad, I'll bet you that's where he's gone."

"That's good, Bobby," Abby said, even as her heart sank. This was in fact, very bad news. The lake area was fraught with pitfalls even for experienced hikers in the full light of day.

"Maybe that's why he hasn't answered his grandma's messages," Bobby said. "You can't get a signal in some places out there because Mount Ortiz blocks the signal from the tower."

"You're right," Abby said. "It was really good that you remembered this, Bobby. It gives us a good lead on where to look."

Abby called Henry as she went out to the car. "Okay, this is a whole different ballgame," he said after she'd told him what Bobby had to say. "I'll call in some help. We'll get Mary and Nancy to call the volunteers you've already got out there. Some of them can help in a foot search. Everyone will assemble at the turnoff on Wayfarer Point Road."

WITHIN THIRTY MINUTES of her call to Henry, a crowd of volunteers had assembled at the staging area. Deputy Artie Washburn was dividing the area into a search grid and a few members of the local orienteering club were plugging coordinates into their handheld GPS units.

"This may actually be good news, right?" Abby asked Henry. "If Dustin's run away, that lessens the chances he's been snatched, doesn't it?"

"You're assuming one precludes the other," Henry said, and Abby felt a shiver go up her spine. "Parker wanted to come out here, but I've convinced him to keep driving the streets with Lawrence and Rick, for now anyway. If the kid has run away, he might hide if he sees or hears his father. If we don't find this kid quick, I'm going to have some hard questions for John Parker and his mother."

It was almost full dark now and the temperature was dropping. Abby pulled on her coat and changed into her hiking boots as Finnegan sat by the car, calmly watching all the commotion.

Other than the archeological dig site, this side of the lake was in a virtually undisturbed, natural state. Since this season's dig was barely underway, even the site was hard to make out in the deepening twilight.

The moon, not quite a quarter into its waxing phase, cast a pale glow that hardly penetrated the wispy clouds, much less, the densely forested area around the lake.

Henry settled the volunteers down with his reassuring baritone. "Okay, folks, now there's no reason for panic here. This boy's only been missing for a short time and we've still got people driving around looking closer to his house over in town. We don't know for sure this is where he was headed, but it's our best lead. We think it's just a matter of his getting a burr under his saddle and running away from home," he said, then smiled. "Boy hasn't lived here long. Guess he doesn't realize it's harder to run away when you're on a island."

Abby saw a few of the volunteers give a wan smile.

"But," Henry continued, "because he hasn't been on the island long, he doesn't know it well, and that can get him in a heap of trouble. It's easy to get turned around out here in the dark. The temperature's going to keep dropping, and he's likely not dressed for it. Let's stay sharp and get him found so we can all get home."

Abby admired Henry, both as a man and as a law enforcement officer. He'd struck just the right note—urgency, but not panic.

The searchers partnered up with walkie-talkies. Owen Gardiner, who was the volunteer search and rescue supply coordinator, passed out whistles from a plastic box. He reminded each person who took one that they were only to be used if they found something.

Since she had Finnegan, Abby was given the sector closest

to the dig site. She grabbed her backpack and set off. She tried to share the spirit of optimism apparent in the demeanor of the other searchers. It was almost like a social gathering as they carried on conversations while walking their assigned area. But they didn't know everything Abby knew. She had a bad feeling.

It was clear to her that the Parkers lived with fear and suspicion. The question was why? Were they under threat or had they done something that required them to hide from a reckoning?

Abby could hear the marsh birds setting off their siren squawks as other waterfowl, most probably domestic ducks and geese, got too near their territorial boundaries.

As she got nearer her sector, walking along the lone trail that ran between the lake and the highway, she could hear the other searchers begin to call out Dustin's name. But even in that, Abby detected a rather *pro forma* tone, as if finding Dustin safe and sound were a foregone conclusion and it was just a matter of how soon. *Maybe Henry overdid the assurances,* she thought.

She and Finnegan had just entered the wooded area when her walkie-talkie squealed a high-pitched note. She pressed the button and talked to Hugo, her partner, on the other end.

"Yes, Hugo? Has he been found?" she asked, heartened.

"No, Abby, not the boy," Hugo said. "But Owen's found his bike, or at least we assume it's his. Do you know what it looks like?"

"Yes," Abby said. "It's blue, has a crest-shaped emblem of some kind on the front bar up near the handlebars, and I think has black grips."

Abby could hear Hugo relating the information to someone, though not over the walkie-talkie. His voice carried on mists of fog that had started creeping in over the tidal pools and up the rock scree across the highway.

"It's his," he came back over the walkie-talkie. "Was half-hidden under a bush right at the turnoff from the road. The child obviously has no idea about the distances. He ditched his bike at least a mile from the dig site."

"Any clue which way he went?" Abby asked.

The instrument let out a squeal again, and Abby missed Hugo's first few words "...Finnegan, see what he can do."

"Say again," Abby requested.

"I say, how about if we bring Finnegan back and let him see what he can do? We've got a valuable tool in that nose of his, we should use it."

"Agreed," Abby said. "Can you relay that to Henry?"

"Will do," Hugo said.

Abby made her way to Owen's position by going straight through the forest. She kept her flashlight aimed at her feet, on the lookout for rocks, vines or marshy areas. She continued to call Dustin's name every few minutes. A couple of times she stood still and listened, trying to parse out a child's voice from the hoot of owls and the dry, papery flutter of the small brown bats that darted about the treetops, snapping insects from the night's moist air. But she heard nothing human other than the murmurs and calls of other searchers.

A finger of the lake injected itself in her path when she was about halfway to Owen's position. As she stepped over a small rise, Abby hit a patch of duff that was wet with half-composted leaves. She may as well have stepped onto a skateboard. She went down on her side, but fortunately, fell into an area of soft ground cushioned with plenty of leaves and vegetation. Finnegan whimpered, nosing at her.

"I'm okay, boy," she told him. "Nothing hurt, not even my pride since there was no one here to see it." She turned onto her side and was very happy there was no one to observe the spectacle as she had to crab walk into a standing position again, checking carefully to make sure she could find a stable foothold with each small change in position.

She took inventory. "Okay, Finnegan," she said, "nothing broken, nothing bruised, nothing cut or scraped. Just a dirt bath." She bent over to sweep the mud from her pants leg and her flashlight beam fell on something that didn't belong in the brown, gold and green palette of the forest. A patch of bright blue. She walked down to where the object was half sunk in the mud. She recognized it immediately. On several occasions she'd seen Dustin stare down at it as if it held the solution to all his troubles. His blue sneaker. It was mired deep in the mud and Abby had a hard time prying it out. It was still tied.

Abby aimed her flashlight beam, along the trajectory of the toe of the shoe. She saw a complementary footprint a little farther along in the muck. She continued to follow the footprints, while switching on the walkie-talkie and telling Hugo what she'd found. "Pass it on to Henry, but tell everyone to circle around and come in from the north end so we don't trample on any footprints."

But she needn't have bothered with that. Once he was out of the mud, Dustin had been on dry forest floor. Abby suspected even an experienced signcutter would have a hard time following the trail under these conditions, and they couldn't wait for the clear light of day.

She squinted, bending over at the waist and shining her light in a slow arc, looking for signs of broken stems, compressed vegetation or indentations in the duff of the forest floor. After about five or six feet, she could see nothing to indicate which way the boy had gone.

She turned to Finnegan and had him sniff Dustin's shoe, but with the hundreds of competing odors in the decaying muck on the shoe, she didn't have much confidence he'd be able to sort it out.

Finnegan seemed to understand what she wanted. He sniffed the shoe, then sniffed at the ground. He got to about the same place she'd run out of clues and stopped. He turned toward her, sniffing at the shoe again, then putting his nose to the ground.

He zigzagged back and forth but moved steadily forward. After a couple of minutes, Abby realized he was headed for the edge of the lake. Her breath seemed to catch in her throat. It was so dark in here. She knew that just over a small promontory of sandstone, there was a straight drop into the lake, but Dustin would not have known that. She began to call out his name again, this time louder. It echoed in her ears as a plea.

She heard someone approaching to her left and turned to see Henry coming at a trot across the forest, dodging salal and thimbleberry bushes.

"Oh, Henry," she said, "I don't like the looks of this at all."

"What have you got?" Henry asked.

She showed him the shoe and retraced the path to where she and Finnegan had both lost the trail.

Henry walked ahead to the promontory and Abby followed. It almost took her breath away when they came to the edge. Compared to the ocean cliffs, this was no drop at all, eight or ten feet at most. But this end of the lake was one of the many old limestone quarries from back in the early 1900s, when limestone had been carved out of the islands and sent back to the mainland for the production of Portland cement. Unlike the more gentle, sloping end of the lake where there was a sandy beach for swimming and recreation, this end of the lake was deep and treacherous.

"Is the boy a good swimmer?" Henry asked.

"I have no idea," Abby said, staring down into the black water, dread uncoiling in her stomach.

"Okay, well, let's not get ahead of ourselves," Henry said, turning to call out to the rest of the volunteers who were closing in on the location.

Henry quickly reorganized the search grid, concentrating on areas near the lake's edge and outward. "It appears he was moving away from the dig site, so maybe he got turned around, or maybe he was trying to get back to his bike. In any case, he's probably getting cold and hungry by now. Let's find him and get this kid home to a warm bed."

There was no casual conversation as the searchers moved away this time. The atmosphere had changed dramatically. Abby and Henry stayed together, searching along the lake's edge. The sharp angle of the promontory gradually gave way to a rock scree, then to a marshy bog lined with cattails.

As they picked their way along, Finnegan snuffling at the ground, they both were startled by a sound and instinctively turned their flashlights upward. Abby spotted a double-crested cormorant, known locally as a shag because of how their feathers drooped when they opened their wings to dry them. He was perched in a scraggly fir and looked prehistoric, looming above them, his wings spread like a pelt cape. Abby spotted one of the characteristic stick-built nests, shaped like a sloppy haystack. A part of her mind went automatically to trying to remember figures from her annual bird count before a splash in the water nearby jolted her back to the present.

She swung her flashlight to catch the silver flash of a small fish breaking the surface of the water, his body twisting as if overcome with joy at being airborne.

For the next two hours they traipsed the woods, calling out for Dustin and stopping to listen for a reply. All they got in return was the hooting of owls and the forlorn sounds of the foghorns from the boats in the far distance.

As she and Henry rounded the southern end of the lake, Abby caught sight of something floating in the water. She yelled to Henry and as he turned, they both aimed their flashlights at the small head. Abby's heart seemed to stop as she pictured Dustin's shock of blond hair. Then the head slowly rose to reveal two black eyes. The river otter flopped onto his back and began pirouetting in the water.

Abby bent over and let out a gush of air, fighting nausea.

Henry came over and patted her on the back. Finnegan nuzzled at her leg. Henry told everyone to meet back at the staging area, where Owen had arranged for hot coffee and sandwiches to be delivered.

Abby didn't want to go; she didn't want to waste time. But she knew Henry was right when he said they would be of no use to Dustin if they lost the strength to sustain the search.

The wet leg of her jeans had created a line of what seemed like frozen flesh down her right leg; she felt faint with hunger and fear. She realized, too, that Finnegan needed food, fresh water and rest. He was not a young dog.

The mood was somber, with an overlay of jittery anxiety as the tired volunteers ate, taking mechanical bites of their sandwiches. They drained bottles of water and clasped hands around steaming cups of coffee with considerably more eagerness.

Some put on extra socks or got heavier jackets from their cars, but Abby didn't want to take the time. As soon as she'd eaten and fed Finnegan, they went back out.

Abby and Finnegan went back to the area where she and Henry had left off the search. Henry went north to check the dig site.

It was now after midnight and Abby felt the increased threat of each passing minute. Her legs were beginning to feel leaden because of the cold night air and the challenges of hiking the forest in the dark—holding back a little with each step in case a foot happened to fall upon a patch of slippery half-rotted madrone leaves or an ankle-turning cone or rock.

Suddenly Finnegan began to pant heavily. He sniffed at the ground with interest, rocking back and forth from paw to paw as his nose examined a pile of leaves.

"What is it, Finnegan?"

He whined and looked at Abby expectantly.

"Lead," she told him and he turned and started down to the water's edge. Abby scurried over rocks and around tree trunks, trying to give Finnegan his head while still maintaining her balance.

"Good boy, Finnegan," she encouraged. Under her breath she muttered, "Please, don't let him just be on the trail of a raccoon or a muskrat."

Finnegan slowed, feeling the pressure she was putting on his harness as she struggled to keep up. "On, boy," she urged, "lead." He put his nose to the ground again and his tail started to wag like a windshield wiper, but Abby could see nothing of interest in the sweep of her flashlight. "Dustin," she called. No response.

Finnegan led her to the edge of a large red flower currant bush. Still she saw nothing. She looked up the trunk of the majestic Douglas fir behind the bush, wondering if Finnegan had treed a squirrel or a raccoon, but he went down on his front legs, his rump up in the air, and rammed his nose in under the bush. Abby bent down cautiously. That's when she saw the toes.

With shaking hands, she swept aside mounded leaves and needles. She uncovered a bare foot. It was cold motionless. Abby choked back a scream. As she pulled away more leaves, she saw a blue sneaker. "Dustin!" she sobbed.

He moaned, then startled, trying to scramble backwards away from her, but the trunk of the big fir stopped him. "Don't take me, please. Don't take me away," Dustin pleaded, holding his hand up to shield his eyes from her flashlight.

Abby moved the light to the side, "Dustin, it's okay. It's me, it's Abby. I've got Finnegan with me."

"Finnegan?" Dustin said. The dog nuzzled at him and his wild eyes softened and his breathing became regular.

"Dustin, we've been very worried about you. Everyone's been looking for you," Abby said. He had scratches on his arms and face. He had clearly had an unfortunate encounter with some stinging nettle. His shoeless foot was like ice, and his hair was matted and tangled, but other than that, he seemed to be okay.

"I . . . I got lost," he said as Abby brushed him off and shrugged off her coat to put around him. She unzipped her bag for the extra pair of socks that she always carried and slipped both of them on his bare foot, massaging it.

"I thought I was going back to my bike," he said, his voice drowsy. "But then it wasn't where I thought. I got stuck in the mud and I thought it was going to pull me under, like quicksand or something. I lost my shoe."

His voice had become flat and quiet. Abby was afraid he might be in shock.

"It's okay now, Dustin," she said. "Now listen, I'm going to stand up and blow my whistle." She showed him the silver whistle hanging around her neck with her flashlight. "That's my signal to the others that we've found you."

She stood and let out three quick shrills, then used the walkie-talkie to tell Hugo. She tried her cell phone, hoping that she could get through to Mary so she could alert the Parkers, but as she expected, she couldn't get a signal. She knew Henry would be here as soon as humanly possible, and he would have his deputy call with the good news.

"Okay, Dustin, we're going to get you home now," she said. "Can you walk?"

"Oh, I'm in so much trouble," Dustin said, his voice quaking.

Abby knelt and put her arms around him. She could feel his small body vibrating as he shivered, both with cold and trepidation about what he faced back home, Abby was sure. "Right now, your dad and your grandmother are just going to be relieved you're okay. The rest, you can work out later," she said soothingly.

Now his body convulsed in great sobs. "No, you don't understand. They're going to be so mad. I just wanted to see the longhouse and all." He stopped for a beat, then let out a wail. "And I want to see my mom."

Abby gathered him to her. She heard feet crashing across the forest floor as the volunteers converged on them. She smoothed his hair and murmured words of comfort. "It's okay, Dustin. Everything's going to be okay."

The sobs waned and he let out a series of moans. "Could we—" he began, "just for right now, could we pretend my name is Nathan and you could call me that?" he asked.

Abby frowned, but she continued to stroke his hair. "Sure," she answered. "It's okay, Nathan. Everything's going to be fine."

CHAPTER ❦ EIGHTEEN

Mary PUT A COFFEE CUP into the sink and saw that her hand was shaking. "Good heavens," she said to Nancy, "You'd think the time for shaking would be past now that we know Dustin's okay."

"I know what you mean," Nancy said. "I think we had too much coffee and too much adrenaline. I don't think I'll be able to get to sleep for a while."

"Poor Abby looked so exhausted, "Mary said. "I'll bet she has no problem falling asleep."

"I wouldn't think so," Nancy said. "She looked as if she could barely make it up the stairs." She stacked all the notes and lists on the kitchen table that she and her mother had been tending throughout the evening. They had fielded calls, then waited through the long silences, willing the phone to ring again.

Mary washed the last of the cups and set it into the dish drainer. "And my poor wonder dog is so tired he's snoring. Listen."

Nancy cocked her head to the side and smiled. "He's a hero —again."

"He's a hero to me every day," Mary said, gazing across at Finnegan who was curled up on the rug, his breath rising and falling with a soft, nasally flutter.

"Nancy," Mary said, "I know it's late, but since we're both too wired to sleep, could we have that talk?"

Nancy sighed. "Yeah, Mom. I think it's high time."

They moved into the living room, careful not to disturb the sleeping Finnegan. Nancy curled up on the couch, tucking her feet underneath her. "I can't imagine what the Parkers have been through tonight," she said. "I think I'd truly go mad if anything happened to one of my children."

Mary nodded. "And the bad news is, you'll feel like that forever. When you're a mother you never stop worrying about your children. The good news is, they're worth every minute of it."

"I don't want you to worry about me, Mom," Nancy said. "That's why I didn't want to talk to you about any of my little troubles."

"I'm not trying to pressure you into talking to me," Mary said. "I just want you to listen." She took a deep breath and began to tell Nancy about the darkest time in her marriage.

"You and Zack were small and not yet in school. I was frequently tired and distracted and didn't have much time to myself. The house was smaller then; it was before we added on. It was a challenge to keep you two occupied and out of your father's hair while he wrote.

"Then there was the issue of money. There was never enough. Your paternal grandparents, as you know, had cut your father off completely when he refused to go into their clothing business to follow instead his dream of being a writer.

"When things got really tight for us, your dad was seriously considering giving up his writing, crawling back to his parents and asking to be let into the business.

"I was against it. I knew he'd be unhappy selling clothes for a living and giving up his writing. And I knew how badly his parents had hurt him by turning their backs on him when he wouldn't let them control his life. Plus, I didn't want to leave Sparrow Island.

"But your father felt he was failing me—and you and Zack too. We fought that year. A lot. Especially at the first of every month when the bills rolled in."

"I—I had no idea," Nancy said, stammering.

"We tried hard never to argue in front of you and Zack. Not that we didn't respectfully disagree sometimes."

"How did you fix it?" Nancy asked.

"With help," Mary said. "I didn't want anyone to know we were having trouble and neither did Jacob. Your father was so proud, he never wanted to ask anyone for help. But finally I couldn't take it anymore, so I talked to Mom and Dad about it."

"What did they say?"

"They asked me if I had told Jacob how I felt," Mary said. "I said of course I had. I was a little indignant about it." She smiled at Nancy. "I mean, all Jacob and I had done was talk about it. Argue about it," she corrected. "But then Mom looked me in the eye and said, 'Yes, but have you told him how you *feel*?'"

"Well, hadn't you?"

"I thought I had," Mary said. "But when I really thought it over, I realized we'd argued over all the logistics and the bills and everything that was wrong, but I hadn't shared a lot of things with Jacob. I hadn't told him how proud I was of him as a writer and that I wanted him to continue doing the thing he loved. I hadn't told him that I would feel sick if he caved in to his parents' oppressive demands because he had to support me. I thought about what your Grandma and Grandpa Stanton had said all that night. The next day I loaded you two into the car and took you to spend a day at the farm with them. I told your father we needed a day off, just the two of us. I packed a picnic and we went out to Paradise Cove and stayed there all day, talking, really talking, about what we wanted out of life. We talked till we were hoarse."

"And that one day fixed everything?" Nancy said, her mouth twisted into a sardonic smile.

"Of course not," Mary said. "But that one day got us back to thinking and planning as a couple. It was us against the troubles again; we didn't let them get between us. It took a while, but we built from there.

"One of the things I shared with your father that day was that I'd always wanted to have a flower shop. I was a little afraid to tell him because it seemed like such a silly idea. Here we were already struggling financially. It seemed ridiculous to even talk about trying to start up a business. But your dad didn't see it that way. He said my dreams were just as impor-tant as his. He encouraged me, and the next year, with a small loan from Grandma and Grandpa Stanton and a rather large chunk of our hard-earned savings, I opened Island Blooms."

"Wow," Nancy said, "I never realized . . ."

"We wanted to provide stability and a sense of security for you and Zack," Mary said. "But you're an adult now. I wanted to share these things with you because I want you to know that out of some of the darkest times can come a much richer and deeper commitment to one another and to your shared hopes and dreams. That was the gift your grandparents gave to me. So now I'll pass it on and ask you, have you told Benjamin how you feel?"

Nancy frowned. "He knows how I feel."

Mary smiled. "That's what I thought, too, or at least I thought your dad surely should know how I felt. But he didn't at all. I think we were both shocked to find out we'd held so many misconceptions about what the other one was thinking and feeling."

Nancy's frown deepened. "You know, Mom, it's amazing how much of what you're telling me parallels what Ben and I are going through. You know how much he loves his job. He really thinks he's doing some good for the world with this environmental watchdog agency he works for. But we're certainly never going to be rich from it. I have to keep working for us to make it."

"Nancy, if it's money that's the problem, maybe I could help you a little," Mary offered.

"Thanks, but it's not a temporary-bind kind of problem. The thing is, I have a dream I'd like to pursue too."

She told her mother about her desire to write and illustrate a children's book about her and Finnegan. Mary felt tears sting her eyes. "Oh, Nancy, that's a marvelous idea. Your dad would be so proud and pleased."

"Well, I'm not sure Ben would be," Nancy said. "I'd have to cut back my hours to find the time, and there's no guarantee anything would ever come of it."

"There are no guarantees about anything in life," Mary said.

"You say you're not sure Ben would be in favor of this. Do I take that to mean you haven't told him?"

"No, I haven't," Nancy said. "It seems selfish to be thinking about what I want when we're already having such a hard time making it."

"A parallel, indeed," Mary said. "The thing is, Nancy, Island Blooms turned out to be a successful little business. But even if it had flopped, I think your dad and I would have been glad we went for it because by then, we were back to being a team again."

"Another parallel," Nancy said, "is that Ben's parents keep after him to come into the family business. The more they see us struggle, the more pressure we get. And Ben won't tell them no."

"Is he interested in going into their sporting goods business?" Mary asked.

"Not remotely," Nancy said. "We'd have to move to Minnesota, and not that there's anything wrong with their business, but Ben just doesn't want to spend his life selling running shoes and baseball bats. He feels what he's doing is worthwhile, that it's making a contribution to the health of the planet and to the world our children will inherit. And so do I."

"Have you told him that?" Mary asked.

"He knows that's how I feel," Nancy answered.

"Okay, Nancy," Mary said. "I'll say no more. You know I'm here if you need me for anything. I'll do whatever I'm able to do to help you. Just promise me you'll think about what I've said. And please, Nancy, talk to Benjamin."

"I will, Mom," Nancy said, letting out a long breath. "I promise."

CHAPTER ❦ NINETEEN

ABBY HAD BEEN EXHAUSTED when she got home in the wee morning hours. She'd fallen asleep the minute her head hit the pillow. But she'd also had so many things roiling around in her brain she awoke just before dawn and couldn't go back to sleep again.

It was in that twilight phase between waking and sleeping that something finally clicked. She didn't have the whole picture, but she had a part of it. She got out of bed, flipped up the lid of her sleeping laptop and tapped a few keys to wake it up. She waited for her eyes to adjust to the light of the screen, then typed in a search. She wasn't at all surprised by what she found.

Now, as she dressed, she hoped what she was about to do was right. There was always a fine line between helping out and butting in, and when people perceived you were doing the latter, it could sometimes get ugly. But she couldn't stand idly by, not with what she knew now.

The house was quiet when Abby left a note on the kitchen

table and slipped out, hoping to leave everyone to some well-earned sleep.

She walked through the doors at the Sparrow Island Medical Center at 7:20. She talked briefly with the receptionist, then walked back toward Dr. Randolph's office.

They met in the hallway. The doctor greeted Abby with a raised eyebrow. John Parker was walking just behind her, making notes on a clipboard. He looked up and saw Abby and seemed startled.

Abby asked after Dustin.

"He's not too much worse for the wear," John said, "but we've still got a lot of talking to do. I don't know how to thank you for finding him."

"You can thank me by having breakfast with me," she said, hoisting a paper bag. "I've got bagels and coffee."

"Oh gee, I'd love to," John said, "but we're pretty busy today."

"Nonsense," Dr. Randolph said, giving Abby another raised eyebrow. "You can certainly take some time to have breakfast with the woman who rescued your child, John." She gave Abby a long hard look that said she'd be expecting an explanation later. Abby hadn't been able to tell her much when she'd called her earlier that morning. But Dr. Randolph had trusted her enough not to ask questions.

"Shall we go out in the courtyard?" Abby asked John.

He looked as if he felt trapped, but said, "Sure, of course. I can take a few minutes."

They settled at a concrete table flanked with two curved benches. Abby took the bagels and napkins out of the bag and passed John's across. They talked for a moment about Dustin and how Ellie was doing with the stress as they tended to coffee condiments, then Abby dove in.

"Tell me, John, how's your job going here at the Medical Center?"

"I like it here," John said, looking off at the flower bed bordering the edge of the courtyard. "It's going very well, I think."

"Good. Well, as talented as you are, do you ever feel that maybe you aren't doing all you were meant to do, John? Or should I call you Dr. Donovan?"

His head snapped up and his eyes frantically searched the courtyard. "Did Dustin tell you? Or did *he* get to you? Are you with Stanford?"

"Dustin didn't tell me anything," Abby said, scowling. "And what do you mean Stanford? As in the university? I worked at a university for years, but it was Cornell, not Stanford."

"Not the university—the man," John snapped. "Stanford Elsworth."

Abby held up a hand. "I'm not *with* anyone. I'm just who I've represented myself to be since we first met, which I think I can safely say is not the case with you. I don't have any agenda here and I don't know all of what's going on, but I know something's wrong."

"Then how—how, I mean . . ." John stammered, then began to fidget. He couldn't seem to decide whether to get up or stay seated.

"The incident with Duncan Grady aroused my curiosity," Abby told him. "And along the way, I noticed things that just didn't seem to add up about your family. I don't know if you're aware of this, but there have been people on the island asking a lot of questions."

"About what?" he asked, now growing still.

"Well, for one thing, that chessboard you sold at the co-op," Abby said. "Apparently there are a couple of guys who have been pretty intent on finding out who crafted it."

He leaned his head back and let out a breath. "What have I done?" he asked. "I should have given that up. Of all the selfish things . . ."

"That's not all of it," Abby said. "I've noticed other things. Last night I heard Ellie call you Greg. I knew from a friend of mine who works at St. Mary's hospital that the emergency room doctor who developed that little trach kit that's been credited with saving so many lives was named Dr. Donovan. This morning I remembered I'd seen the name on the site—Dr. Greg Donovan. It didn't take much from there to find a photograph of you and to find out a bit about your life."

"If you found me, he can't be far behind," the man Abby now knew as Greg said, running a hand through his dark hair. He was shaking. "Sounds like he's already got guys here, at the very least. We'll have to move again."

"I'm not going to ask you why," Abby said. "I'm going by my own instincts here and I hope I'm right. You seem like a good man, and I feel sure both you and Ellie want what's right for Dustin. Or perhaps I should say Nathan."

"Did you get that off the Internet too?" Greg asked, sounding tired and discouraged.

Abby ignored the question. "I'm just going to say that I can't imagine a situation where it would be right to keep a boy from his mother unless she was harming him. If this is a custody dispute or a marital disagreement, I hope you'll examine your heart and stop to think about whether what you're doing is right. That's all I wanted to say."

Greg sighed and pushed his untouched bagel aside, leaning

on the table. His eyes looked hollow with exhaustion. "What you must think of me," he said at last.

"If you want to tell me about it, I'm a pretty good listener," Abby said. "Though I'm not a licensed counselor," she added with a wan smile.

Greg shook his head slowly. "I am, you know," he said at last. "A licensed counselor, I mean. I was a social worker before I decided to go back to med school. I thought if I became a doctor, maybe I'd earn my father-in-law's respect. But that wasn't enough for him either. He wanted me to be a surgeon. That's when I started doing the veneers as a hobby, to improve my hand-eye coordination. I thought if I became a respected surgeon, he'd let up on Lena and me. That's my wife—Nathan's mom. I thought maybe then he'd stop making our lives a misery, but it didn't work. Do you know who Stanford Elsworth is?"

Abby shook her head. "I can't say I do."

"He's a businessman. Sounds pretty innocuous, doesn't it? He's a very successful businessman," Greg said tilting his head to one side. "That still sounds okay. But what he really is, is a predator. His big thing is acquisitions, which is a sanitized word for destruction. He looks for ailing companies, goes in and picks them up for a song, then tears them apart, keeping what he wants and throwing the rest away. The trash heap he leaves behind is made up of men and women who have given their sweat and loyalty to the original companies for years. There's no thought at all given to the devastation he brings to these families or communities. He leaves a trail of destruction in his wake and gets richer and more powerful with every conquest."

"He doesn't sound like a very ethical man," Abby said.

"The man's not acquainted with the concept," Greg said bitterly.

"I met Lena when she was doing volunteer work with a literacy group. That was her mother's influence, by the way, certainly not her father's. Her mother was a lovely woman. She died shortly after I met Lena. Anyway, we fell in love, but her father let it be known that I was definitely unsuitable. I came from a blue-collar family, which to Elsworth translated as the wrong side of the tracks. He wouldn't give his permission. So we eloped."

Abby waited patiently as Greg seemed to be lost in his own thoughts.

"That was the last time Lena ever defied her father," he said at last. "The man's done nothing but interfere and try to run our lives ever since. When Nathan came along, it got worse. Stanford wanted a say in how Nathan was raised. He wanted him raised as an Elsworth, not a 'shanty Irish Donovan,' as he put it. He constantly undermined the moral values we were trying to teach Nathan. I wanted the man out of our lives, but Lena just couldn't stand up to him."

"Did that break up your marriage?" Abby asked.

"No, not yet anyway," Greg said. "Not legally. Stanford told Lena constantly that if we didn't do as he said, he'd cut her off without a penny. That didn't bother her; Lena's not materialistic. But when that didn't work, he told her she'd be dead to him if she didn't honor his wishes. That she couldn't take."

"That doesn't explain why you're living here under false names and why Nathan can't see his mother," Abby said.

Greg nodded. "One day everything just came to a head when I overheard a conversation between Nathan and his grandfather. Nathan's a small boy, and you've no doubt noticed not very athletic. But he'd found out he was pretty good at rope climbing. They did this in their phys ed class at his school. You know, big long rope with knots tied along the way, the kid scrambles to the top as fast as he can and rings a bell. Well, anyway, they were having a field day and giving out trophies to the fastest kid in each event. Nathan wanted that rope-climbing trophy so bad he could taste it. He told his grandfather about it, but he said he didn't think he could win because there was another boy who was always faster than him. Stanford asked what the other boy's father did for a living. Nathan told him he was a teacher. Stanford's response was to peel off a hundred-dollar bill from his wallet. He handed it to Nathan and told him to offer it to the kid to throw the race. These were nine-year-olds!"

"That's terrible," Abby said.

"It gets worse," Greg said. "I told Nathan he was to do no such thing and I handed the money back to Stanford. I told Nathan that was unethical and unsportsmanlike. I told Stanford he was teaching Nathan the wrong lessons and I wanted it stopped. He erupted! He said I was an idiot and naïve and that I should recognize this as the practical solution he thought it to be. He said this way both boys would get what they wanted. The teacher's kid would obviously welcome the money and Nathan would get his trophy. He said if I couldn't see the beauty of that, I had no business raising an Elsworth heir. He was blind-hot angry that I'd contradicted him in front of Nathan.

"He came to see Lena the next day and told her he didn't approve of the way Nathan was being raised and that he intended to take matters into his own hands. Lena had no idea what he meant at the time, but the following day Stanford took Nathan out of school and was halfway to the airport with him before the school called to double-check to make sure his grandfather was supposed to pick him up."

"Where was he going with him?" Abby asked, working to suppress a gasp.

"Who knows?" Greg said with a shrug. "He has homes in Switzerland, the Bahamas, Dubai and London, and apartments in other places all around the world. The only reason he didn't make it out of the country with Nathan that time is because the hospital's on the airport side of town and I was able to intercept them."

"Do you think he intended to kidnap him?" Abby asked.

"I don't need to speculate," Greg said. "He told me he intended to get the boy out from under my influence—my 'namby-pamby' influence, I believe were his exact words—and that one way or the other he'd succeed."

"Did your wife know about this?" Abby asked.

"Yes, of course. I told her. And I told her she'd have to make a choice. That she'd have to cut her relationship to her father. It scared her, but she agreed. Then two weeks later I came home unexpectedly—I'd left my PDA at home—and found suitcases by the door and Lena and Nathan's passports on the table. When I confronted her, she said her father was never going to let up and if she didn't go with him, she'd lose Nathan. She was near hysterical. I couldn't reason with her. I got Nathan and went to my mother's. The next day, someone tried to snatch him out of my mother's front yard. That's when we went on the run."

"How did you get false identities?" Abby asked.

"I told you, I was a social worker," Greg said, giving a disgusted grimace. "I worked with troubled youth. Some of them became troubled adults. We don't win them all. I'm afraid I used the services of one of my failures to get new identities for us. But that meant giving up my license to practice. This is as close as I could come."

"Have you gone to the authorities?" Abby asked.

"No, I can't," Greg said. "I consulted a lawyer. This isn't a custody dispute. Lena and I are still married and have equal custody of Nathan. If she wants to take him out of the country, I can't stop her. I know I'll never see him again if Stanford gets him under his complete control. The man has money and power."

He stretched his back and looked up at the sky. "So, another move. Too bad. We liked it here. Lena would like it here too."

"Are you in contact with her?" Abby asked.

"I call once a month to let her know Nathan's okay and that he misses her, that we both miss her. I use a prepaid cell phone. I try to call when I know I'll get her answering machine because it tears my heart out to talk to her."

"Well, this explains why Ellie—I'm sorry, is that really your mother's name?" Abby asked.

"Yes." Greg nodded. "Sort of. Her name's Eleanor, not Elise, but she goes by Ellie. Ellie Donovan."

"Well, this explains why Ellie wants to keep such a close watch on Dustin. On Nathan," Abby corrected.

"Yes, it's a terrible burden on her I'm afraid. It kills her to see my marriage torn apart. She loves Lena like her own daughter. And she feels just sick about keeping Nathan from her. But I don't know what else to do. I have to save my child. After what happened at her house, she sees Stanford or his men around every corner. I can't tell her she's paranoid, because he has a whole security force working for him, SES, Ltd, and they're very good at what they do."

"Oh dear," Abby said. "That was the name on the credit card the fellow used to buy your chessboard."

Greg sucked in a breath. "We'll definitely have to move on. He's found us again."

"Maybe," Abby said. "But you are on a island here. It wouldn't be easy for them to get to Nathan. Surely there has to be some way to work this out," Abby said.

"Everything rides on Lena," Greg said. "As long as she won't stand up to her father and get him out of our lives, this is how it has to be."

"You said earlier you didn't know how to thank me for finding Nathan last night," Abby said, looking at him thoughtfully. "Well, here's how you can thank me. Try again. Try one more time to talk to your wife. If you still love her, tell her so. Tell her that her son misses her and loves her. You've made tremendous sacrifices to keep Nathan with you and to keep him safe. Now you must do everything you can to save your family. You have to give her something to be strong *for*. Promise me you'll do *that* and your debt to me will be squared."

Greg ran his hand through his hair again and let out a gust of breath. "I'll take it under advisement, I really will. But you don't know this man. Right now, I think I'd better go start making plans to get us out of here."

CHAPTER ❦ TWENTY

THE NEXT COUPLE OF DAYS went by fast for Abby. She was very busy at work. They completed the remainder of the repairs in the museum and the conservatory and they nailed down the plans for the video booth, including a new addition. Thanks to Bernadette, who had volunteered her time and signing skills, there would now be an inset video signing the presentation narrative.

Apart from her work duties, Abby had been doing her best to keep a dispirited and friendless Bobby McDonald busy. Dustin/Nathan was not allowed to leave the house. Bobby assumed he was grounded, but Abby suspected it was more complicated than that.

Abby had kept her promise to tell no one the Donovans' story, but she was worried about them. She'd done a little research on Stanford Elsworth and found that, if anything, Greg had been too generous in his characterization. She half expected the Donovans might simply vanish and no one on Sparrow Island would hear from them again. She hoped and prayed that Greg would honor her request and contact his wife, but she wasn't at all sure he would. She could hardly blame the man for wanting to safeguard his child.

Abby had called her friend Diane back to ask for a character reference on Greg Donovan. Diane had nothing but good things to say about him. In fact, she fairly gushed about what a good and caring man he was. When Abby asked if she knew Stanford Elsworth, Diane had said, "By reputation only, and I'd like to keep it that way."

As she pulled into the garage on Wednesday afternoon, Abby was exhausted. Nancy and the children would be leaving tomorrow, so things would settle down to a more milder pace at home, but she was still worried about the Donovan family too.

As she entered the house she found Nancy tidying up the kitchen, upbeat and smiling the most genuine smile Abby had seen since she'd arrived.

"You look happy," Abby said.

"She is," Mary answered, sorting through drawings the children had made to choose the day's new refrigerator art. "We all are."

"Ben and I have been talking—for hours," Nancy said, grinning.

"And she means that literally," Mary said. "It's a good thing I have that unlimited calling plan."

Nancy gave her a look and cocked her head. "I know we have a lot of things to work out, but it feels like we're making a whole new start. Never let it be said I don't know when to take good advice," she babbled on. "I finally told Ben that it was bothering me that he wasn't being up front with his parents. He was completely taken aback. He said he was trying to keep his options open because he thought that's what I wanted, to have a bailout plan if money got too tight. And I found out he's been sending out resumes for another job that might pay more, even though it was making him sick to think of leaving the job he loves. I never knew he'd done that. That's what was making him so irritable."

"Did you ever ask him what was bothering him?" Abby said.

"No, I did not," Nancy said, "and yes, it's ridiculous. I see it now, now that I'm out of the day-to-day and can get some perspective. We were trying to second-guess one another and read one another's minds instead of talking honestly."

"I don't know about ridiculous," Abby said, "but it's certainly a human failing. Your mother and I did that for a long time too."

"Really?" Nancy said, "You two? I always thought you two were so simpatico."

Mary and Abby both laughed. "We are," they said at the same time.

"Mostly," Abby added. "Now, anyway. But our communication hasn't always been the best. These days we work hard on avoiding misunderstandings and we talk. A lot."

"Well, Ben and I have realized that's one of our problems. Between all our activities and the kids, the only time we have to talk is late at night when we're both exhausted. But we're going to change that. My friend Rachel Watts from next door—you remember the Watts, Mom. They have Carly and Steven who are roughly the same ages as Emily and Nick. Anyway, for months now she and I have been talking about swapping babysitting services so we can have a 'date night' with our husbands. Now I'm determined we're going to follow through on that instead of just talking about it."

"That's a great plan," Mary said. "You know, even though we had your grandparents here as eager babysitters, for the longest time your Dad and I didn't take advantage of that because we had it in our heads we had to have some event or special occasion in order to ask them—and we were too broke for many of those activities. Then one night your grandmother offered—no, it was more like she *insisted*—that we go do something, anything to give her some time with you kids. Your dad and I took a walk down to the marina and just watched the boats for a while and talked and talked and talked some more. There was something about being out of the house, where every which way we turned we were reminded of our responsibilities and the never-ending to-do list. It was freeing. After that, we made it a weekly event."

"Weekly?" Nancy said. "I remember you and Dad going for a walk almost every night after dinner. Usually while Zack and I were doing the dishes—and arguing."

"Well, by then we needed to get out of the house more often," Mary said, laughing.

"Well, the other thing is, I finally screwed up my courage and told Ben about my idea for the children's book. Mom, Abby, he was great! He didn't hesitate a nanosecond. And the more we talked, the more I realized I can make time for this. I can't cut back my hours at work, but I've told the kids they have to choose just one activity to be involved in this summer. I thought they'd be upset, but it turns out half the stuff they were doing—dance lessons, T-ball, gymnastics, soccer—they were just doing because other kids were doing it. They weren't really enjoying it all that much. They're happy as clams to pick one and have more time at home. And they'll be even happier once they learn about our last item of big news," Nancy said, lowering her voice to a whisper.

"What's that?" Abby asked. "How much more can there be?"

"I told you we talked for hours!" Nancy said. She put her fingers to her lips and looked toward the stairs. "I think we're getting a dog," she said. "There's a black Lab named Noah, a service dog who's going to be retired. We've put in our application to adopt him."

"Noah," Abby said, "now there's a name full of hope and promise."

Nancy laughed. "I hadn't thought of that, but yeah, it seems destined, doesn't it? But it's not for sure yet, and we want to surprise the kids, so mum's the word."

The children came clopping down the stairs. "Okay, Mommy," Emily said, "we have all our things in a big pile so we can pack."

"Great," Nancy said. "Let's go get started. You know we leave early tomorrow morning. Daddy says he can't wait to see us!"

The children squealed, then raced back upstairs. Nancy laughed as their footfalls on the stairs made a syncopated percussion. Abby glanced over at Mary and saw there were tears in her eyes, but she knew they were tears of relief.

The telephone rang and Abby picked it up. She listened for a few minutes, then said, "Yes, of course. You'd be very welcome. Okay, see you in a bit."

Mary looked at her questioningly.

"That was . . ." Abby began, then hesitated. She didn't want to say John Parker because that would feel like she was being dishonest with Mary, but she didn't want to betray his confidence either. "That was the father of our runaway boy," she said, keeping her tone light. "They'd like to come by for a few minutes. He said they wouldn't stay long."

"They'd probably like to give you a medal," Mary said. "Or maybe they're bringing Finnegan a new chew toy for his part in the rescue."

"Maybe," Abby said lightly, but she was wondering exactly why they *were* coming. To say good-bye?

Abby excused herself and went up to change clothes. She did want to freshen up, but mainly, she wanted to avoid being in the room with Mary. It was difficult for her to keep things from her sister. She thought of how Ellie must feel, living a lie alongside her son and grandson. It had to be incredibly difficult to sustain. Now she understood why Ellie had been so withdrawn.

Abby washed her face, then changed into khaki pants and a pretty lavender blouse Mary had given her for Christmas. She could hear Nancy and the children talking excitedly in the next room. She smiled to herself and went to her jewelry box to retrieve something, then went in to Nancy.

"I want you to have this," she told her niece, opening the clasp on a necklace chain and holding it out to her.

"What is it?" Nancy asked.

"It's a pendant that was given to me by your grandfather and grandmother when I went away to Cornell."

Nancy took the gold pendant in her hand. "It's two doves," she said. "It's beautiful. But I can't take this Aunt Abby, it must mean a lot to you."

"Yes, it does," Abby said. "Which is why I want you to have it. Your grandparents gave it to me because the dove is a symbol of promise and new beginnings. It was a dove that brought back the olive branch to Noah." She gave Nancy a wink.

Nancy glowed. "I will treasure it, Aunt Abby. Thank you."

Abby fastened the necklace around Nancy's neck and kissed her on the cheek. "Incidentally," she said, "doves generally mate for life!"

Abby went downstairs, her foot hitting the bottom step just as the doorbell rang.

As she opened the door, she found Greg Donovan, Nathan, Ellie and a tall, dark-haired woman she didn't know standing there.

Greg smiled broadly. "Abby, I did take your request under advisement," he said. "Let me introduce—"

"This is my mom," Nathan cut in, grabbing the slender woman around the waist.

Greg tousled his hair. "Yes, exactly what I was going to say. This is Nathan's mom and my wife, Lena Donovan," he said.

"And my daughter-in-law," Ellie said, touching the woman's arm. "Lena, this is our friend Dr. Abby Stanton."

"It's very nice to meet you," Lena said, extending her hand. "I understand we have many, *many* reasons to thank you."

"Oh, please," Abby said, stepping back. "Where are my manners? Please come in." She was trying to get grounded, but her brain was freezing up. She held up a hand to stop the guests in the hallway and turned to Greg. "I've kept your confidence," she told him, keeping her voice low. "But I won't lie to Mary, or to anyone else, so I'm not quite sure how to handle this visit . . ."

Ellie reached out to take Abby's hand. "You've learned a little signing," she said. She made a series of gestures, but Abby couldn't get it.

She looked quizzically at Ellie who repeated the series, this time more slowly. Abby searched her mind as she repeated the motions herself "Begin," she said, making a motion that resembled a key being turned in a lock. "Again?" she said, making a final motion.

Ellie nodded.

"That's what we'd like to do," Greg said. "Make a fresh start here. We'd like to speak with Mary if we could. Our next stop is the McDonalds' and eventually we'll make our way to everyone we've met on the island."

"Mom wants to meet Bobby," Nathan said. "I told her all about him. Mom's going to stay here with us and we're going to live here and be a regular family again."

Abby looked at Greg. He looked at his wife and she smiled, but it was a smile filled with regret. Abby could see that. "We've got a long way to go," Greg said, "but we had that frank talk you suggested. We both know what we want now and we're willing to work to hold on to it."

Abby stepped back and led them into the living room where Mary was, smiling as she saw Nathan's face, lit by the purest happiness, though scratched and still suffering from his encounter with the stinging nettle. He and his mother couldn't seem to stop hugging one another.

Mary listened carefully as Greg gave her a truncated account of what he'd told Abby a couple of days earlier. Abby could see that Mary was trying to hide her shock.

"I'm so sorry, Mary," Ellie said. "I felt terrible about deceiving you, but you have to understand, we felt we had no choice in this. We couldn't lose him."

"No apology needed," Mary said. "I'm just sorry you've all been through this. I'm so very happy that things are looking up now and that you'll be staying on the island. Now we'll have a chance to become friends without all these impediments. My daughter's upstairs with the kids, packing, but we were planning to have a simple supper in about a half hour. We'd love it if you'd stay and eat with us."

Greg started to decline, but Ellie cut in, "Actually, Mary," she said. "Nathan and I would be thrilled to have supper with you. Maybe afterward he and his friend Bobby could visit a little while. I know they have lots to talk about. And Greg and Lena you can have a chance to talk to the McDonalds, then maybe go somewhere and really talk and reconnect."

Lena turned to her mother-in-law, "But I want to be with Nathan," she signed and spoke aloud, "and with you, all of us together. I've missed you all so much."

"And I've missed you too," Ellie said, reaching out to touch Lena's cheek, "but we have the gift of time now. If we're to rebuild, we have to start with the foundation, right?"

A LITTLE WHILE LATER, Ellie, Mary and Abby sat out on the deck, watching the sky mellow into purples and pinks as the sun seemed to float lazily down to meet the ocean.

Bobby and Nathan were out in the yard with Finnegan between them, each one petting the dog as Nathan explained his rather unusual life experiences to Bobby. Abby could see Bobby staring ahead, somber, trying to take it all in.

Nancy was inside, minding a pot of soup on the stove as she and the children set the table for their last night on Sparrow Island—for this eventful trip anyway. She, too, seemed to be trying to get her mind around the Parker/Donovans' plight.

"They have a long way to go," Ellie said, "but I believe they can make it. Lena's father has disowned her. Completely turned his back on her after she told him that from now on she was making her own decisions. The first decision, she told him, was that if she ever found Greg and Nathan, they would be a family again, and he would not be welcome in their home —or anywhere near Nathan."

"How can you be sure he won't keep trying to take Nathan?" Mary asked. "I mean, heaven forbid, but he sounds like a determined man."

"Oh, indeed he is," Ellie said. "But Lena has a brother, David, who works for their father. David's horrified by what his father has tried to do. He's promised Lena he'll let her know immediately if their father gets it into his head to stir this up again. He assures her that their father's so angry with her that he has washed his hands of her and her whole family, at least for now."

"Sounds like that's not such a bad thing. Terribly sad, but a great relief for them," Mary said.

"So, she's been looking for them all this time?" Abby asked. "It was her, not her father?"

"Yes," Ellie said. "Well, with some help from her brother. Unbeknownst to their father, he's been using the company's security arm to help Lena find us. As desperate as we were to hide Nathan, that's how desperate she was to find him. They were getting close. The same day that Greg called Lena, they reported to David that they'd located us here in the San Juans and were closing in. We would have run again if Abby hadn't been so persuasive." She reached over to touch Abby's knee. "Thank you for that . . . and for everything. Both of you, for your generous hands of friendship and for everything you've done for us. Again, I hope you'll accept my sincerest apology for not being honest with you."

Abby struggled to remember the signs she'd been studying. She raised her hands and made the sign that she thought matched her spoken words. "You're forgiven," she said.

Mary reached over, touched Ellie's arm and said, "Of course, you're forgiven." She tried to repeat the gesture Abby had made.

Ellie laughed, loud enough to make the boys look up from their conversation.

Abby frowned, "What is it? What's funny?"

"I read your lips fine and I'm glad you forgive me, Mary, but"—she pointed to Mary's hands—"you just asked me if I want to buy something. We're going to have to work on your signing skills."

Mary looked at Abby and they all started to laugh.

Ellie asked if one of them would drive her out to see Goldie the next day. "I'd like to explain myself to her in person," she said. "Make a new start with her too. I'm happy that we'll be staying on here for a while. I've grown so fond of the place in this short time,. Now that I can call my daughter and my two other grandchildren and even have them come out to visit, I think I could be very happy here. There will be lots of adjustments for Lena and Greg. They have a lot to work out. I want to help as much as I can with Nathan, though I think I'll try to find a place of my own. The last thing they need is interference from another in-law."

"Lena seems very fond of you," Abby said. "She's learned signing. Was that for you?"

Ellie nodded. "I love her dearly. That's one thing that's made this so hard. I felt awful keeping Nathan from her. It made me heartsick every single day, but I just couldn't see any way out of it. She says she understands, and I believe she does now that she's been without Nathan for all these months. We all have a lot of hurts to mend."

"Sparrow Island is a wonderful place for new beginnings, I can attest to that," Abby said.

"So can I," Mary said as she cocked her head toward the dining room where Nancy and the children could be heard laughing. "And so can a lot of other people."

As they all turned to gaze out at the sunset, Abby could just make out two figures strolling along at the water's edge—Greg and Lena. The sun was low now. The light struck the madrone tree at an angle, the rust-colored bark turning to an orange glow. Lena, her dark hair blowing in the easy breeze, reached out and took Greg's hand. He gathered her into his arms and they both stared out at the sea.

Mary raised her teacup and turned toward Ellie. Abby did the same. "To Sparrow Island and to new beginnings," she said. The clink of the china cups carried like a musical chime on the velvety evening air.

"I can hear that sound in my memory," Ellie said softly. "It's a beautiful sound."

A NOTE FROM THE EDITORS

This original book was created by the Books and Inspirational Media Division of Guideposts, the world's leading inspirational publisher. Founded in 1945 by Dr. Norman Vincent Peale and Ruth Stafford Peale, Guideposts helps people from all walks of life achieve their maximum personal and spiritual potential. Guideposts is committed to communicating positive, faith-filled principles for people everywhere to use in successful daily living.

Our publications include award-winning magazines such as *Guideposts* and *Angels on Earth*, best-selling books, and outreach services that demonstrate what can happen when faith and positive thinking are applied in day-to-day life.

For more information, visit us at www.guideposts.com, call (800) 431-2344 or write Guideposts, PO Box 5815, Harlan, Iowa 51593.

duplicitous 153